DAMAGED

DAN SCOTTOW

Print ISBN 978-1-913419-24-0

This one is for my mum. I wish she could be here to see it.

A SUMMER'S AFTERNOON, 1995

PALMERSTON, HAMPSHIRE, ENGLAND

The scorching sun beats down on a balmy July day. Birds chirp and twitter from the woods behind the garden, and the delicate scent of roses and freesias from the well-kept flowerbeds drifts through the air. A squirrel scuttles across the top of the fence. It pauses on top of the gate, sniffing the air, alarmed by some distant sound in the undergrowth, then continues on its journey before ducking down the other side of the fence, out of sight.

Helen Abbott smiles as she sees her daughter Alice and her best friend Emily splashing each other with water from drinking bottles at the bottom of the garden. Helen is hanging laundry on the clothesline and the fresh smell of fabric softener and washing powder drifts into her nostrils. Alice wears a fluorescent pink bikini. Helen was unsure about letting her have it, but it isn't too revealing, and she still looks like a little girl, rather than a child trying to be an adult.

Emily, always the more modest of the pair, wears denim cut-off shorts and a plain white T-shirt tied into a knot to expose her midriff. The wet fabric clings to her skin as she spins around, laughing. She dodges around the legs of the swing set, narrowly avoiding a further soaking from the bottle of water that Alice sprays towards her.

A wave of noise and laughter and excitement rushes past Helen as the girls run into the house, giggling and screaming.

'Be careful you don't slip on the kitchen floor, and don't get water everywhere please, girls!' Helen calls to them, but they don't hear.

She reaches her hand up to her face, wiping a bead of sweat from her brow. She picks up a pair of Alice's knickers. Pink and white polka dot with a tiny pink satin bow stitched to the front. Helen wonders sadly how long it will be before Alice outgrows such childish clothes, and Helen smiles to herself sadly as she pegs them to the line. From inside the house, she hears the phone ring. She pauses for a moment but the girls are clearly oblivious and the phone continues to ring, unanswered. Helen sighs and makes her way inside.

As she picks up the receiver, she hears her husband Jim's voice on the end of the line and she smiles again. He's calling to say he will be a little late home from work and not to bother waiting for him to eat. They exchange pleasantries before hanging up. Helen walks into the downstairs loo to fetch a towel. She dabs at her forehead and looks at herself in the mirror.

The blow dry she had earlier that morning is already starting to look dishevelled from the heat. She tuts, smiles and reaches up to tuck a strand of silky hair behind each ear, revealing her diamond stud earrings; an anniversary gift from Jim the year before. She knows it is not the done thing to feel such pride and contentment with one's life, but still she wonders, *does it get much better than this?* The sound of two twelve-year-old girls thundering up the stairs shakes her from her reverie. She chides herself for feeling so smug and heads back out to the garden.

Helen crouches to pick up some more of the laundry, but as

she stands, something occurs to her. She looks along the line of washing she has been hanging out but sees that Alice's knickers are gone. She frowns and looks back at the laundry basket. She bends over and rifles through the damp washing, but the knickers are definitely not there.

Feeling slightly uneasy, she straightens, glancing around the garden. The back gate is wide open. She shakes her head and strides over quickly to the fence. Stepping into the narrow lane behind the gardens, she looks up and down the path but there is nobody there. She steps back into her garden, firmly closing the gate and locking the two heavy bolts.

She tells herself she must mention this to Jim when he gets home, then heads back to the task at hand. When she is finished, she heads inside to start on dinner. She uncorks a bottle and pours herself a cool fresh glass of crisp white wine. *Yes,* Helen thinks, *life is good, and damn anyone who judges her for admitting it.*

By the time Jim Abbott arrives home from work later that evening, Helen has finished the bottle and the incident with her daughter's underwear has completely slipped her mind.

1

Present Day

I am going to die here.

I open my one good eye. My head pounds, blood is crusted over my cheek. The smell in the room is unbearable. I try not to make any noise but I can feel the body against my back and I let out a cry. The smell of decomposing flesh is more than I can bear and my squirming sends flies clouding and buzzing around me. I attempt to move but my wrists are hand-cuffed together around a pipe from a boiling-hot radiator.

Panicking, my eyes dart about the room, taking in the scene. Dimly lit by a small bedside lamp, I see clothes strewn all over the floor and furniture upturned. Drawers have been emptied of their contents. The cuffs are on my wrists tight, cutting off the circulation. The flies settle, but the hum continues. The body has been lying close to the radiator, which has sped up the rate of putrefaction.

There are flies everywhere. A maggot wriggles across my

arm. I can't brush it off. I try to knock it away with my head. I feel it on my lips... sticky, wriggling. I whimper. I spit. The pain radiates from the centre of my face and travels in waves through my head. I think my nose is broken, cartilage crunches as I screw up my face, trying to assess the damage that has been done. Everything hurts.

I inhale and the putrid air makes me gag. All I can hear is the loud buzzing of the flies. The rest of the house lies eerily silent.

Am I alone?

I've been drifting in and out of consciousness. Did the front door slam shut? Or have I just imagined that?

The smell... it's everywhere. I can even taste it. The flies swarm around me. I try to calm myself, but as I realise the gravity of my situation, fear begins to set in. I'm totally at the mercy of the person who has cuffed me to this radiator, although I'm not sure that mercy is a word in their vocabulary.

One thing I am sure of is that if I do not find a way out, I will end up like the rotting corpse beside me.

Nobody knows I'm here. Nobody's coming to help me.

I scan the room again as best I can from my position. I can't sit up... the cuffs are chained close to the floor.

I try to reposition myself to get a better view of the room, but I slip. A rotting bloated face is now in front of mine. The skin is a discoloured green. The tongue and eyes protrude from the face, making it look distorted... somehow unreal. I struggle and my face brushes against it. I feel something on my skin. I try to roll over again to get away from the body. It's difficult and hurts my wrists, hurts my whole body, but I don't care. I manage to turn myself away. The smell is like silage and spoiled meat, bad bins, but far, far worse. I see the rank puffy decomposing face again as I close my eyes, and I vomit. I can't help myself and the bile splatters down me, mixing with the blood on my blouse.

I compose myself again and search the floor around me for something... anything that can help me escape. A small rucksack lies on the floor, a metre or so away from me. I stretch out my leg as far as I can. I can almost reach it, but not quite. I try frantically to hook it with my toe, but it's no use. It's too far. The millimetres may as well be miles.

I scream in frustration then regret it as I remember that my attacker could still be in the house. I lie for a few seconds, listening, too terrified to even breathe. I hear nothing. Just the buzz of the flies. I allow myself to let out a long steady breath.

I have to stay calm or I'll never make it out of this alive. The intense heat from the radiator almost feels as if it is burning my skin. I'm sweating profusely. It runs into the cuts and grazes that cover my body, and they sting. Sweat, blood and vomit run down my face, plastering my short hair to my skin. I sob uncontrollably. I close my eyes and resign myself to my fate. Suddenly I think of Alice, my sweet lost childhood friend. And this is all it takes. A moment of clarity and I realise I must at least try.

I know I'll probably die here tonight, but I am damned if I am going down without a fight.

I turn my face towards the radiator. The pipe is thin... it doesn't look strong.

I can't manoeuvre my legs around enough to kick at it, so instead I grasp the chain of the cuffs in my hands and pull as hard as I can. It's agony as the metal cuts into my wrists again, but this is the least of my worries. I do it again. The cuffs clatter against the pipe over and over, but I don't care about the noise I'm making anymore. I'm certain if anyone were still in the house, they would have been up here by now. The pipe moves slightly. I put all my strength into pulling on the chain, yanking it over and over again, trying to break the pipe away from the radiator.

My skin burns as it brushes against the scorching hot pipe,

but the pain makes me pull harder. The cuffs slice deep into my flesh. I pull as hard as I can, but it's no good. I can't get enough purchase to break the pipe. My body slumps. I have nothing left.

I need the toilet. I don't even try to stop it. I piss myself and it seeps into the carpet around me, mixing with blood and vomit and God knows what else.

My whole body stiffens.

A noise from somewhere within the belly of the house. I hold my breath for a second. I hear footsteps slowly advancing up the stairs. Definite. Purposeful.

Someone is coming.

The terror drives me to one final attempt at the pipe. I pull, crashing the links of the cuffs against it. I scream. I use every last bit of energy I have to try to break the pipe. I can't feel the pain in my wrists anymore. I can't feel anything but fear. Adrenaline has taken over.

As the door swings open, crashing against the wall, the flies swarm and buzz around the room like thick black smoke.

The figure looms in the doorway, looking annoyed. As my attacker steps inside, I receive two hard kicks to my ribs, as a telling, no doubt. 'What the fuck do you think you're doing?'

I knew I was going to die here.

2

Two weeks earlier

I often dream about Alice, even now. With no knowledge of how she would look these days, I see her as I knew her. A twelve-year-old girl. If a small child can be beautiful, then Alice was. In my dreams, she never speaks. I wonder if this is because I can't really remember her voice. It's been such a long time. She wears her mauve check dress with the pleated skirt.

The dress that everybody recognises from the picture.

Her blonde hair blows in the wind, a pale pink ribbon tied over the top of her head in a bow, the loose ends of the ribbon trail behind her in the breeze. She gazes at me with a sad lonely longing in her eyes. My parents always used to say that Alice's beauty had ultimately been her downfall. But we will never really know for sure. It's more than likely that this is the case. Ugly children rarely get taken.

I'm packing a small bag, but I'm not really concentrating on the job, so I'm just putting in random things. Every now and then I'll think better of something and take it out. I'll take what's necessary. Two things that I'll definitely take are my childhood diary and a small scruffy bear. His name is Toby. I've read the diary so many times that I probably know most of it by heart, but after twenty-five years, memories are sometimes inaccurate. It's a good idea to have a first-hand account of everything as it was then.

The bear belonged to Alice. She didn't give it to me as such, but I took it from her room a few weeks after she disappeared. I remember how I had guiltily hidden it under my jumper the last time I was in her room. Her parents might have missed it. Perhaps they would have gone to look for it one day and wondered if she took it with her, wherever she was. If they did, they never asked me about it in the weeks before I left. I was so scared of getting found out that I used to keep it hidden away in a shoebox under my bed. Now it sits on top of my chest of drawers.

As I pack, my mind wanders back to the meeting at work, a week earlier. I had arrived into the office as usual, ten minutes late on a Monday morning after what had been a sadly uneventful weekend socially. I knew as soon as I reached my desk that something was going on. There was a buzz, an excitement around the room. The editorial team for the magazine were rushing about like headless chickens, gathering papers, pads and pens.

Dillon, another of the writers, rushed over to my desk, dropping a cinnamon Danish pastry down in front of me. 'Meeting. Boardroom. Now!'

I cocked an eyebrow as I picked up the Danish, taking a bite.

'A kid's gone missing in Hampshire. Quite close to where Alice Abbott lived. The boss thinks we can write a fairly good piece about the two cases, drawing comparisons.'

As soon as the words left Dillon's mouth, I stopped chewing, unable to swallow. My mouth was too dry. Dillon turned and scurried off towards the boardroom. I stood, following him slowly.

As I entered the boardroom, the meeting had already begun. I took the only remaining seat at the end of the table as the editor, Dave, eyed me, annoyed.

He made a big show of looking at his watch. 'Nice of you to join us, Emily.'

I sat down and listened as he relayed the details. A ten-year-old girl, Becky Clarke, had left her grandmother's house in Carrington on Sunday afternoon and set off on the five-minute walk back to her parents' house. She never arrived. Dave joins the dots for anyone too stupid. Carrington, in Hampshire, is less than a ten-minute drive from Palmerston, where Alice Abbott (and I) lived. Any mention of Alice Abbott sells magazines and papers. Even now. If we make a suggestion that the two cases might somehow be linked, it's a no brainer for sales figures. Alice's abductor was never caught.

'Apparently, the main suspect in the Alice Abbott case still lives on her street, next door to the mother. It's mental. I want someone in Palmerston this afternoon. This is a big story.' Dave was so excited that little droplets of saliva were flying from his mouth as he ranted.

I didn't look up from my notepad as I mumbled, 'I know the Abbotts.' The room went silent and all eyes were on me. 'I used to live over the road from them.'

I glanced at Dave; he was staring back at me, with a look of disbelief. I continued, 'In fact, Alice was... a very good friend of mine. I could call Helen Abbott, see if she'll talk to me.'

Dave's jaw hung open for a moment. 'And you've never thought to tell me this before because...?'

The question lingered in the air for what felt like forever before I replied. 'Because I didn't feel it was relevant.'

After Dave got over his initial anger that I had kept such a gem from him for seven years working beneath him, he decided that I most definitely needed to go back to Palmerston. He'd sourced Helen Abbott's phone number and insisted I call her immediately. I dialled slowly, nervously. This woman had been like a mother to me as a child, but now I dreaded speaking to her.

The phone rang for a good minute before it was answered and her voice came down the line. Crackly from a bad connection. She sounded older for sure, but unmistakably her. A warm familiarity washed over me at the sound of her voice and I pictured her standing in her kitchen, folding laundry. Always immaculate, even if she was doing housework.

'Hello?' She sounded almost confused. Something in her voice told me she was not used to receiving phone calls these days. She sounded hesitant, as if she was always expecting the delivery of some bad news.

'Hi, Mrs Abbott... I... I'm not sure you'll remember me (a lie, I know she definitely will), but it's Emily Blake. I used to live across the road from you when I was a child.'

The line was silent for such a long time that I wondered if she was still there.

'I remember. Of course I do. What can I do for you, Emily?'

'I'm so sorry to get in touch out of the blue like this, but I need to ask you a favour...'

3

Alice Abbott and I were inseparable. I'm sure that back then, most people didn't know which of us was Alice and which was Emily. We were simply 'Alice and Emily'. Everybody knows now though. Her face was in every newspaper for months, if not years. Even now, you'll see her pop up in the news for some obscure reason. She was one of the most recognisable children in the world due to the media frenzy that surrounded her disappearance. Everyone knew who she was yet nobody knew her, but to me she was more than a face in a newspaper. She was my best friend. She was funny and kind. Together we made plans, as only little girls can. We would be friends forever and nothing would ever separate us. And the sad thing is we believed it. I think we would still be close now if things had not happened the way they did.

Alice and I couldn't have been more different physically. She was tall, slim and pretty with blonde hair. I was shorter, stockier, plainer and dark. I'm sure people saw two pretty girls when they passed us in the park, but I think I was a by-product of Alice's beauty. As if in a way she could make anything seem more attractive simply by being near it. I didn't mind. It worked for me and I liked it.

Our brothers used to play together, although Alice's brother Tom was a few years younger than Adam, who was eleven. As far as I know, they are still in touch. I don't hear much from Adam these days. In the months following the abduction, my parents decided to leave Palmerston far behind them.

My brother hated being taken away from his friends, his home and everything he had known in his life. In turn he grew to hate everything about Alice, who he blamed entirely for us having to leave. He got into numerous fights at his new school and eventually my parents sent him away to a strict boarding school. He felt that they had abandoned him, and as he got older he stopped coming home for the holidays.

After that, our relationship was strained at best. We have drifted apart. We send Christmas cards and the odd text message, but nothing that could be described in any way as a close relationship. I couldn't tell you the first thing about him.

Lots of people moved away from the village. But Adam felt *he* was the only person it was happening to. In reality, it no longer felt like the safe attractive place it had once been in people's minds. Nobody wanted their precious child to be next. At the time I didn't understand everything that went on, but having studied it all in great detail, I suppose there was a sense of guilt amongst many of the parents who had been there that night. Palmerston was a largely unknown village. It had nothing going for it and was quite unremarkable in any way. But it was rural, peaceful and safe, so people liked to live there. Alice's disappearance more or less put it on the map for most people.

It had been a friendly close community. A house on Pear Tree Close would once have been a very desirable residence. These days, however, people would probably change the subject rather than admit to living there. Many of the residents had children. They were all aspiring to a better life than their parents had. They would take it in turns to host parties that went on into the small hours of the morning, safe in the knowledge that their little ones were tucked up without danger in their four-bed semi across the street, or a few doors down.

Or so they thought.

In hindsight, it was astonishingly bad parenting to leave young children alone in a house while you were over the road getting drunk, but at the time it was inconceivable that any harm could ever come to any of us. Although Alice and I were older by then, they had been doing it for years, since we were very small. Some of my earliest memories are of being woken in the early hours by either my mum or my dad opening the bedroom door and poking their head in. The smell of alcohol from them would be very strong, but at the time I didn't really understand or know what it was. I would pretend to be asleep and they would click the door shut, sneak down the stairs, and I would hear the front door open and close as they returned to their revelry. If my parents were hosting, we would be packed off over the road to Alice's house, and vice versa.

Those were the best times, although as we got a little older, we just wanted to stay at home and join in the fun. Sadly, we were never allowed. It was during one such party in the summer, when I was twelve, that the incident occurred. It was a balmy late August evening. A dry bank holiday, as far as I can remember, was a rare thing, but this particular weekend had been glorious.

The usual crowd had decided on the spur of the moment one Sunday evening that it was too good an opportunity to waste. It was the turn of the Aitkens at number forty-eight to host. Adam and I were left to our own devices, as were Alice, Tom and many of the other youngsters on Pear Tree Close. Children aged from two to teens were left unattended as the parents revelled and drank champagne together. A babysitter was unheard of. Unnecessary. A mother or father would take it in turns to pop home every few hours to look in and make sure everything was okay, which of course it always was. The parents with the older kids, like us, sometimes didn't bother. Nothing interesting ever happened in Palmerston.

Until *that* night.

I was perched on the windowsill in my bedroom at number twenty-three, looking across the street to Alice's room, the red plastic phone pressed to my ear. The sound of crickets chirping filled the air and the rich scents of summer lingered. It was hot, and I felt happy. I remember thinking that life was good. That misguided belief that only children can have, that you are entirely safe. Before the whole world turns to shit around you.

The sounds of muffled music and bad singing in chorus drifted through my window from a garden further down the road. Alice gave a wave. I remember looking at my clock as she told me she was heading to bed soon. I can see the giant gold Casio watch hanging on my bedroom wall as vividly as if it were in front of me now. It's funny how some details remain so clear but others dissipate. I can still see her pink pyjamas. Her hair pulled back in a loose ponytail. It was ten thirty. I had checked on Adam. He was in bed reading a comic by the light of his Batman torch. Alice said goodnight, and that was the last time I spoke to her.

The last time I saw her.

I put the phone down and pulled the curtains closed, climbing into my bed, kicking the covers away from me. It was hot and stuffy, even with the window wide open, but I think I drifted off to sleep fairly quickly.

I remember waking at some point, around one o'clock. Something had roused me. Had there been a noise? Or is this something I have now invented? Making my way to the window,

I peered through the curtains, surprised to see a light still on in Alice's room. A shadow moved past the window behind the curtains and then the light went off. Puzzled, I got back into bed and was soon fast asleep again.

When I awoke the following morning, I opened the curtains expecting to see Alice's already open. She was always up before me. Her mother was much more insistent on an early rise than either of my parents. But today her curtains were still closed. There were police cars parked in the street, outside her house, and the front door to number twenty-two was wide open. Some men were standing around out the front of the house. I know now that one of the men was Detective Mills, who led the investigation into Alice's disappearance. A few uniformed police officers were knocking on doors up and down the road. Alice's mother came to the front door of her house and looked out. She was crying. She glanced up at my window and I waved, but she just looked away, closing the door slowly.

I remember rushing down the stairs to find my parents sitting in the kitchen. They were mid conversation but they stopped talking as they heard me rushing down the hallway. As I entered the kitchen, they both looked at me with a sadness in their eyes that, until that day, I had never before witnessed in them. My mother sat me down and told me that Alice was missing. Her parents had gone to wake her that morning and her bed was empty.

A policeman came to the house not long after that. He had asked me some questions. 'Was Alice unhappy about anything?', 'had we argued recently?', or 'had she mentioned that she might want to run away?'

I didn't want to answer the questions. I just wanted to know where my friend was.

· · ·

As I understand it now, her father had popped home roughly around midnight and stuck his head in both of the kids' rooms, finding them safely sound asleep. He had then returned to the party until two o'clock, when he and Alice's mother returned home together. Given the late hour, they decided not to disturb the children and headed straight to bed.

Alice's mother had knocked on her door at eight to wake her, only to find the bed cold and empty. The back door as always was unlocked. This was not unusual in our little street. My parents rarely locked the front or the back door. The rear gardens on Alice's side of the road were adjacent to a wooded area which eventually opened out onto the next residential street. Each garden had a tall fence, with one gate leading onto a path that ran the length of the road. The investigating team later discovered that the Abbotts' gate was open. Neither parent could remember if this had been shut before they left for the party, but said that it would be unusual for it to be open as it would bang in the wind at night if left unbolted, disturbing both their own sleep and that of their neighbours. The gates have two bolts on the garden side, one at the top, one at the bottom. The assumption was that somebody had climbed into the garden, unbolting the gate for a quick escape. Whether this was an opportunistic wanderer or something more planned, nobody knows.

All the neighbours were questioned. The focus turned to Alice's parents for a while. They were demonised for leaving children alone in the house. The press suggested they had killed her, then tried to cover it up. This turned out to be a costly mistake for more than one national newspaper. Forensics found no evidence of foul play within the house, nor could they find anything to suggest that anyone had entered the property. No hair or skin samples, no footprints, no DNA.

In the days after Alice was gone, the police received a phone call from a resident claiming to have seen a man in the street.

This sparked a number of reports from various neighbours, agreeing that they too had seen an unfamiliar man in the days leading up to the bank holiday weekend, though any descriptions were extremely conflicting. Some said he was tall, others short, one said he was of ethnic origin, others were certain he was white. My brother, Adam, along with a group of local children who had been playing in the woods during that weekend, also claimed a strange man had been watching them, and had even tried to talk to them.

As time went on, everyone became a suspect, because quite frankly, the police had nothing. The atmosphere in Pear Tree Close deteriorated from a friendly close-knit community to a paranoid untrusting place where people were all suspicious of each other. Children no longer played out in the streets.

My parents were questioned further after we moved away. You can understand how this could look suspicious, but of course it came to nothing. Every neighbour not at the party came under scrutiny, and eventually eyes turned towards the Abbotts' next-door neighbour, Alan Gillespie. Gillespie lived alone with his dog at number twenty-four. He had no wife, no children and as far as anyone could tell, no friends. The perfect scapegoat when a young girl vanishes without a trace. The police questioned him on numerous occasions.

Over the years I've read many articles about the case, and in the eyes of the press, Gillespie was guilty. It didn't matter if he was or not, the papers had made up their minds and the public agreed. His life was ruined. He became an outcast; he lost his job. He was subjected to a number of attacks. He had 'paedophile' spray painted in large red letters across the front of his house. He also claims his dog was poisoned, although the police seemed to ignore this at the time. On one occasion he was assaulted by a gang of parents in the middle of the street. Nobody helped him. People looked on and continued with their daily routines because they were sure; he had taken Alice and deserved what he got.

The police could find no evidence linking Alan Gillespie to Alice, or the house, and eventually they had to let him go free, but the public still blamed him. Despite this, he has never left Pear Tree Close. He still lives in the same house, next door to Alice's mother. The thing that troubles me with the theory of Alan Gillespie's guilt is that I never remember him being creepy in any way. He was a kind man who kept himself to himself. I used to stroke his dog sometimes when I saw them out for a walk. The old Alsatian would roll over onto her back and let me rub her belly. I can't remember what the dog was called. I didn't even know Gillespie's name before I came across it in the papers years later.

I've read hundreds of cuttings, newspaper articles and online forums regarding the case. I've read witness statements and police testimonials. Nobody had any reason to link Gillespie to Alice's kidnapping aside from idle gossip. As far as I can work out, he had never upset anyone, had never fallen out with the neighbours, but when the shit hit the fan, the families closed ranks and anyone who wasn't one of them was in the firing line. Gillespie was the obvious man to point the finger at. He was not at the party with the rest of them. He did not socialise. He was not married and had no family, which made him different. And we all know how people are terrified of those who are different.

With no evidence and no conviction, the case was left unsolved. Alice's parents have raised thousands of pounds in charity to try to track her. If you say the name Alice Abbott to anyone these days, chances are they will know who she is. The little girl who was never found. Most people have come to the conclusion that she is dead, and when I analyse it rationally, this is probably what I believe too. There was a time when you couldn't go anywhere without seeing her face on a poster, in the papers, or on the news. If she were out there, then somebody would have recognised her.

Every now and then a case comes into the news that gives me new hope. A girl who has been missing for thirty years manages to escape the underground dungeon in which she has been held captive, and is found. Another in America has been living with a sect, disguised under a burka, and paraded around in public for years. A woman in Germany has been living in her father's garage for forty years and has given birth to five of his children. Nobody was even aware that the woman existed. A handful of stories like this have made their way into the press over the years, and each time I wonder if Alice is still out there somewhere. I wonder if she is in pain. Does she remember me? When I think of the possible alternatives, sometimes I pray that she *is* dead.

4

Twenty-five years does its best to numb the pain, but I would be lying if I said that I had moved on. Without closure, I've been unable to accept that she is gone. I think of her often. When I see a pretty blonde girl in the street, or when I am getting dressed in the morning and my eyes wander past Toby, the bear sitting in the corner of my room on my dresser. In reality I've known a life without Alice far longer than I ever knew one with her.

I sometimes wonder what life would have been like if Alice was still here. I wonder if we would still be friends, or if we would have fallen out over something trivial. I wonder if my brother and I would be closer. I also think about my parents. The whole messy affair affected everyone in different ways. My parents were always very wary after Alice disappeared. I was never allowed out on my own, and we were never left without a babysitter. My mother wouldn't even pop to the local shop without getting a neighbour to sit in with us. Even when I was in my teens, she would insist on a sitter rather than entrusting me to look after Adam. I used to resent her for that at times. I felt that she thought I couldn't be trusted to protect my brother. My parents changed a great deal in the years after we moved. They lost their spark and became more introverted. They rarely socialised and didn't really make any new friends. I don't think anyone who knew Alice, or was involved with the investigation, came out the other side as the person they would have been.

For me, it formed a big part of the adult I am now. It inspired me to study investigative journalism at London's Birkbeck University. I had graduated with a first-class honours degree, but never used it to get a first-class job. I've always somehow felt I don't deserve one. We all suffer from imposter syndrome from time to time. My insecurity has always prevented me from applying for jobs that I probably should have. Instead I spent years drifting between posts at trashy magazines and tabloid newspapers, writing stories about sheep worrying, and local business men who were caught with their trousers down, until eventually finding a job at *Yours, truly!* magazine, the exclamation mark at the end of our title sums up everything about us. 'Real stories about real people' is our strapline. To say that this is one of the classier publications I've worked on isn't really saying much, but it is an easy job, and it pays the bills, so there I've stayed for the past seven years. I've tried to get on with life, but I don't think my life is what it could have been.

I'm thirty-seven and single. I have little interest in a relationship. I dabbled of course, when at university, but found that on the whole boys and men always want more than I'm able to give them. Nowadays, men hit on me often. I pretend not to notice, so people think I am aloof or stuck-up, maybe even unfriendly. I don't really care. I suppose I would be classed as attractive. I've grown into my features, I'm no longer a clumsy-looking dumpy girl. I realised in my early twenties that shorter hairstyles suited my face shape more, so that is how I keep it. It also takes far less time to dry after a shower so it works for me on many levels.

When I was young, I think I very much lived in Alice's

shadow. Next to her, I used to always feel dull and unattractive. But now, I can easily command a room when I walk in, whether I want to or not. My body is by no means that of a glamour model. I was never blessed with large breasts but nonetheless, men still stare at me. I don't stare back. To even catch their eye usually gives them the false impression that I'm interested, and then they don't leave me alone.

I don't own my flat. I don't own my car. I have lots of money in the bank because I never spend it on anything other than the essentials. I go to work and I come home. I sometimes meet up with some 'friends' from university, but this is a rare occurrence. To be perfectly honest, any relationships I formed at university have fallen by the wayside in recent years. Most people my age are married with babies or small children to obsess over. I'm the exception in my circle. More and more, as we met for dinner or coffee, my eyes would glaze over as they would regale me with the latest tales of what their kids had been doing. I would smile and nod, and they'd be oblivious to the fact that I wasn't in the slightest bit interested. Either that, or they knew and didn't care. It's such a shame that when people have kids, they lose every shred of their own personalities. It's probably an unpopular view, but I find people all become so very dull after they give birth. It makes me wonder what we used to talk about *before* the babies and husbands came along. These days I have little in common with anyone I used to socialise with, and I would rather stay at home and read a good book than spend an evening in a noisy bar listening to people talk about potty training.

I don't really make new friends. I find most people annoying, or boring, or both, and can't be bothered making small talk at work. I don't have the need for social interaction that most other human beings crave. I think that a great deal of this is shaped from the experience of losing my friend. The fear of losing someone you love is a great deterrent from actually allowing yourself to become close to anyone.

Truth be known, I had given up trying to discover what happened to Alice many years ago. I put a great deal of my twenties into researching the case, looking into all leads, suspects and lines of enquiry. I was obsessed. Everything led to a big fat nothing. Alice had vanished. Nobody had seen her. Nobody knew where she was. This was the sad but accepted truth of the matter. It's just one of life's great mysteries. I'm nervous about returning to Palmerston, but in a way it may help to bring me some closure on the whole sad affair.

As I pack, my mind drifts to the conversation I had with Alice's mother a week earlier on the phone. It must have been very hard for her, speaking to the grown-up friend of a child she never got to see become an adult. She sounded sad when I told her the reason for my call. Of course she insisted that I should stay with her. She has a spare room, and hotels in the area can be expensive. I declined the offer at first, not wanting to sound too eager, but eventually it was agreed. I'm welcome to stay as long as I need to. Dave actually did a little victory dance when I told him.

I place my laptop and my iPad into the carry case, close it and zip it up, placing it neatly onto the bedside table. Sitting on the edge of the bed, I start to feel nervous. I don't know what I expect to find after all these years. I should have returned a long time ago. I was always fond of Alice's mother, but after Alice was gone, we were awkward around each other. I suppose I was a constant reminder of what she had lost. Sometimes, I would catch her staring at me with a look that I could only describe as anger, maybe even hatred. When my family moved away, it must have been a relief for the Abbotts, although they would never have admitted it. Did Alice's mother ever wish it had been me? Probably, in the same way that my parents were glad it was not.

I climb into bed. In the morning I'm going home.

Closing my eyes, I see Alice's face as I drift off to sleep.

5

Driving into Palmerston, I'm surprised at how unfamiliar it all looks to me. I half expected it to awaken feelings and memories locked away for many years, but in reality I feel nothing. I could be anywhere. The rain drums down onto the roof of my car, the rhythm slightly soothing and hypnotic. I feel as if I've never been here. This place is nothing to me. And then I reach Pear Tree Close.

As I drive down the street towards Alice's house, things become slightly more familiar. At first glance not much has changed from my cloudy memory. The red-brick houses look older, the maple trees more established, but in general it is as I recall. Expensive-looking *fairly* modern town houses (modern being a *fairly* relative term, in comparison, that is, to the rest of Palmerston), that should look out of place in the village surroundings. They are pretty in a way, but a world apart from the period cottages and thatched roofs that adorn the rest of the village. But somehow they fit. Ivy has grown up the sides of the once-new red-brick walls. The surroundings have almost engulfed the buildings, trying to make them a part of itself.

As I make my way towards the end of the street, towards our

houses, I start to see the signs of decay. The once well-mani-
cured lawns look less so these days. Some of the houses have
overflowing plastic bins out the front. To my right, I see the tall
trees of the woods behind towering over the houses. I drive past
number twenty-four and my eyes fix firmly on the front of the
house. Alan Gillespie's house.

I scan the building but see no signs of life or movement
within, yet I know he is probably in there. He has become somewhat of a recluse over the years. Is he standing in the gloomy
front room, watching my car as I drive slowly past his window? I
push the thought from my mind as I park up outside number
twenty-two. Where Alice used to live.

Climbing out of my old battered silver Mondeo, my eyes flick
to the other side of the street... my childhood home. A red sports
car sits in the driveway. It looks somewhat out of place in these
run-down surroundings. The window frames have been painted
dark green, and somebody has added fake leaded lights. The
cheap self-adhesive kind. A mass of ivy climbs up much of the
front of the house but apart from this, it looks the same.

I stand and stare at the house, once so familiar. I search
within myself for some warmth, some wonderful childhood
memory, but all I feel is empty. Any good memories have been
drowned by the horror of what happened across the road at
number twenty-two. My eyes wander up the front of the house
and come to rest on what was my bedroom window. A vase of
artificial flowers sits on the windowsill where I once sat and
waved across the street to my friend. The last time I saw her.

I shake my head and look back down towards the front door.

I notice the net curtain to the left of the door move.

Is somebody watching me?

I turn back towards Alice's house. The same old gate I
remember creaks open on its hinges. The gate is rusty, the paint
flakes off in patches. I feel its rough surface against the skin of

my hand, and I recall how house-proud the Abbotts had once been. I shiver, wrapping my arms tightly around my body as I walk down the path. It was so familiar to me, but now it seems like an alien landscape. I used to spend so many hours playing happily on the perfect front lawn. The sound of children laughing is nowhere to be heard now. The care and pride that used to be taken in the presentation of the house and its gardens is nowhere to be seen. The lawn is overgrown and patchy. Weeds strangle what little plant life is left alive in the beds, while rubbish and carrier bags lay strewn across the garden. I take another tentative look over my shoulder towards my old house, and again I see the net curtains shift.

I am definitely being watched.

I don't know who lives at number twenty-three these days, but I make a mental note to find out.

I turn back towards the door, feeling self-conscious. I press the bell firmly. The familiar chime echoes through the house, before the sound of shuffling footsteps can be heard coming down the hallway. As the door opens, I barely recognise the old lady standing in front of me. Limp wavy greying hair hangs messily around a face whose wrinkles belong to someone much older than her sixty-or-so years. She is dressed in shabby jeans that were once blue, and a crumpled old grey shirt. A cheap-looking grubby black cardigan is pulled tightly around her; arms folded across her chest. Her toes poke through holes in the end of her slippers.

Her eyes survey me, looking for something she recognises.

They stop above my chest as she notices the half heart-shaped pendant that hangs around my neck. I've worn it every day since I was ten. Alice had the other half. A weak smile appears on Helen's lips but fails to travel as far as her eyes.

'Emily,' she says, almost in a whisper. It's a statement rather than a question.

I smile at her and she steps forward, enveloping me in a tight hug. A familiar scent fills my nostrils as I relax into her embrace. In that moment, two people are getting something that has long been missing from their lives. For me, the warmth of a mother's hug, for her, the feeling of a daughter in her arms. I don't know who pulls away first, but the moment has passed.

'Please, come in. The kettle's on. I was just going to make some tea.'

She takes my coat and hangs it on a row of hooks on the wall. As she stands aside, I get my first glimpse inside the house. I stare at the old hooks, and for a moment I'm eleven again, and a wave of sadness washes over me. I compose myself and follow her down the unlit hallway. I remember the house as if I had just been here yesterday. I know its layout like the back of my hand. To the right of the front door is a small toilet. Opposite on the left of the hallway is the living room. I see magazines strewn across the floor in the doorway. Further down to the right is a small dining room, opposite the staircase, and an under-stair storage cupboard. At the end of the hallway is a large kitchen diner with French doors and a picture window looking out to the garden.

The rain beats against the glass windowpanes of the front door behind me. I note that the house is mostly unchanged from when I was last here in terms of decor. The same pictures hang crookedly on the walls. Alice as a baby. Alice and Tom in their school photo, toothy grins beaming out; I vaguely remember the day these pictures were taken. Alice's mother had put Alice's hair into two pigtail plaits and secured them with red ribbons. Alice had shaken them out ten minutes before the pictures were taken, leaving her hair wavy and kinked. I remember thinking how beautiful she was, and so I had copied her, but my hair just ended up looking messy, and my mother would tut and comment every time she looked at the picture for many years to come.

The same old wide striped cream and brown wallpaper hangs below a battered dado rail, although now the paper is tinged yellow with nicotine stains and peeling at the corners. The plain cream carpet looks a dirty shade of brown, stains and marks and the odd cigarette burn cover its surface; a noticeable path is worn away in the centre of the hall. The house smells of cigarettes, grease and sweat. Helen Abbott never smoked when I was a child. Her husband, Jim, would sneak the odd one, but *never* in the house. I would sometimes see him from my bedroom window, huddled outside the front door, puffing away. If he saw me he would wave and try to hide the cigarette, as if he was embarrassed.

Helen has certainly let everything go to seed.

I remember her always being immaculately turned out. She would wear designer clothes with expensive-looking accessories. I remember once Alice and I getting into a great deal of trouble when we were about eight or nine, for going into her mother's jewellery box to play with a beautiful necklace which turned out to be antique diamonds worth a fortune. A family heirloom. I wonder if it's lying upstairs in the same old jewellery box, gathering dust.

The glamour of Alice's mother was a stark contrast to my mother's Plain-Jane way of dressing. My mother wore trousers, or leggings, a lot. You only ever saw her in a dress or a skirt at special occasions, and when she did wear them she looked awkward and uncomfortable. As a child I used to be so jealous of Alice and her family. Her stylish mother, the spotless house and the brother who obviously adored her. Sometimes, I would fantasise that my family would disappear, leaving me behind, and the Abbotts would step in, taking me in as one of their own.

Careful what you wish for, I think, as my parents' faces flash into my head.

Children never realise how good they have it. The grass is always greener on the other side, and I feel more than a little ashamed as I recall my childhood reveries.

As I look around at the state of the Abbotts' house, all I feel is sympathy.

6

As we enter the kitchen, I glance over the table, through the grimy picture window out to the garden and the woods beyond. The garden is untidy and overgrown. Weeds cover the lawn, which is at least a foot high. An old brick barbecue up against the fence is mostly hidden beneath a blanket of ivy. A bird feeder dangles beneath an overhanging branch from next door's garden, the fat balls within it the only sign that anybody inhabits this space. A few chaffinches and pigeons flap greedily around it. A squirrel sits on top of the fence, waiting patiently to steal whatever is left behind.

Helen follows the direction of my gaze.

'So many birds round here. I love watching them. So innocent...' she trails off.

'I was sorry to hear about you and Mr Abbott,' I offer sadly. I had read in the news a few years earlier that they had separated.

Her face doesn't change. 'I wouldn't waste too much energy worrying about him,' she mutters.

'Are you still in touch?'

She shakes her head sadly, a distant look in her eyes.

'He walked out, five years ago. Said he was going to buy cigarettes... never came home. I've not seen or heard from him since. He left all his things. When it became clear he wasn't coming back, I boxed them up and put them away.' She pauses. 'Neither of us really... you know... we both struggled for many years... after, Alice...I mean to say... we...' She searches for the right words and looks out of the window, clearly embarrassed.

'You both had a lot to deal with... it would take its toll on any relationship. It must be very lonely in this house without him.'

'I have Tom. And the birds, of course.'

'Does Tom visit a lot?'

'He still lives here... never moved out,' she says with a sad look in her eyes.

This comes as a surprise. Most details of the Abbotts' private lives were reported in some tabloid, but for the most, Tom's life has been of little interest to the press. Apart from one time when he had got into a fight with a girl outside a nightclub. It had gone to court, but eventually the case was thrown out. I had no idea what he was doing with his life aside from this incident.

Helen continues. 'He has suffered a great deal. He's never really been able to accept what happened. He couldn't bear the guilt of having been in the house when she was taken. He was asleep in the next room, as you know. Blamed himself for a very long time, still does to some degree, I think. He dropped out of school very young and works in the coffee shop near the church. I don't suppose you'll remember it. Lovely scones.'

The words come out of her mouth like she is reciting a well-learned script. As if she is apologising for the perceived failures of her troubled son, or perhaps even worse, her failures as a mother.

'He doesn't remember anything about that night, you know. He's blocked it all out. He was only eight. I think whatever he saw has been lost forever. The police tried hypnotism, and psychologists, but there's nothing there. Just a void. We kept him out of the press as much as we could. The general consensus is that he slept through it all... but I'm sure he saw something. Who knows what. The doctors call it psycho something or other. Apparently it's quite common after a traumatic experience. He has terrible nightmares, even now, but he can never remember them when he wakes up. He screams and cries in his sleep. It's terrible to hear. Perhaps it's better he never remembers.' She pauses, as if she feels she has said too much. 'He's at work just now, but he'll be home this evening. He's been... looking forward to seeing you. He remembers you fondly.'

'It'll be good to catch up with him,' I reply. 'I think Adam's still in touch with him.'

'Your brother? Yes. He turned up here one day, years ago. I didn't know who he was at first, but when he told me, I could see it. It's his eyes... they haven't changed.' She pauses, a look in her eyes that I can't quite read. 'I'm... glad Tom has a friend. He didn't have anyone for such a long time. People didn't know how to behave around him.'

She doesn't volunteer anything further. She puts a cup of tea in front of me, placing a plate of biscuits on the table next to it. I take a bite of a stale digestive, then place it back on the plate awkwardly, trying not to screw my face up at the musty taste. I suspect the packet of biscuits has been open and sitting in the kitchen cupboard for some time.

The rain has abated so I go out to collect my bag. As I approach my car, I notice a girl standing on the other side of the street, watching me curiously. She's in her twenties and has blue streaks in her long tangle of black hair, a stud in her nose and a ring through her bottom lip. She is painfully thin, and her features are awkward. She wears far too much make-up and cheap-looking plastic jewellery. Her knees poke though ripped black jeans and a tatty crocheted jumper hangs loosely over a red crop top, exposing her ribs and belly button, which is also pierced. He skin is adorned with large scrawling tattoos. A withering rose here. A skull there. Some words I can't make out. I feel old as I look her up and down.

When she realises I'm watching, she turns and hurries away down the street, ducking into a driveway at the other end. She pulls a key from her pocket and enters the house without giving me another glance. I can't help wondering what Helen thinks of her neighbours these days. When I go back into the house, she's waiting at the bottom of the stairs.

'I hope you don't mind, but you'll be in Alice's old room.'

She avoids my eyes as she turns and heads up the stairs.

I follow her, but I know where I'm going.

At the top of the stairs is a long narrow landing. A tatty red and brown paisley carpet adorns the stairs and the floor. Helen and Alice's bedrooms are at the front, looking across the street towards my old house. Tom's room is to the left, opposite the family bathroom, both overlooking the garden and the woods beyond.

Helen turns right at the top of the stairs, stopping outside the bedroom door on the right of the hallway. She opens it, stepping to one side with a small hand gesture indicating, as if I wouldn't know.

I half expect the room to be the same as it was when I was last here, with Care Bear wallpaper and New Kids on the Block posters on the walls.

Instead I am faced with a plain white room, devoid of any character. An old-fashioned wooden wardrobe in the corner is the only thing I recognise, although the stickers that once adorned it have been carefully scraped off. Clinical crisp white bedding covers the single bed against one wall, a heavy-piled cream carpet covers the floor.

This room is pristine.

There's not a speck of dust on the dresser opposite the bed, or indeed anywhere in this space. The contrast of this room from the rest of the house is unbelievable, as if this is the only room that gets attended to. A vase of large white lilies sits on the windowsill in front of wide white wooden venetian blinds. A few of the petals have fallen onto the carpet. Helen hurries over and picks them up. The pungent perfume of the flowers wafts out through the open door, like horse piss.

As she watches me, she holds the corner of her cardigan in one hand, fiddling with the threads between her fingers. 'We didn't change this room for a long time. I wanted it to be the same as it was... if she came home. Jim decorated it not long before he left. He said enough was enough.'

Helen's eyes drift towards my tiny bag.

'There should be plenty of space for your things in the wardrobe and the drawers there, but if you need anything, just let me know. You'll find towels in the airing cupboard at the end of the hall, and there are toiletries in the bathroom. Feel free to use whatever you want. I'll let you unpack.'

She turns to leave.

'Mrs Abbott, thanks so much for your hospitality. I appreciate this must be very difficult for you.'

She faces me again. 'Life goes on. Even if we sometimes don't want it to. Please, call me Helen.'

Another weak, unconvincing, smile.

She leaves me, closing the door softly behind her.

I put my case down on the bed, glancing once more around the room. Part of me is relieved that it's so different to how it was when I was a child, but a part of me is slightly disappointed. Crossing to the window, I see to my surprise that the blue-haired girl is standing at my car, nosily peering through the windows. She tries the handle of the driver's side door, finding it locked. I take a step back so I can't be seen. I take out my phone, snapping a picture of her. She looks nervously around her, then up the driveway to Alice's house. She shakes her head, stuffs headphones angrily into her ears, then hurries away, fishing around in her pocket for her phone. She hammers away at the keyboard as she leaves, typing a text message, I assume.

Odd, I think. I'll need to keep an eye on that one.

I return to my case and begin to unpack its contents. Taking the diary from the top of the pile, I slide it under a pillow on the bed. I open the wardrobe, noticing that on the inside of the door there's a small patch of graffiti scratched into the wood, towards the bottom. 'Alice and Emily – '89' it says in crude carved letters. A little pointy heart is scratched underneath it. I don't remember doing this, although I suppose I must have been present. I wonder if Helen knows it's there, or if it was supposed to be erased with the rest of Alice's history in this room.

It doesn't take me long to put my things away. I place my laptop onto the dresser. I take Toby, Alice's bear, and sit it on the pillow. It's grubby from being handled many times, and looks out of place in its divested surroundings. I take my diary from under the pillow, flipping through its dog-eared pages. I stop at the last entry.

In large angry tear-stained letters, I have scrawled, over and over, 'WHERE IS ALICE?'.

7

I make my way downstairs, looking for Helen. I find her in the front room, sitting in a tired old armchair by the window. The covering of the chair is almost threadbare, and the fabric on the tops of the armrests is so worn that the stuffing pokes out through holes. She doesn't hear me come down the stairs. She is muttering to herself, shaking her head, picking at the threads with her fingers.

I cough so she realises I'm there and she looks up at me. Her eyes are red and sore looking. I can see she has been crying.

'Are you all right?' I ask, hoping that I'm not the cause of her upset, but knowing that I most likely am.

She rubs at her eyes with her left hand and swats me away with the other. 'I'm fine. It's just... Seeing the young woman you've grown up to be, it makes me wonder what Alice would be like now.'

She brushes her hair away from her face with her hand, tucking it behind her ear, and for the first time I see a trace of the Helen Abbott that I once knew.

'If it's going to be too hard for you, I really don't mind finding a hotel.'

'Nonsense, I won't hear another word about that. I'll be absolutely fine.'

She looks around, taking in the piles of papers and dirty mugs, the crumbs on the floor.

'You'll have to excuse the mess. I've let everything get a bit on top of me since Jim left.'

I'm embarrassed. I don't know what to say, so I shake my head and smile.

I feel I must break the silence.

'I'm so glad you agreed to talk to me. My boss is very keen to hear your thoughts on the new situation. I wasn't sure how you would feel about it all.'

'I'll do what I can, but I don't really know if I can be of any help with your story, I'm afraid. I don't follow the news much these days, so can't say I know anything about this little girl who's been taken. It's twenty-five years since Alice disappeared. It's unlikely these cases are linked, if you ask me.'

'My editor is keen to go down the route that whoever took Alice is still at large... and of course, Alan Gillespie still lives next door. It's mad that he stayed here after everything that happened.'

Helen stands up, shuffling towards me. She stands very close. I can smell her stale breath and body odour. 'Alan Gillespie is innocent. He's harmless. It's shameful the things he's had to endure over the years.' She shakes her head.

'You feel sorry for him?' I'm somewhat surprised by her reaction.

'Yes, I feel *very* sorry for him. I don't condone anything that has been done to him. Not in Alice's name, and certainly not in mine. We have become companions over the years. That might sound odd to you, but he needed a friend. And so did I. Do you know, at the weekend, after it emerged about that girl going missing, someone put dog mess though his letterbox? You can't imagine what it's been like for him. I saw him out there, on his hands and knees, scrubbing it away. It was shameful! People round here don't have a clue what that poor man has been through.'

'Why doesn't he just move?'

'Why should he have to?' Helen retorts.

'You don't think he had anything to do with Alice's disappearance then.'

'Of course he didn't. Alan Gillespie is a loner, but that is all.'

'I read that someone killed his dog.'

She shakes her head again. 'It was disgraceful, I tell you. Someone fed the dog oven cleaner. The poor animal was in agony. That stuff ate away at her from the inside. Alan had to put her out of her misery in the garden. There wasn't time to get to the vet.'

'Most people seem to think he was guilty.'

'Most people are very foolish. The only thing he was ever guilty of was being an outsider. The police never found anything to link him to Alice, and God only knows they tried. Alan is innocent.'

'But surely you have to admit that it's at least a possibility.'

'He's innocent.'

There's an uncomfortable silence and I struggle for something to say, then I remember the curtains twitching across the street as I arrived.

'Who lives in my old house?' I enquire nonchalantly.

Helen's eyes don't shift. 'It's changed hands so many times over the years I've lost track. I don't really take a lot to do with people anymore.'

I get the impression from her tone that she doesn't want to discuss this any further, so I leave her to her own company and return to my room.

8

S andie Jackson is sitting at the dressing table in her bedroom as she applies her lipstick. She is not too old for 'Ravishing Red' despite what her daughters persistently tell her.

Her blonde hair is tucked neatly into a tidy 'up-do', her flawless make-up complementing her features. Who cares if a woman her age isn't supposed to wear that much make-up? It makes her feel good.

She wears a knee-length royal-blue shift dress, just short enough to show off her shapely legs well, but not so short that she looks cheap.

Appearance is everything she tells herself as she slips her feet into a pair of black pumps.

She makes her way across the bedroom, opening the floral curtains to the new grey day in Palmerston. The pavements are shining wet, it has been raining all night, and the deluge shows no signs of letting up any time soon.

She sighs and goes to turn away, but something catches her eye. Across the road, Helen Abbott's front door is opening and the old goat is standing in her doorway, peering out into the rain. Sandie smiles to herself as she takes in Helen Abbott's attire. She is wearing her usual filthy jeans and tatty old cardigan. She pulls the garment tightly around her body, as if it will somehow protect her from the elements. Her limp greasy greying hair falls lifelessly around her face. She glances up and sees Sandie staring at her from the bedroom window. Sandie makes no effort to move out of view.

Let her stare, she thinks, shaking her head.

Helen Abbott quickly closes her front door as Sandie turns away and heads out onto the landing. She makes her way down the stairs. Her home is long overdue some redecoration. She hasn't touched it since she moved in. It had been freshly decorated for the sale, and the old owner's choice of decor did not offend her taste. It wasn't important to her at that point. She had other goals to achieve. She had never planned to live there for very long, but months had turned into years, and here she was, almost five years later, still in the same small house that did not suit her at all.

She rarely had friends round to visit as she was too embarrassed. Her daughters could not understand how a woman who takes so much pride in her appearance, could take so little pride in her home. They were mortified when she sold her detached mansion house in a leafy suburb, only to move into what they saw as a far-inferior property, in this, of all streets in town. But the house is just a base. Nothing more. Somewhere for her to sleep, and keep an eye on things. As soon as she has her answers, she will leave this life behind her. But for now, she can't.

She heads into the living room and, standing at the window, twitches at the long net curtains with her slim fingers. The rain is battering down. It bounces off the pavement in front of her waterlogged front lawn. The last of her summer flowers are looking sorry for themselves in the downpour.

She sighs again to herself, a habit she is very aware she does too often, and shakes her head, letting the lace drop from between her fingers. She brushes past a pile of *House and Home* magazines on the coffee table, making her way down her narrow hallway to the kitchen. She can never understand how anyone manages to live in such small houses long-term. She constantly feels like a hamster in a cage, *but each to their own*, she thinks.

Flicking on the kettle, she takes a cheap mug out of the cupboard and spoons in two heaped teaspoons of instant coffee, then pours in some skimmed milk from the fridge. As the milk splashes into her cup, she sees lumps floating in it. Raising the bottle to her nose, she takes a sniff and the rank smell of sour milk fills her nostrils. She gags, turning to the sink to pour the contents away. She picks up the mug, rinsing it under the tap, then starts the process again. She's not fussy. She can drink her coffee black.

She strolls back to her front room and leans against the wall next to her window. Coffee in one hand, she pulls at the net curtains again. Helen Abbott is once more standing at her door, peering out through the rain, a glum slightly worried expression on her haggard old face.

Sandie can sense that something is going on.

Helen Abbott is rarely seen these days. She tends to keep herself shut away in her dark house, only venturing out for essential trips, so to see her twice on the same day in the space of twenty minutes is an odd occurrence in itself. Sandie sips her bitter black coffee as she watches her neighbour. Helen looks as if she is waiting for someone. She glances anxiously up and down the road, then checks her watch. Aside from her neighbour, Alan Gillespie, and of course her oddball son who, although in Sandie's opinion is far too old to be doing so, still lives at home with his mother, she never has any visitors.

Nobody comes to see Helen Abbott. Nobody cares anymore.

She shut herself off from the world and made no attempt to

be polite to her neighbours. She doesn't speak to Sandie if she passes her in the supermarket, or even in the street. In five years, she has hardly said as many words to her. Sandie tried at first. Helen's front door was of course the first Sandie knocked on when she moved in. She pretended not to recognise her, or have any idea who she was, and feigned the usual 'I've just moved in over the road...' spiel that she had practised so it sounded believable, but Helen Abbott had put an end to Sandie's plan before it had even begun. She simply looked her up and down, then closed the door in her face.

Sandie had tried a few more times to speak to her over the next few weeks, but Helen Abbott had made it abundantly clear that she had no desire to be friends, making Sandie's goal much harder to achieve. And here she was, no closer to the answers she sought, still stuck in this shithole of a neighbourhood, alone. Her friends had all fallen by the wayside over the years as she had dedicated herself wholly to her cause. It had become somewhat of an obsession. It was unintentional of course. She used to tell herself that she could walk away at any time if she chose to do so, but she doesn't bother trying to convince herself that is true these days.

Sandie could not tell anyone what she was really doing in Pear Tree Close. Not even her friends. Of course, none of them could understand her leaving the luxury of her beautiful home on the good side of town, and moving into the dump in which she now resides. But Sandie Jackson has her reasons, and she could not risk Helen Abbott finding out who she was. She had been very careful to make sure of that.

Sandie hears a car pulling up outside, across the road. She hurries back to the window, pulling once more at the edge of her net curtain, being careful she is not seen. Nobody likes a curtain twitcher... especially in this neighbourhood. A beat-up old silver Ford Mondeo has pulled up outside the Abbott house. Sandie makes it her business to know every car that frequently visits Pear Tree Close. She knows the relatives. She knows the drug dealers. She even knows the cars that belong to the random casual sex partners of some of her neighbours. This car, she has never seen before, of that she is absolutely certain. Sandie watches with more than a mild interest as a short-haired woman in her mid-thirties climbs out of the vehicle. She is pretty and petite, with very short dark hair. Why these young women have to cut all their hair off these days mystifies Sandie. If one of her daughters were to arrive at her door with that style, Sandie would be mortified. Of course, the likelihood of either of her daughters visiting her here is slim to none.

The mystery woman is wearing tight stonewashed jeans and a black sweater with a short black leather jacket. She has that casual cool appearance that seems unplanned, but in reality she has probably stood in front of a mirror for hours trying to perfect it. The woman turns briefly and stares right towards Sandie's house. Sandie is so surprised that she quickly drops the curtain. The woman turns and slowly makes her way through Helen Abbott's front gate and up the garden path. She glances over her shoulder back towards Sandie's house again, catching Sandie a second time.

Sandie panics and drops the curtain once more, this time spilling her coffee on the clean carpet. She rubs it in with the toe of her pump, then pulls back the curtain again. Helen Abbott is standing at her door, arms folded across her chest. She eyes the woman coldly as they exchange a few words, and then the strangest thing happens. Helen steps forward and gives the woman an awkward hug before inviting her inside, closing the door behind them. Helen Abbott very rarely has visitors, and even less that she chooses to hug. Sandie stays at the window for what seems like a long time, but nothing of any interest happens out in the street. She looks up at the rain pouring from the dark brooding sky, and knows that something odd is going on. She doesn't know what yet, but she plans to find out.

Sandie perches on the arm of her chair, and as she does so, she sloshes some more coffee from her mug, but this time it spills down the front of her dress. She sighs and tuts, then hurries upstairs to change.

9

I make my excuses and go out towards the kitchen, taking my leather jacket from the hook on the wall as I pass through the hallway.

Unlocking the back door, I step out into the garden.

The smell of wet pavement fills my nostrils.

There are broken paving slabs directly outside the door, which are green and slimy with moss and bird shit. The garden feels desolate and although the air is not cold for September, I shiver. In the middle of the garden sits the old swing set, rusty and unused. The seat rocks gently back and forth in the wind, chains creaking. I pass it and let my fingertips brush over the cold metal. Twigs crack under my feet in the long grass.

My foot treads into something soft and the smell of shit drifts up from beneath me.

I feel devoid of any emotions as I approach the gate at the back of the garden. Crouching down, I examine the corroded bolt. I take some photos, then stand to do the same with the top bolt. They are heavy and solid. I work them open, scraping my knuckles in the process. The latch is stiff but the gate opens surprisingly easily. I turn back towards the house, taking a few more photos, then out towards the lane again, snapping a couple of pictures in each direction, and then out into the woods opposite me.

There are piles of black plastic bags outside on the ground, the smell of rubbish and rotting vegetables is almost unbearable.

A fox or some other wild animal, I assume, has been at the bags, and the contents are strewn around the overgrown path. It's narrow, less than a metre wide. My memory of it is different... I thought it was wider. A low wire fence has been erected across the way, separating the woods from the path. This is relatively new. When we were children, you could walk straight into the woods. I cross the gravel, stepping over the fence.

As I venture into the woods, the air feels cooler and damp. Brambles catch at my jeans, through the denim to my legs. Pushing my way through overgrown ferns and tree branches, something scratches at my ankle. I look down to examine the damage, but the light is too dim.

The tall trees are denser than they used to be, blocking out most of the daylight. I venture further into the woods, taking a few photos as I go. I turn back towards the houses, but the view is obscured by the undergrowth and trees. If you didn't know that the houses were there, you would think you were in the middle of a vast forest. I turn back into the woods and continue the journey.

'Where are you, Alice?' I whisper to myself.

I take a few more pictures, reviewing them as I walk. They are too dark, just a mass of black and the odd shaft of light filtering through the dense branches. I activate the flash on my phone and try again.

Somewhere close by a twig cracks. Movement in my peripheral vision. A rabbit perhaps. Too big. A deer? I hope. A crow caws from somewhere within the dense undergrowth. The sound echoes around the woods.

I suddenly feel very uneasy.

Am I being watched again?

I tell myself it was just a deer, over and over. I'm so scared that I find myself saying it out loud.

My hand is trembling.

I shine the beam from my phone torch around me in an arc but see nobody. The undergrowth is thick, there are plenty of places for a person to easily stay out of sight.

I push my way back towards the path as fast as I can, thorns tearing at my face and arms as I rush towards the light and I climb back onto the path. My heart's pounding and I'm breathing heavily.

More twigs crack behind me.

I am being followed.

I swear under my breath. I've only been back five minutes and I'm already scaring myself.

'Hello?' The sound of my voice is swallowed up by the thick heavy damp of the trees.

I shout, more assertively than I am feeling. 'Is there someone there?'

Silence.

I take a couple of hurried steps down the path, looking over my shoulder to ensure nobody's following. The path is clear.

I'm not looking where I'm going and I put my foot in something brown, slimy and very smelly.

I slip, landing in a heap on the floor.

The palms of my hands scrape painfully along the gravel and I bang my knee hard on a gate before it swings open.

A tall man stands looking down at me.

'If you've come back to put more shit through my door, you can bugger off.'

Alan Gillespie is in his eighties. He has a serious-looking face with cool grey eyes framed by dark circles. He is thickset. I can tell from looking at him that he used to take care of himself. He has a large solid frame and he looks powerful.

'I'm sorry, I'm not here to cause you any trouble, I assure you.'

He regards me with suspicion. I hold my hands up to show they're empty.

'I'm staying with Helen Abbott and I was... exploring, I suppose.'

Gillespie's face changes. An expression of sadness fills his eyes. 'You're Alice's friend.'

'Yes. My name's Emily Blake.'

'Helen said you were coming.' He holds his hand out, pulling me up from the ground, and I feel the strength from his arm as he does so.

There's mud on my knees. Tiny specks of blood are making a mottled pattern on my hands.

'You'd best come in, so we can get you cleaned up.'

'It's fine really, they're only grazes.'

'There's mud and gravel in those cuts. You'll get an infection.'

I glance down at my upturned hands, brushing leaves and mud from my clothes.

Gillespie looks at my face more closely. He turns and retreats down the path towards the kitchen door.

I follow him, bolting the gate firmly behind me.

As he makes his way across the garden towards his back door, I stop and listen at the gate.

Is it my imagination, or can I hear bushes rustling?

I crane my neck towards the gate, holding my breath.

Footsteps, sprinting away down the gravel path.

10

The house is not at all how I imagined it would be. As dirty and unhomely as Helen Abbott's place is, Gillespie's is warm, cosy and inviting. It smells of fresh coffee and bacon.

He takes a pot of coffee from a percolator on the kitchen side, pouring two cups. He adds milk and sugar to both without asking, sliding one across the worktop towards me. As I drink, he opens a cupboard beneath the sink, taking out a small green first aid box. He removes a little bottle of surgical spirit and pours it onto some cotton wool. Taking each of my hands in turn, he wipes the wadding gently over the grazes. They sting and I close my eyes, sucking in breath through my teeth. His touch is soft as he carefully cleans the wounds. He takes two small squares of gauze dressing and straps them onto my hands with surgical tape.

Placing the box back under the sink, he notices I'm watching him.

'Are you scared of me, Miss Blake?' he asks softly.

I pause for a second before I respond. 'No, I'm not. Should I be?'

He chuckles to himself but his eyes show no humour. 'Depends who you ask.'

'I'm well aware of the allegations against you, Mr Gillespie.'

'I'm sure you are.'

He studies me for a while, looking me up and down.

'So, what are you doing back after all these years?'

'You're probably aware that a young girl has disappeared quite close to here, and the media interest in Alice's case has resurfaced. The magazine I work for wants to run a feature on the two cases, and with my personal knowledge of the area, my editor thought I might be able to get some exclusive material from Mrs Abbott.'

'Yes, I know the official line, but you know as well as I do that it's highly unlikely these two cases are related. So why are you *really* back? Why now?'

I am caught off guard by the directness of his question.

'It's my job to ask questions. To rule out if there is a link, or look for similarities.' I pause for a second. 'And I suppose I'm also still looking for Alice. I need some closure.'

'You won't find her out in those woods, that I can tell you for sure.'

'What happened to Alice, to all of us, has affected so many people, including me. I want to know what happened, so I can move on. I don't want to go through my whole life not knowing. I can't.'

Gillespie studies my face, and I can tell he's pitying me.

I look him in the eye before I speak again. 'Can I ask you a question?'

Gillespie folds his arms in front of his body and leans onto the kitchen work surface, making himself more comfortable. 'You can ask.'

'What do you think happened to Alice? Where do you think she is?'

'That's two questions.'

I hold his gaze.

'What do I think happened to her? That's easy. She's long dead. I don't think that was the intention. Someone saw her, and wanted her. She was a beautiful girl. A bad person saw her, maybe saw you both, playing out in the woods, or walking to school. He wanted her, and he took her. He waited patiently, watching, and when he saw his chance, he went into that house and took her while she was sleeping.' Gillespie takes a sip of coffee before continuing.

'He took her as a plaything, but with the media storm that surrounded her kidnapping, there was no way he could keep her. It would have been impossible. She would have been recognised by everyone back then. So I think he would have panicked and gotten rid of her.'

All I can hear is the ticking of a clock from another room. And my thumping heartbeat.

Blood pulses in my ears. I look down at my hands. Small spots of blood are seeping through the dressings. I know what he's saying is probably true, but it's a blow to actually hear somebody say it out loud.

'As for where she is, that's a bit trickier. The police searched extensively for a long time. Teams were out everywhere for miles, but they never found a shred of physical evidence anywhere, but if you want my opinion, the best bet is the downs.'

The downs were a few miles from Palmerston, and were known these days as the South Downs National Park. It's a vast expanse of land, stretching for roughly ninety miles from Winchester in the west to Eastbourne in the east, crossing three counties, and about six hundred square miles. The police concentrated a great deal of their time searching the downs, but with such a large area to be covered with limited resources, it was hopeless.

'If you wanted a small body to disappear anywhere around here, that would be the place to do it. There are woods, there are hills and fields. There's no way anyone could ever hope to find her up there. The police can vouch for that.'

I had to admit, this would have been my guess, from what I had read of the surrounding areas. It would be quite easy to hide a body, and if you dug deep enough, then it would be unlikely to be disturbed by scavenging wildlife.

I picture Alice's pale limp body in a hole in the ground, earth piled on top of her.

Alan catches the look on my face. 'But what do I know? I'm just an old man. What about you? Do you think she's still alive?'

'I don't know the answer to that question. My mind changes all the time. But realistically, probably not.'

We sit without speaking for a while.

Tick. Tock. Tick. Tock.

The clock is the only sound in the room.

'It was a tragedy what happened to that family. Helen Abbott was a fine figure of a woman. She was the envy of all the other women on this street. But now... It's a pure shame.' He shakes his head. 'And don't get me started on that son of hers.'

I cock my head.

'If you think she's a mess, you wait 'til you see him. Hardly surprising really. Sleeping in the next room while your big sister is stolen away by some... pervert.'

'I can't imagine the damage that's done to him.'

'His mother tells me he wets the bed. A man that age... It drives her to despair. Still, he didn't have the best life after Alice was gone. His parents, they never got over it. I don't suppose you ever do. How could you? They all had their own personal guilt to deal with, I think. But he was just a small boy. He couldn't have changed anything. This street used to be a haven. It's funny how one split second can decide the fate of so many different things. Ripples.'

Alan Gillespie's gaze drifts to the window, and he seems to be somewhere else for a moment.

'Mr Gillespie, I saw a girl out in the street by my car. Can you tell me if you know who she is, please?'

I take out my phone, showing him the picture I took of 'Blue Hair'.

Gillespie shakes his head again.

'Lily,' he says solemnly. 'Now there's a sad one.'

Gillespie strides across the kitchen and heaves himself down onto a chair, taking a few gulps of coffee. 'You probably will have known of her back then. She was just a baby; seven or eight months. Her parents were the Aitkens.'

The Aitkens were the family who hosted the party on that fateful evening. I remember they had a new baby. She was adorable, and Alice and I used to rush over to see her whenever we saw Mrs Aitken pushing her pram down the street. Her smile could melt my heart.

'Most of the other families with kids moved away over the years. Not a place to raise children anymore, though we seem to be getting a few now. Anyway, her parents stayed put. She didn't have any pals. She grew up a very lonely girl. Her father suffered with severe depression. Threw himself from Beachy Head when she was five. You can imagine the effect that would have on anyone, but on a young girl, it was devastating. Then when she was fifteen, her mother was diagnosed with terminal breast cancer.' Another pause while he finishes his drink.

'Lily nursed her for two years and watched her waste away to nothing. With no other family, she bore the brunt of that responsibility herself. When her mother passed away, she inherited it all. The house, the money. That was her one blessing. I don't generally listen to village gossip. I know better than most people what it can do to someone, but I believe she fell in with a very bad crowd. People turning up at the house at all hours. Dodgy deals going on at the door. That girl never had a chance. Like I said, ripples.'

'She seemed very interested in my car, should I be worried?'

Gillespie shrugs. 'The girl is trouble, but she's not stupid.'

'So, this girl who has gone missing, Becky Clarke, you *really* don't think there's any connection to Alice?'

'Do I hell. It's been twenty-five years. That's one heck of a hiatus if it's the same guy. Why wait that long?'

'But it *is* possible?'

'Anything's possible. But I'd say it's extremely unlikely.'

'I need to look into it for my story. Do you know much about what's happened?'

'Just what it said on the news. She left her grandmother's house on foot to make the short walk home. Never made it. It's totally different from what went down with Alice in my opinion. It's a different style. But there are a few unsavoury characters on my radar. More than you'd think for a quiet village. I've had a sniff around. After Alice, I like to keep my eye on things. Mud sticks and all that. I've done my fair share of investigating over the years. You'd be surprised what you can find out if people think you're one of them.'

Gillespie stands to refill his coffee cup. He holds the pot up towards me, raising an eyebrow.

I shake my head.

'These people, they tend to know each other. They like to exchange tips, among other things. I truly expected over the years to hear something about Alice, but there's never been a whisper. None of the local perverts that I've come into contact with know a thing. There's this one guy I've spoken to over the years, he's definitely a wrong 'un, but kids aren't his style. You could do worse than to talk to him. He might know something.'

'Have you spoken to the police about this guy?'

'He's nothing to do with Alice. He's not old enough for a start, but as I said, he's not into kids. He just likes girls... a bit too much though. Besides, I don't think it would be particularly good for me to admit I've been talking to perverts, given my history. I'm not friends with the police, Miss Blake, and the police are definitely not friends with me. There are folk who worked on the Alice Abbott case who are still there, and they would *still* very much like to see me in jail, if they could get anything to stick.'

Gillespie scribbles something on a sheet of paper, tears off the corner, handing it to me.

'The guy you need to speak to is called Eddy. Don't know where he's living at the moment, but you'll be able to find him at the pizza delivery shop up on the high street. He's the manager. Just be very careful. He's not a nice man, and he'll definitely be into you. Then again, that might work to your advantage if you want to get some information out of him. He won't talk to me.'

'So, what makes you think he'll talk to me?'

Gillespie looks me up and down slowly. 'He'll talk to you. Trust me.'

I glance down at the paper. On it is written simply 'Eddy', then 'Pizza-Go-Go'.

I fold it up, tucking it into my jeans pocket, then looking at the clock on the wall, I stand from my chair.

'I should get going. I don't want Mrs Abbott to worry.'

'Nope, that woman has had more than her fair share.'

11

I leave Gillespie's, taking a right turn onto the street back towards my temporary home. The rain falls heavily again. The smell of wet tarmac is all around me. Having spoken to Alan Gillespie, I am surer than ever that he has nothing to do with Alice's abduction. I understand Helen Abbott's staunch insistence that he is innocent. She's spent far more time around him than I have.

As I make my way along the pavement towards the gate next door, a car pulls up on the street behind me. It's noisy, as if the exhaust has blown, and there's a distinct rattle as it slows down. The breaks make a high-pitched squeal as the car rolls to a stop. The smell of petrol fumes is overwhelming.

A youngish man, early thirties, gets out, slamming the door. It doesn't close properly the first time, so he tries again. Third time, the door stays shut, more from luck that engineering, I think. He turns towards me and I see that he's carrying a paper bag under his arm.

As he walks it becomes apparent that we're heading in the same direction.

He keeps looking at me, nervously. He's slim with sandy

blond hair which hangs messily all around his face. He's wearing blue jeans and a baggy bomber jacket over a rust-coloured jumper.

We arrive at the gate in front of the Abbott house together, but rather than letting me walk through, he scurries up the path ahead of me, fumbling around for his key.

'Tom? Is that you?' I call after him.

He glances nervously over his shoulder. He doesn't make eye contact.

'Do I know you?' He sounds nervous.

'I'm Emily. Do you remember me? I was Alice's friend. I used to live right over there, across the street.' I turn and point towards my old house.

He drops his keys on the path in front of him, turning to face me. He still seems unwilling to look directly at my face. 'Yes. I remember you.' His eyes flick up, then down to my feet. 'Your hair is… different. It's short.'

I raise my hand to my head, ruffling my spiky dark hair. 'Yes. I haven't had it long for years. I cut it all off when I was at university.'

'It's nice. I… I like it,' he says quietly, and his cheeks flush.

He bends down to retrieve his keys. As he turns, the front door opens. Helen Abbott is standing on the other side. She looks at Tom, to me, then to her son again. Stepping out onto the path, she puts a hand on his back, ushering him into the house.

'You two will catch your deaths standing out here in this deluge!'

She steps towards me, taking my wrist with a vice-like grip that is much stronger than I would have expected, pulling me towards the door. She half shuts the door, looking up and down the street, before closing it fully and putting on the security chain.

'Tom, go upstairs and change out of your work clothes.

Supper will be ready soon. Alice, will you join us for something to eat?'

Tom and I stand in silence, embarrassed by her mistake.

'This is Emily, Mum.'

Helen looks confused. 'I know that. That's what I said.'

I exchange a look with Tom, shaking my head slightly, but he doesn't get the message.

'You called her Alice.'

She looks to me, then down at the floor. The colour drains from her face. 'Did you bring me some scones home?' she says, clearly annoyed with him for pointing out her mistake.

Tom holds up the bag and offers it nervously towards her. She snatches it from him, shuffling into the kitchen, muttering away indecipherably and shaking her head.

I go up to my room to change into some dry clothes.

When I return, Tom and Helen are sitting at the dining table in the kitchen. The dull evening light is fading fast outside and an eerie halo hangs above the trees to the rear of the house. The garden is enveloped in dark shadows that move with the wind. A large green cast iron casserole dish sits in the centre of the table. I remember it from when I ate here as a child.

I take a seat opposite Tom, who glances at me, then back down to his hands.

We eat for the most part in silence. A tasteless beef stew. Watery and under seasoned. As I force down the food, trying to look like I'm enjoying it, it occurs to me how odd this situation is. Three people who were once so familiar to each other, now like total strangers. Awkward and uncomfortable. As I look up from my chipped plate, I see Tom's eyes dart away from my direction.

He looks back towards me and I smile. His eyes dart away

again, down to the end of the table where his mother is picking something from between her teeth with her little finger.

'Mum tells me you're writing about Alice.'

Helen Abbott's eyes are fixed on me and do not leave my face.

'That's right, Tom. I'm a journalist, and I work for a magazine in London. We're doing a piece about what happened to Alice.'

'Is it because of that little girl who went missing down the road at the weekend?'

'Yes. With that case being so close to here, people are drawing obvious links to Alice. So I'm going to try to find out if the two cases are related. I also think it'll help to give me some closure.'

'Are you going to try to find Alice?'

Tom speaks with the innocence of a young boy, full of hope. As if he expects me to say yes. I look at his mother. She just looks sad.

'I don't think so. That's not why I'm here. I need to look into the suggestion that this new disappearance might be related to what happened here when we were children. It's unlikely, but I wouldn't be doing my job properly if I didn't at least look into it.'

'I think she's still out there. At least, I hope she is. I don't like it when people say she's dead.'

'Anything's possible.' I hope this sounds more convincing than it feels to me. 'Your mother was telling me you don't remember much about the night it happened.'

Tom looks at his mother, who shifts uncomfortably in her seat. 'No. I know Alice came into my room. I was reading a comic. She wanted to make sure I was okay. I went to sleep after that. The next thing I remember, it was the following morning and Mum was shaking me in my bed, asking me where Alice was. I wish I knew what happened. I've tried so hard, I really have. But it's not in there.' He looks down at his plate, rubbing his eyes.

'Don't worry about it, Tom. Chances are you slept through whatever happened. You were very young. But if I can help you think of anything about that night, I'd like to try. I can help you, and you can help me maybe. It would be good to talk to you for my story.'

There's a crash as Helen's water glass falls to the floor and smashes. She stands up, cursing. 'I'm such a clumsy old fool these days. Tom, will you fetch the vacuum cleaner.'

Tom rushes to the kitchen. I hear the sound of a key turning in a lock, then footsteps going down wooden steps, and I remember the basement. Alice and I used to play among the laundry baskets and storage boxes, hiding from Tom and Adam, whispering about boys from school. I wasn't allowed into the basement in my house, but Mr Abbott would usually let us play down there, as long as we didn't touch his tools and things.

'Tom doesn't need to remember anything. I think it's best that he forgets and tries to move on with his life.' Helen stares down at the table as she speaks.

'Oh, I'm sorry. I just meant that–'

Her eyes dart up towards me as she cuts me off. 'I know what you meant. But please don't. He is damaged enough as it is,' she snaps.

Tom scurries clumsily back up from down below, struggling with the old hoover. He and Helen busy themselves with cleaning up the glass and clearing the table, so I retire to my bedroom.

12

I take out my phone and look back through the photos I took in the woods. I scroll through with my thumb, assessing the quality.

I freeze.

Something in one of the pictures catches my attention, so I grab my iPad to examine the pictures on the larger screen.

I zoom in on the area of trees off to the left.

Is that a person?

Lurking behind the trees, a few feet into the distance, is what appears to be a shadowy figure.

I spread my thumb and finger across the screen, zooming in further.

It's looking towards me.

I can't make out any features, but it's definitely a person.

I take a screenshot of the enlarged picture, then dial a number.

She answers on the second ring. Cathy is a doctor in London. We lived together when we were both in the first year at university. To say we were friends is pushing it a little, but we have a mutually beneficial relationship. She helps me with medical enquiries for stories I'm working on, and I feed her any gossip I hear about her hospital in the press circuit. We exchange some meaningless small talk, enquiring about each other's lives, but neither of us is really particularly interested. I get to the point.

'Do you know anything about an amnesia condition? Psycho something or other?'

'Psychogenic amnesia?'

'That's it, I think.'

'Hmmm… hold on.' I hear her moving across the room, and then flipping through the pages of a book. 'Not my field of expertise by a long shot I'm afraid, but I know the basics. More often than not it's linked to post-traumatic stress. It's usually caused by severe stress or psychological trauma on the brain. I assume you're talking about situation-specific amnesia? That's where the memory suppression occurs as a direct result of something severely stressful. Some rape victims, or people involved in a natural disaster, for example, will block the event from their memories. It's a kind of self-preservation if you like.'

'Do the memories ever come back?'

'That's a tricky one. Some do, some don't. The memories are there, but they're buried very deep in the person's subconscious. Some repressed memories can return spontaneously, years or even decades after the event. They can be triggered by a smell or some other stimulus. Sometimes they can be accessed using psychotherapy or hypnotism. Of course, it can sometimes be very difficult to distinguish a true suppressed memory from a false one, without corroborating evidence. There was a case a few years ago, where a hypnotherapist in the States was finding that every one of his patients was starting to remember being sexually abused as children. He was somehow creating the memories in the course of his therapy, but it turned out only one of them had actually been the victim of an assault.'

'So people can create memories as well as suppress them?'

'Exactly. But it's very dodgy ground. As with any self-preservation technique, it's sometimes better that these memories don't come back. People suppress them for a reason. The result of remembering can be extremely unpleasant. People who access repressed memories can suffer from severe anxiety and, in some cases, even suicide.'

'Is it possible to fake it?'

'I suppose anything is possible… but I would imagine it would be unlikely. It would be very difficult anyway. People are usually put through rigorous tests to establish if there is a real case or not. But as with anything, if someone is a good enough actor, then yes, theoretically, I think they could potentially pull it off.'

'So, an eight-year-old child–' I begin to ask.

She cuts in. 'No chance. A child's brain wouldn't be capable of passing the tests. Of course, there is the odd exception with some forms of autism, or child geniuses, for example, but in my professional opinion the chance of an eight-year-old managing to fool doctors into believing they were suffering from psychogenic amnesia over a prolonged period would be highly, highly unlikely.'

I thank Cathy for her help. We make loose plans to meet for a drink when I return home, though we both know, as we say it, that this will never happen. I hang up.

I open my laptop, make a few notes about my conversation with Alan Gillespie. Then close it and place it back onto the dresser.

Pulling my phone out to look again at the photo of the figure in the woods, I tap my nail on the screen. 'Who the hell are *you*?' I say out loud.

I turn off the lamp to the side of the bed, then crawl towards the window, peeking through the blinds.

Lily, the blue-haired girl, is leaning against my car, smoking a cigarette.

She is looking up at my bedroom window.

I don't think she can see me, but I shrink away from the window anyway.

Collapsing onto the bed, I pull the covers up around me and lie in the dark room, but I don't close my eyes.

All around me I see shadows that seem to be forming malevolent shapes around the room. The pungent smell of the lilies is overwhelming.

I stare at the shafts of moonlight, cast onto the ceiling and wall through the gaps in the blinds, and imagine Alice lying here, twenty-five years ago.

I wonder what she was thinking as she lay in her bed, in this very room that last time.

Did she hear a door open downstairs?

Did she hear footsteps creeping up the stairs, then down the landing towards her room?

I stare at the bedroom door and imagine the handle turning.

In my mind, a dark figure floats in, crossing the room towards the bed. Two long arms reach out towards Alice and she screams, but a thin spindly hand covers her mouth, stifling the noise.

As I shake myself from this rumination, returning to the present, I hear muffled shouts and whimpers coming from Tom's room.

I'm not the only person in this house who is having trouble sleeping tonight.

13

Sandie Jackson parks her car in her driveway, having returned from an early morning trip to the supermarket to buy fresh milk, amongst other things. She steps out onto the paving slabs, glancing over towards the Abbott house. There is movement behind the net curtains. The woman did not leave the Abbotts' last night, and her car is still parked on the street outside. The situation is getting stranger by the minute. Sandie can't recall Helen Abbott ever having had an overnight guest.

The day before, Sandie had also seen the shorthaired woman coming out of Alan Gillespie's home, but she had been watching the place for hours and had not seen her go in. This left the only explanation being that the girl had entered through the rear gate, from where it backs onto the woods. Alan Gillespie receiving a visitor was even more odd than Helen Abbott receiving one... but the same visitor to both residences made this a very strange turn of events indeed, and even stranger still was a visitor who enters Alan Gillespie's through the back door. Sandie was even more sure now that something significant was going on in Pear Tree Close. Finally, after years of waiting, *something* has happened.

She opens up her umbrella, turning towards her front door, then has a better idea. Glancing around to make sure nobody is watching her, she leans into her car, opens the glove compartment, and removes a couple of fuses from the fuse box. She closes the glove compartment, tosses her umbrella into the footwell, and shuts the passenger door. She stands in the rain, letting her mascara run down her face. When she feels she looks suitably bedraggled, she runs across the road to Alan Gillespie's house and knocks on his front door.

After a few minutes, the door opens and her neighbour eyes her suspiciously from the doorstep. He looks her up and down, somewhat confused by the arrival of a bedraggled rain-soaked female at his front door so early in the morning. Sandie can't imagine that Alan Gillespie gets too many attractive women knocking on his door at any time of the day after the rumours surrounding him and the disappearance of Alice Abbott. No smoke without fire, she tells herself.

'It's Alan, isn't it?' Sandie tries to sound as upset as she can manage.

'That's right.'

'I'm Sandie, I live over the road from you.'

'Yes, I know who you are.'

'I'm really sorry to bother you, but I don't suppose you know anything about cars?'

'What seems to be the trouble?' There's a note of suspicion in his voice.

'I don't really know. I'm not very good when it comes to engines. I came out to go to the supermarket, but it won't start. I wondered if you would mind taking a look at it for me? I need to be somewhere after the shops and I really can't miss the appointment.'

Sandie reaches up and brushes her wet hair off her face, keeping eye contact with Alan Gillespie the whole time. She looks at her watch to emphasise her story.

Alan Gillespie reaches behind him, grabbing a jacket and a hat from the coat hook on the wall, then steps out into the rain, closing the door behind him.

'I'll take a look, but it's a long time since I have done any work on cars. I can't promise I'll be able to help.'

'Oh, thanks so much. That really is very sweet of you.'

Sandie smiles at Gillespie over her shoulder as they hurry across the street. She opens the car, popping the bonnet for him, and he props it up, fishing around underneath.

He tells her to try starting the car. She does so and nothing happens.

She stands and joins him in front of the car, looking down at the engine. He is scratching his head and seems puzzled.

'It's not even turning over,' he mutters.

'Is that bad?' she asks, trying to sound as stupid as she can.

He shoots her a sideways glance but does not say a word. He fumbles around under the bonnet as Sandie watches.

The rain drips from every part of her. She shivers, wrapping her arms around herself to try to keep warm.

'Why don't you go and wait inside,' Gillespie says. 'No point in us both getting soaked to the skin out here.'

'Oh no, I couldn't do that. Besides, I'd like to see what you do, so I know if this happens again.'

He shrugs. 'Suit yourself.'

Sandie watches for a few minutes before she speaks again. 'Was that your daughter I saw leaving your house yesterday?' she asks, trying to sound nonchalant.

Gillespie looks at her. 'Excuse me?'

'The lady I saw leaving your house yesterday. I just wondered if she is your daughter.'

'No, she's not.' Gillespie offers no further information.

'I've not seen her around here before, that's all. She's very pretty.'

Gillespie straightens up and looks at Sandie. 'She's a friend of Helen Abbott's. She's staying with her for a while.'

'Oh,' Sandie says innocently. 'I didn't know Helen *had* any friends.'

Gillespie gives her an irritated look. He stands up and closes the car's bonnet. 'She's a very old friend. She was her daughter's best friend actually. Used to live in your house as a matter of fact.'

Gillespie's eyes do not leave Sandie's the whole time. He gives nothing away with his expression, but she feels he is testing her.

'In my house? Is that so? Well I never. And what is she doing here now?'

Alan Gillespie takes a handkerchief from his back pocket, wiping oil from his hands.

'You said your car wouldn't start and you were on your way to the supermarket?' he asks calmly.

'Yes, that's right,' Sandie responds nervously.

Alan Gillespie's eyes flick towards the car's windscreen. 'Can you maybe explain to me then why you have two bags of shopping on the front seat of your car, and your engine is warm?'

Sandie feels her face flush at the realisation that she has been caught out.

He turns to walk away, then stops, turning back towards her briefly. 'Mrs Jackson, I know we've not really spoken since you've moved in, but I can tell that you're not stupid, and I think you will probably know why I don't join in with neighbourhood gossip. If you're so desperate to know what Emily Blake is doing back in Palmerston, then I suggest you knock on Helen Abbott's front door and ask her yourself, rather than making up some bullshit story about your car not starting. I'm sure she'd be happy to tell you. I think we're done here, don't you?'

Alan Gillespie strides away across the street and in through his front door, closing it behind him without looking back once.

Sandie feels extremely foolish. She is usually so careful in her investigations, but excitement and desperation had caused her to act recklessly. She will have to be far more cautious from now on. Her mistake had been to assume that Alan Gillespie was a doddery old man who could be easily manipulated, but he is obviously far shrewder than she had realised. It had been stupid to so badly underestimate the subject of her scrutiny. A schoolgirl error. But it was one she would not make again. And so what if she had been caught out? She had achieved what she wanted. She had the information she sought. The girl staying with Helen Abbott is called Emily Blake, and she is the childhood best friend of Alice Abbott, the missing girl from the street. Jim's daughter... presumed dead.

Sandie smiles sadly as she remembers Jim Abbott taking a photo of his daughter from his wallet and handing it to her.

'She was very beautiful,' she had said as she passed it back to him.

'Yes, she was,' he had agreed, before folding it into quarters and slipping it back in between the pockets of the old leather. The fold marks on the photograph were very defined, as if it had been unfolded and folded up again many, many times.

So now Sandie has a name, and she is even more intrigued. What would bring this woman back here to this desolate hellhole after twenty-five years? Sandie turns and hurries down her path and into her house. She heads up the stairs, dripping all over the carpet as she goes. Her blouse is off over her head before she reaches the bathroom. She throws the sodden garment into the washing bin in the corner, then unzips her black pencil skirt, letting it slip down over her shapely legs. It flops with a wet slap onto the floor. A puddle is forming around her on the tiles. She removes her sodden knickers and throws them on top of the pile of clothes.

After taking a quick shower to warm herself, she saunters along the corridor to her bedroom, throwing open the wardrobe doors. Sweeping her hand along the rail of clothes, she picks out a thick black jumper dress with long sleeves, pulls it on over her head, then climbs into a pair of tall black leather knee-high boots. She scrapes her damp hair back from her face, pulling it into a tight bun. She hates having her hair up, but it's far more practical, especially with the weather as it is.

Glancing at herself as she passes a tall mirror next to the bed, she hurries out of the room, gliding down the stairs. After such a long time without anything happening, she had almost forgotten why she was here, but within the last twenty-four hours, the fire inside her had been reignited, and she felt more determined than ever to find the answers she so desperately needs. She glances out of the window, glad to see that the rain has finally stopped.

As she watches, she sees the front door across the road open and Emily Blake hurry down the path, in the direction of her car. Sandie's eyes dart towards the clock on the mantelpiece. Midday. She grabs her car keys from the sideboard where she left them and hurries out to her car. She pulls the fuses from her pocket and carefully slots them back into their casings. Emily doesn't notice her as she pulls her car away from the side of the road and drives down the street. Sandie starts her engine and follows, keeping a safe distance.

14

The sound of thunder wakes me from my sleep long before my alarm. Heavy rain batters against the window. I can hear noises in the house, coming from downstairs below my room.

Somebody is already up.

I decide there is no point in trying to return to my slumber. Drowsily, I make my way downstairs, carrying the bunch of lilies from my windowsill. There is nobody in the kitchen so I shove the stinking flowers into a carrier bag, burying them at the bottom of the dustbin in the corner of the room. I fill the kettle with water, flipping on the switch. Opening a few cupboards looking for mugs, I find them eventually above the cooker hob.

As I wait for the kettle to boil, I try the door to the basement. It's locked. I look around for the key but it's nowhere to be seen. I hear the button on the kettle click and I make myself a cup of black coffee, then head down the hallway. Tom is sitting in the front room eating a bowl of cereal. We exchange morning pleasantries and I sit on the small sofa opposite the window.

I see a key on the mantle above the old electric fire.

'Is that the key to the basement?' I nod towards the shelf.

'Yeah, but Mum doesn't like people going in there. She says there's rats. She's put poison down, so she says it's not safe for people.'

'We used to play in there, me, you and Alice. Do you remember that?'

Tom doesn't reply. He looks away awkwardly.

'It's just in case I need to hoover. That bedroom is so clean, I'd hate to get any mess on that beautiful carpet.'

'They should have left it. Alice won't like it when she comes home and it's all changed.'

'Tom, I'm not sure Alice is ever coming home. You have to know that, right?'

'You think she's dead like everyone else, don't you?' He sounds hurt.

'I don't know. Nobody knows. But it's been a very long time. And she has never made contact. Why would she do that? If she is alive and out there somewhere, why wouldn't she let us know?'

'I don't know. Maybe she can't. Maybe she's locked away somewhere. Or maybe her memory is broken, like mine. Maybe she doesn't even know who she is.'

'I guess that's a possibility.'

I notice Tom is holding something, a card of some sort. He's turning it over and over in his hands. 'What's that you've got there?'

He looks down as if he had forgotten he was holding it. 'It was on the mat this morning. She must have put it through the letterbox last night after we went to bed.'

He stands up, handing me the card.

It's a child's birthday invitation, with cartoon drawings of dolls and other toys on the front. Someone has written 'Lily' in large letters in a space above the words 'IS HAVING A PARTY'. Inside the card, messy handwriting scrawls a brief message from someone who likes to overuse exclamation marks.

Tommy baby!! It's my birthday party, and I'll cry if I want to!!!! Come along on Friday night, my place from 9. FANCY DRESS!!!!! Lil X. PS. Bring your new (girl)friend??!!!

Tom looks embarrassed.

'You don't have to come if you don't want to. I'm not sure I'll go. I certainly won't be wearing fancy dress if I do.'

'No, it might be fun. Would be good to meet some of the locals. I can see what people have to say about the situation, for my story. I'm not doing anything else tonight anyway.'

Tom gives me a strange look. 'Adam will be there,' he says awkwardly.

I'm confused. 'Lily knows Adam?'

Tom pauses, looking slightly uncomfortable, like a child who has said something they know they shouldn't have. 'They're sort of going out. They've been together a few years... on and off. They're terrible together, but he keeps going back to her. God only knows why. She smells of cigarettes.'

This surprises me. I guess I'd never really thought of my brother as an actual person with friends, let alone a girlfriend. I had wrongly assumed that his inability to build a relationship with me or our parents was indicative of his view on relationships in general. I don't know how I feel about seeing him. Especially in these circumstances. I wonder if Lily knows who I am. Tom continues, 'He has *really* bad taste when it comes to girlfriends.'

I cock an eyebrow at him. 'Girlfriends? Plural?' I struggle to hide my surprise.

'Adam is *very* popular with the ladies. Just all the wrong ladies.' Tom is interrupted by what sounds like a crash of crockery from upstairs, then coughing. He looks embarrassed as he glances up at the ceiling. 'She sleeps in late most days. Says she doesn't see the point of getting out of bed just to sit in her chair.' He checks his watch. 'I have to go to work but I'll be home around seven. If you want to go over the road, then we can pop along after Mum's made dinner.'

'It's a date,' I say.

I regret my choice of words immediately. Tom blushes, jumps to his feet and almost runs out to the hallway, grabbing an old tracksuit jacket. He slams the door behind him as he leaves, then I hear the racket of his car driving away.

I cross to the fireplace, lifting the key from the mantle. I turn it over in my hand a few times, running my fingers over its smooth form and biting my bottom lip.

I return to the hall, hold my breath and listen. I can't hear a sound from Helen upstairs, she must have gone back to sleep, so I decide to risk it.

I make my way as quietly as I can down the hallway to the kitchen.

I unlock the door, pulling it open with a loud creak.

Reaching round the corner, I fumble for a switch and am glad to find it. It is cold and has a greasy film on it. A bulb flickers in the darkness below me, casting shadows up onto the bottom of the wooden staircase. The dim grey daylight barely illuminates the top few steps. There are cobwebs in the corners of the doorframe. Cold bare brick is exposed down the side of the staircase. A damp musty smell floods my nostrils.

I wipe my hand on my jeans as I step down tentatively.

As my foot touches the third step, there is another loud creak.

I freeze.

Terrified, I listen for any signs of life from the house.

Still there is only silence.

The hairs on the back of my neck stand up. Why am I so afraid? I played in this basement many times as a child, but the knowledge that I'm not supposed to be in here has changed the whole dynamic. It feels forbidden. But why?

15

I get to the bottom of the stairs to find the space completely changed from the image in my memory. What was once a cosy and intriguing play space has become a desolate waste ground. Boxes are piled up all around me. A blanket of thick dust covers everything. I see the vacuum cleaner Tom had fetched the night before, sitting in the corner by an old chest of drawers. The carcass of a long-dead mouse lies in the middle of the floor, lit by a narrow shaft of light struggling in through a small window on the wall above my head, at street level. The overgrown front lawn obscures the view, blocking most of the light that should be filling the dark basement.

I reach to my left, brushing the dust from the top of a box.

The word 'ALICE' is written in capitals in thick black marker. I pull the flaps of the box open, revealing neatly folded clothing. I rummage in the box, finding a pale blue scarf. I remember Alice wearing this, and I feel sad. I push the clothes back into the box, folding the flaps closed. I walk to another pile of boxes with the word 'JIM' in the same black marker. I open the top box.

I note that this one has not been packed with as much care, if any. The contents are screwed up inside, and a musty smell comes from them. Just old clothes and shoes mainly.

Beyond the piles of boxes, the space opens up into a larger room. There are old chairs, suitcases, children's toys and crates of board games. I see dusty mousetraps dotted around the edges of the room. There is an old tool bench up against one wall, with drills, saws and screwdrivers scattered around on its top.

Leaning against the wall at the end of the bench stands a shotgun. I don't remember this from my childhood, but it probably would have been locked safely away back then, with young children in the house. I vaguely recall that Jim Abbott used to go hunting from time to time. He took Tom and Adam with him one Sunday, and when Adam arrived home later that afternoon, he was all excited, claiming to have shot a rabbit. My parents were furious, my mother especially so. She abhorred violence.

Strangely, unlike everything else down here, the gun doesn't appear to have any dust on it. As I take a step towards it, I hear footsteps above me. Helen is awake, and in the hallway. I run back up the stairs, flicking the light switch off as I pass it. I close the door as quietly as I can, locking it stealthily.

I spin round, turning my back to the door. I am breathing heavily from the sprint up the stairs, and my clothes are covered in dust and dirt.

She is standing in the kitchen, glaring at me.

'Good morning, Helen. Did you sleep well?' I ask as cheerfully as I can manage, trying to hide the key behind my back.

Her eyes dart to the basement door, then back to me, suspiciously.

'What have you been doing down there?' she asks frantically. She gives me a weak smile, then says more calmly, 'I'd prefer it if you stayed out of the basement, please. There's rat traps and poison. It's not safe. Not safe at all.'

'I'm sorry. I was just having a look. I remember Alice and I used to play down there. I hope I haven't upset you.'

Helen quickly crosses the kitchen, holding out her hand. For the key. I give it to her.

'No, no... It's not a problem, but I would rather you stayed out of there if you don't mind. It's just storage, nothing of interest anyway. Very dusty though. Filthy really. It's not healthy.'

She flips on the kettle and holds up a cup towards me. 'I'm making a drink if you would like one.'

I refuse the offer and retreat upstairs to the relative safety of my room. I feel like a naughty child who's been caught somewhere they shouldn't be, which is ridiculous. Helen told me to make myself at home, and that's what I was doing. I catch a glimpse of myself in the dressing table mirror. A dark smudge of dirt is streaked across my cheek, and there's dust in my hair. I feel dirty from having been down in the cellar, and suddenly feel the need to be clean. Grabbing my towel, I head down across the landing to the bathroom. I throw my dusty clothes in a heap on the floor, turning on the shower.

I hear the pipes knocking around me noisily as the shower springs to life.

This house is devoid of any warmth, I think, as I reach for the cheap apple-scented shampoo from the shelf. I lather more than is necessary into my short hair, keen to wash away the muck from the basement.

The homeliness that this house used to possess is long gone. It is just four walls and a roof.

And dust. Lots and lots of dust. I suspect it holds a few secrets too. Something about Helen's behaviour since I arrived has been off. She seems nervous, like she always has to consider very carefully what she says before she says it, in case she says too much.

I close my eyes, rinsing the shampoo from my hair, and

picture the shotgun leaning against the wall. Everything in the basement was thick with dust, but not the gun. I wonder why.

16

After the incident in the kitchen, I feel slightly awkward about being around Helen, so rather than join her downstairs, I sit in my bedroom. I can hear pots and pans being slammed about, and the occasional loud thud from downstairs. She must be preparing another tasteless meal. The storm shows no indication of easing, so I resign myself to having to stay in the house for now. As unappealing as that prospect is, the rain outside is even less so.

I choose to stay dry.

Pulling my phone from my pocket, I send a text to my brother.

In Palmerston. Sorry didn't let you know sooner. Have been invited to your gf's party tonight, so I guess we can catch up later?

To my surprise, the reply comes almost straight away.

It's short and to the point.

Ok.

No inquiry as to what I'm doing here. No small talk. Adam does not appear to have changed.

Maybe he's busy. It occurs to me that I don't even know

where he's working these days. The last time we actually spoke face to face was six years ago. I know the exact date. August twentieth. A date I can never forget. I feel more nervous about seeing Adam than I had been about Helen, but then again, I had time to prepare for that meeting. Last time we spoke, things didn't go so well, but under the circumstances, it was hardly surprising. I wonder if he thinks about that day. I wonder if he still has a chip on his shoulder. I will find out tonight no doubt.

Around midday the rain stops, so I take the opportunity to get out of the house.

I drive to the high street, finding a parking space near the old library.

Alice and I used to spend many of our Saturday mornings in this building. We would hide from each other between the rows of shelves, pretending to be interested in the dusty old books upon them.

As I head towards the high street, I pass a row of down-market food establishments.

One in particular catches my attention.

The shabby looking shop front is adorned with handwritten offers on neon coloured sheets of card, cut out into jagged star shapes advertising special deals for the day, stuck in the dirty window.

In large red letters above the door is a sign that reads 'Pizza-Go-Go – Quality food FAST!'.

Nothing about the shop suggests quality.

I pull the folded scrap of paper from my pocket, confirming that this is the establishment that Alan Gillespie had told me about the previous day. I pass the doorway, ducking into an alley.

Pulling out a compact mirror from my handbag, I apply some lipstick and mascara. I rub a touch of lipstick on each cheek, then ruffle my hair, pushing my short fringe one way, then back the other. Deciding it's as good as it's going to get, I undo an extra button on my blouse and head back towards the pizza shop.

I glide nonchalantly into the shop, glancing at the menu above the counter. A short fat spotty teenager stands behind the counter in a pair of bright yellow trousers, a white polo shirt and a dark green apron. Greasy ginger hair is plastered to his face underneath a yellow cap. He wears a name badge that looks like a big slice of pizza.

It reads 'My name is: KEVIN. I'M HAPPY TO HELP', although I note that he looks far from happy in any capacity.

'Hi. Welcome to Pizza-Go-Go. What can I get you today?' he asks in a monotone unenthusiastic drone, which confirms he is less than happy to help.

Then he looks at me and his face brightens. 'Would you like me to tell you about today's specials?' he asks in a much friendlier tone.

I give him my biggest smile. 'Hi, Kevin. I'm actually looking for Eddy. Is he working today?'

'Yeah, he's out in the staff room on his break. He'll be back in about half an hour. Can I help instead?' His voice is full of hope.

'I'm afraid I really need to talk to Eddy.'

I glance over his shoulder towards the kitchen area. To the right is a doorway with a small sign telling me it's the staff room. I lean onto the counter, watching his eyes wander slowly down towards my unbuttoned blouse. 'Is he in there?' I point to the door through the back.

'Yeah, would you like me to get him for you?'

I lift the hatch in the counter, pushing past Kevin, my feet sticking to the greasy floor. 'No, that's fine. I'll just go on in to see him.'

'Hey, you can't come through here... it's not allowed!' Kevin is panicking. He's clearly not used to dealing with situations like this in his daily routine.

'Eddy won't mind, I promise.' I rush through the door before Kevin can stop me.

As I push the door shut behind me, I turn the key, locking Kevin out.

He bangs on the door, shouting.

I turn around to find a tall skinny man in his late thirties standing staring at me quizzically.

His face is initially confused, but as he looks me up and down, he smiles.

The man licks his lips. He has short tidy hair, thinning on top. He wears thin wire-framed glasses and the same yellow and green uniform as Kevin, but with the addition of a bright yellow tie and a name badge that says 'MANAGER: EDDY'. A thin moustache decorates his upper lip.

'Can I help you, miss?' His eyes are fixed on my chest.

'Oh hi. Are you Eddy?' I flash him a smile.

His smile broadens and he blushes. 'That's me. Do I know you? I'm sure I'd remember a face that pretty.'

I giggle like a teenaged girl, feeling slightly ashamed and somewhat out of my depth, but it's too late to back out now. 'My name is Jessica.'

Kevin's banging on the door, asking Eddy if he should call the police.

Eddy shouts back to him. 'It's fine, Kev. Go back to work!'

I hear him waddling away outside the door.

I continue. 'I'm looking for some information, and somebody told me you're the man who might be able to give it to me.'

Eddy looks nervous, but he smiles again. 'Who might that be then?' His eyes wander down my thighs.

'I'm sorry, Eddy, but I can't reveal my sources... Nobody would ever trust me if I did that.' I wink at him, then worry that I might be overdoing it.

'What is it you want?' he asks slowly. He sounds intrigued, but slightly worried.

I take a few steps closer to him, keeping my eyes fixed on his. He's sweating.

'I'm trying to find somebody,' I say. 'Someone who might be able to give me some information about little girls going missing in the area.'

He looks nervously around the room. 'I don't know anything about that. I think you need to leave.' He pauses. 'Are you police?'

I smile again. 'Do I look like the police, Eddy?'

I pull my blouse up to show him my midriff. 'I'm not bugged, I promise.'

I pout and cross my heart slowly with my right hand, letting my index finger trail down in between my unbuttoned blouse.

Eddy licks his lips excitedly and I know he's taking the bait, so to speak, so I continue.

'Eddy, I have a problem. I'm really interested in finding out some information about some kids who have disappeared, and I think you might be able to point me in the right direction.'

'Can't help you, I'm afraid. Like I said, I wouldn't know anything about that, and I'm not sure who's told you any different... but they are definitely wrong!' he says in a panic.

A bead of sweat trickles slowly down from Eddy's sideburn, dripping onto his shoulder, mixing with grease and other stains.

He wants to trust me, I can tell, but I don't have him yet.

I take a step closer to him, placing my hand on his chest. I can feel the heat from his body. 'Eddy, you're not in any trouble. I just really need to speak to someone who might be able to help me.' The sweat is pouring off him. I loosen his tie, pressing my body closer to his. It makes me feel sick and I struggle to keep the grimace from my face.

He smells of sweat and cheap aftershave... Old Spice or some such thing. The mixture of smells is quite nauseating.

Despite this, and the terror I feel inside, I try to keep the smile locked firmly in place. 'Come on, Eddy, do me a favour. I really need to get this information. Please?'

My lips are almost touching his. I brush them over his face and stop next to his ear, whispering, 'I can make it worth your while.'

'Yeah?' Eddy asks. 'How?' He looks me up and down again and smiles.

I raise my knee into his crotch slowly and feel him go immediately hard inside his trousers. I reach down and put my fingers onto the zip of his fly. 'I can give you whatever you want, Eddy. Name your price.'

'Prove it,' he says.

I wasn't expecting this. I'm out of my depth and realise I should have come with a plan.

I panic, trying to keep it from showing on my face. I cup my hand over his crotch and give his rock-hard cock a gentle squeeze, release, then squeeze again, a little harder this time. I fight back the overpowering urge to throw up, pulling his head onto my shoulder so he can't see my face. I whisper in his ear again. 'If you want something from me, you have to give me what I want first.'

I giggle again, pushing his head away from me. I remove his cap and run my hand through his greasy sweaty hair. He's breathing heavily, almost panting. He puts his nose into my hair and sniffs loudly.

'You smell like apples. It's nice.' He glances nervously around the room as if somebody might catch us, then continues. 'Kids aren't my scene at all. I think those guys are disgusting.' He looks at me, then continues, 'But there's an old sheet rubber factory just up over the hill in town. It's been closed down for donkey's years, but there's a guy who squats in there, goes by the name of Rab. If anyone knows anything, he will. Though I can't imagine why anyone would want to talk to him. Dirty old bastard.' Eddy smiles, placing both his hands on my buttocks.

I forcibly remove his hands from me and pull away, buttoning up my blouse. I wipe my hand on Eddy's filthy shirt, turning to leave.

'Oi, where the fuck do you think you're going?' Eddy shouts after me.

'Thanks, Eddy, you're a star.'

'But... but, what about...' He looks like he might actually cry.

'No time, I'm afraid, I need to be somewhere.'

I unlock the door, leaving Eddy bewildered and frustrated. I look nervously at Kevin as I pass through the shop. He looks baffled by the whole situation. I grab some sachets of wet wipes from the counter as I pass, tearing them open to cleanse my hands and face.

I feel disgusting.

I exit the shop, stopping at an off licence on the way back to my car. I buy a cheap bottle of Pinot Grigio for the party tonight. At a charity shop next door, a pair of black suede winkle-picker boots in my size catch my eye. I didn't bring any 'going out' clothes, so decide these will do for tonight. As I head down the high street, I can't shake the feeling I'm being watched.

I tell myself that this is stupid.

Nobody here knows me anymore, nor does anybody care about who I am or what I'm up to. But having seen the shadowy figure in the photo from the woods, I am worried. I glance in my

rear-view mirror. There are no cars behind me, and no pedes-
trians on the pavement.

I shake my head and scold myself for being such a wimp,
putting my foot down as I drive back towards Pear Tree Close.

17

W e head down the road to the party at about nine thirty. With a limited selection of clothes, I settle on skinny black jeans and a tight black T-shirt, with the charity shop boots and my leather jacket making it look a little dressier.

Casual is cool, I tell myself, then wonder why I even care.

Tom wears baggy shapeless jeans and a short-sleeved checked shirt that is at least a size too big for him. It looks like it could have belonged to his father. Tom seems awkward and nervous. I can't help feeling sad for him whenever I look at him.

I wonder what his life might have turned out like under different circumstances, what any of our lives might have turned out like.

We could have been happy.

I take the cheap wine I purchased earlier in the afternoon.

Tom takes nothing. Not even a card for the birthday girl.

The front door is open when we arrive, the sound of loud dance music booms out from inside. The house is a dump, but compared to the Abbotts' it's fine. There are people milling around in the hallway. There are some revellers in fancy dress; the usual bunch of slutty bunnies and cats, a few cartoon characters, but the majority are not, so I feel much more relaxed. Tom doesn't seem to know anybody at the party, but that doesn't surprise me. He's socially awkward and I can't imagine him hanging out with anyone. I count about thirty people dotted around the house, but I can't see Lily. I make my way over to a table in the living room, placing down the bottle of wine. I take two plastic cups from a pile. Opening the screw top, I fill one to the brim for myself, and another for Tom. He shakes his head frantically, pushing my hand away, spilling the wine down my top.

'I don't drink. Alcohol is bad,' he grumbles, shaking his head vigorously.

This man is all kinds of messed up.

I shrug and down the wine, tossing the empty cup onto the table. Turning my back to the living room door, I scan the room. There are no pictures on the walls, no ornaments, no photographs. No evidence that a human being actually lives here.

Nothing at all.

Just a tatty-looking sofa with a torn cover, a dining table and a collection of mismatched plastic chairs. As I assess the lack of decor, I hear a voice from behind me.

'Hey, sis. How's things?'

I spin round. Adam's appearance has changed drastically since I saw him last. His shaggy bleached blond hair is now his natural dark brown, cropped stylishly short and neat. He was always big for his age, but now he is toned. His shoulders fill his unzipped leather jacket well, and his defined chest is visible beneath a white T-shirt. Muscular legs show in part through his tight ripped jeans.

From the looks of things, my brother has been hitting the gym hard since I last saw him.

'Adam, hi.' I smile nervously, then totally unexpectedly, he steps forward, hugging me hard.

My body stiffens.

'It's really good to see you, Ems,' he whispers into my ear.

I don't know how to react. I can't remember the last time Adam showed me any affection. I'm touched but baffled. He places a crate of cheap lager down onto the table, peeling one off and opening it for himself. He offers one to me, I shake my head, raising my wine to him. He clinks my plastic cup with the edge of his can, taking a few gulps.

'Hello, Tom,' he says. 'You looking after Emily?'

Tom nods and shrugs.

Adam ruffles his hair. 'You dirty dog! That's my sister!'

I make an unamused face at Adam.

Tom looks embarrassed.

'Aw come on, mate. We all know you've always had a soft spot for my sis here, haven't you?'

Tom turns a deep shade of scarlet and looks at the floor.

Adam continues. 'That's fine, buddy. I don't mind. I had a thing for yours too.' He winks at Tom and grins.

Tom looks hurt and glares at Adam.

I am shocked by his comment.

Adam doesn't even look as if he realises he's said something stupid. 'So, what brings you back here?' he asks me in a way that tells me that somehow he already knows, a slight smile on his lips.

'Mainly work,' I reply, leaving it there. 'So Lily, she looks... *interesting*.'

'She's okay.'

'I've not met her, but I'm sure you'll introduce me tonight.'

He shrugs. 'If you want.'

18

The party is starting to fill out. Someone turns the volume up and the music vibrates through the cheap speakers. I finish my cup of wine and quickly pour some more.

I'm drinking too fast and it's going to my head.

Adam crushes his empty can and drops it on the floor. He opens another, gulping from it. A few people are dancing and the volume of conversation has risen to battle with the music. I peer through the French doors into the garden, and picture the Abbotts sitting out there with the rest of the neighbours, enjoying a glass of champagne on a balmy summer evening, oblivious to the fact their daughter is in danger across the road.

I try to imagine a life without fear. I have always known fear for as long as I can remember. It was hounded into me by my mother's neurosis. 'Never go anywhere alone, Emily. I need to know where you are at all times please,' she used to say.

Adam is milling around, saying hello to a few people, mainly the girls. They all make eyes at him, and I realise for the first time that my brother is popular. He winks at one girl, slaps another's bottom. I wonder how Lily feels about his openly flirtatious behaviour.

As Adam returns to my side, I look at Tom, who's not enjoying himself. He keeps checking his watch as if he's eager to leave.

'You all right, Tom?' I shout to him. He just shrugs.

A tall busty blonde girl across the room smiles at Adam, raising her glass at him.

'Friend of yours?' I enquire with a smirk.

'Old flame.' He sucks in air through his mouth, then chuckles to himself.

'Where's this girlfriend of yours anyway? It's a bit rude not being at her own party.'

I look around the room, but she's nowhere to be seen.

'Oh, she'll be here. She's most likely upstairs powdering her nose.' He winks at me. I shake my head.

I look up at Tom. His face has frozen in a grimace. He is staring over my shoulder. The chatter in the room has stopped.

I turn to follow his gaze, and see why.

Lily is standing in the doorway. She is wearing a long blonde wig and a mauve gingham dress with a pleated skirt. Just like the one Alice had, the one that everyone recognises from the picture. Lily's skin is intricately made-up, with marbled purples and whites. Veins are painted all over her arms, legs and face.

She is dressed as Alice. Alice, dead.

She wears one shoe and carries a teddy bear in her hand, dangling down by her side. She has a pale pink ribbon tied in a bow on top of her head. White contact lenses make her eyes appear lifeless. She smiles around the room, exposing yellowed rotting teeth.

There are gasps. There are whispers. There is nervous laughter.

I shoot a glance at Adam. He's looking furiously at his girlfriend.

'Can anyone guess who I'm supposed to be?' she shrieks, then giggles.

Nobody speaks.

Lily howls with laughter. She's drunk, or high, or both.

Someone turns off the music.

It's Tom. He's clenching his fists, then opening them, and clenching them again.

Tears are welling up in his eyes. 'Do you think this is fucking funny?' he screams.

'Oh come on, Tommy baby, it's a party.'

'The party's over!' he shouts, striding towards her.

Adam jumps in between them, pushing Tom back with one hand, and Lily with the other.

'Tom, I think you should go home, mate.' He turns to me. 'Emily, can you get him out of here, now please?'

I take Tom by the hand and lead him towards the door.

Adam turns to Lily. 'You, get the fuck upstairs and get that shit off your face. Everybody else, out. Party's over,' he snarls.

There are some cries of objection. 'I said out!' he bellows, and I'm shocked by the level of his anger.

Lily tries to walk past Adam but he grabs her wrist. She raises her other arm to try to slap his face, but he catches it with his free hand. He holds her like a rag doll, her flesh turning even paler white beneath his grip.

'You're hurting me, baby,' she says with a smile.

'Good,' Adam retorts. 'What the fuck were you thinking?'

She spits in his face.

He turns to me again. 'Emily, take Tom home, now!'

I hurry out of the house among the stream of guests exiting the party. I can hear Adam and Lily arguing as we cross the road. I steer Tom down the path towards his front door.

He's shaking. 'I can't believe that bitch,' he says through angry tears.

'Don't think about her, Tom, just try to calm down. She's obviously screwed up. Please, try not to let it upset you.'

We stop outside the front door. I pull a tissue from my pocket, handing it to him.

'Here, try to get yourself sorted out before we go in. I don't want your mum to see you like this.'

He wipes his eyes with the palm of his hand. Down the road, I hear Lily's front door slam.

'Do you think Adam will be all right?' I ask him.

'He'll be fine. They fight all the time.'

'Nice. And what about you?'

'I'm pissed off. How dare she? Who does she think she is? What sort of person does that? I know she's a dick, but honestly, that's messed up, even for her. If Mum had seen that, it would have pushed her over the edge.'

'She didn't, so try to calm down and let's go inside. Do you have your key?'

Tom rummages in his pocket, handing me his key. I unlock the front door and we enter the hallway, closing the door behind us. The sound of the television comes from the living room.

Helen calls out over the noise of the telly. 'You're back early.'

I put my hand over Tom's mouth. 'Yeah, it wasn't a very good party. Loud music and a load of drunk kids. We decided to come home.'

'Sounds like you're better off here then,' she calls back absent-mindedly. Her speech is slightly slurred. I think she's been drinking.

I hurry past the living room door, dragging Tom by the hand. I lead him up the stairs and into my room. He stops in the doorway, as if he doesn't want to enter.

'Tom, you can come in,' I say softly.

He edges in, closing the door behind him. I sit on the bed. He stands, looking around the room.

'I don't come in here,' he says softly. 'I'm not really supposed to.'

'Your mum doesn't like you coming in here?'

He shakes his head slowly.

'You need to remember Alice too, Tom. She was your big sister, and she loved you very much.'

Tom glances at Alice's bear on the pillow. He looks confused for a moment.

'That's Toby, Alice's bear,' I tell him. 'Do you remember?'

He shakes his head. I pick the bear up, handing it to him. He looks at it strangely.

'I took it with me when I left all those years ago. I wanted something to remind me of her.'

Tears are welling in the corners of his eyes again. One drips down onto the bear's head. He closes his eyes, hugging the bear to his chest. He smells it, but any trace of Alice is long gone.

He looks very sad, and I feel guilty for letting him see the bear. The muffled sound of the telly comes through the floor from downstairs, with the occasional loud cough from Helen.

'I want to remember,' Tom tells me. 'But when I try, it's just blank.'

I place my hand gently on his shoulder. 'Tom, if there's anything I can do to help you remember, I will do it. You can ask me anything you know. I was a little older than you, so my recollection of it all is maybe clearer. Although I wasn't here in the house.'

He shakes his head. 'I remember Mum and Dad going to the party. Alice and I watched some telly. Then I went to my room. I wanted to play some more, but she was on the phone, to you I think.'

I look at him. 'You remember that?'

'Yes. She was sitting on the windowsill, looking across to

your house, talking to you on the phone. I came into her room and she told me to go away.'

I remember Alice breaking away from the conversation to shout at her brother. 'Get out, brat!' she had said.

'So, Alice tells you to go away, then what?'

'I was upset, because she was mean to me, so I went back to my room. I got out my comics and got into bed to read. I didn't want to see Alice anymore. She hurt my feelings.'

'Right, so Alice told me she was going to bed, that was at ten thirty. Do you know what happened after she was finished on the phone to me?' I ask calmly.

Tom screws up his face as if he's in pain. 'It's not very clear, I know I read my comics for a while. The next thing I remember is my mum crying in the morning, and the police coming. I can't...' He closes his eyes, shaking his head.

He lifts his hand and slaps the top of his head repeatedly. 'I just don't know what happened. Maybe I saw him. I could have told the police. Then maybe they might have found her.'

I squeeze his shoulder gently. 'Tom, I don't think anything would be any different. You were eight. Chances are you probably slept through it all, whatever happened.'

'No,' he replies petulantly. 'I could have saved her. But I'm too stupid. It's all my fault.'

There's a knock at the door. 'Emily, is everything okay in there?'

'Yes. Tom and I are just having a chat,' I reply.

The door swings open and Helen steps in, uninvited. 'Thomas Abbott, you know I don't like you coming in here. Get back into your own room now please!' She points down the landing.

'I don't mind, Mrs Abbott, I told him he could come in.'

'It's not your place to tell him. This is my house and these are my rules, and Thomas does not come into this room. Ever. Understood?'

I'm shocked by her anger. 'Yes, I'm sorry. I didn't know.'

Tom goes to hurry out of the room but I call after him. He turns to face me.

'You can take this, if you want.' I hold up the bear.

Helen's face drains of all colour as she stares, dumbfounded, at the bear.

Tom takes it from me, pushing past his mother. He goes to his own room, slamming the door behind him. Helen stands staring into space for a few seconds, then as if she has forgotten where she is, she looks at me. She gazes around the room sadly, then back at me.

'Be careful with him. He's not had an easy life. He's delicate. He hasn't really dealt with what happened to Alice. He's buried it away, and it causes him all sorts of trouble.'

'Yes, I can see that.'

'He doesn't need you filling his head with nonsense.'

Was she listening at the door while Tom and I were talking?

'I understand, but I can assure you I would never do that.'

'Good. I'll let you get to bed then, dear. Sweet dreams.'

She closes the door firmly behind her. I lay down on the bed and I think of the words of an ABBA song as I stare at the ceiling and wish that I was somewhere else instead.

I can't imagine what had compelled Lily to do something so cruel. I don't know the girl, but it seems that such a thing would only be done to get a reaction, or to hurt someone.

Was the intended victim me or Tom?

Or was it both of us?

Maybe it wasn't for my benefit at all. Perhaps she just wanted to piss off my brother. If that was her aim, then the party had been a roaring success.

It was twisted and hurtful. But the message was clear to me. 'Alice is dead.'

Lily was only a baby when Alice disappeared, so she's grown up with school playground tales about what happened to the girl who lived down the road from her. No doubt, as children do, the story had been embellished, and gruesome details added to satisfy their morbid curiosity.

I shiver as I recall the image of Lily in the matted blonde wig. The dress in hindsight was not correct, but she had done a good job sourcing one that was quite close to the real thing.

I think of poor beautiful Alice, but now all I see is Lily's parody. I pull my phone from my pocket to text Adam.

Everything ok? I type.

A few minutes pass before my screen lights up and the phone buzzes with a reply.

Peachy. Then another message. *Sorry about Lily. She's a bit fucked-up.*

Can't argue with that.

It was a dick move, but I don't think she meant any harm. Wot U doin tomorrow? he types. *Want to meet?*

Yep. Sure.

Great. I'll pick you up about 1.

See you tomorrow.

x he replies.

I'm still slightly awkward with the affection. I don't recognise this person as my little brother, but I'll take it. I decide that tomorrow I'll go to find the old warehouse and speak to Rab. Adam can be my security. I don't think anyone will mess with me while he's by my side. He's built like a brick shithouse.

As I undress and turn out the bedside light, I hear sobbing coming from the room next door. I lay down on the bed, enveloped in darkness, wishing I could do something to help Tom. I fall asleep listening to the sound of him crying.

19

S andie Jackson is feeling restless. She has not been at all happy with what she has witnessed of Emily Blake since she arrived back in Palmerston. Her behaviour has been extremely suspicious. When Sandie had followed her yesterday, she drove to a trashy pizza shop in the town centre. Sandie watched in astonishment from her car across the road as, rather than make her way inside, Emily ducked down an alley next to the shop and did her make-up, before unbuttoning her blouse and breezing into the shop as brazen as anything, and making her way behind the counter, much to the bewilderment of the poor teenaged shop assistant.

She spent around fifteen minutes back there, doing God only knows what.

When she finally emerged from the shop, she re-dressed herself, wiped the make-up from her face and cleaned her hands, then went to the off-licence to buy a bottle of wine, and the charity shop next door to buy what were *admittedly* a rather fetching pair of boots. Something odd was going on with the girl, but Sandie was none the wiser as to what it was.

That same evening, she had gone to a party at the house of

the young miscreant, Lily Aitken. Sandie had never spoken to the girl, but she could tell she was trouble. Any young girl who chooses to dye her hair blue is *bound* to be trouble. There were always dodgy-looking people coming and going from the house at all hours of the day and night. As far as Sandie could gather, the girl did not work, she didn't need to after inheriting a small fortune, along with her house, after the deaths of both her parents.

Sandie's misgivings about the Aitken girl were confirmed later in the evening, when the party was finished prematurely after some sort of fight between Lily and her boyfriend. There was shouting and screaming and all sorts of noises from the house until the small hours. Sandie was quite surprised that Emily had chosen to associate with such a crowd, but she had learned from her dealings with her own daughters not to even try to understand the motivations of the young.

Sandie hardly slept, due to the raucous behaviour of her young neighbour. Sandie stands in her living room, in her usual spot next to the window, twitching at the curtains. It's almost like an addiction for her, or a habit at least. She is about to head to the kitchen for yet another coffee (that's all her life seems to consist of these days; cheap coffee and curtain twitching) when she sees Emily emerge from Helen Abbott's front door. She watches as the woman heads down the garden path and stands on the pavement. She checks her watch and then her mobile phone. She appears to be waiting for someone. Sandie decides this is the chance she has been waiting for, and rushes out of her front door and across the street.

20

The weather is cool and grey, but at least it's dry. I hurry out of the house without saying anything to Helen. I feel uncomfortable after last night's events so I decide to wait outside on the pavement for Adam to pick me up. As I close the door I hear Helen calling to me, but pretend that I've not. I'm standing on the pavement, minding my own business, when an attractive woman in her late fifties comes out of the front door across the road, from the house that used to belong to my family. She's immaculately dressed and made-up.

She smiles at me from across the street and gives me a nervous wave. She has a pleasant face. I look around to make sure she's not waving at somebody else, then return the gesture. She crosses the street and approaches me. Her blonde hair is smooth and glossy, and her floral dress is classy and well pressed. She is a stark contrast to Helen Abbott's drab existence, but in a funny way reminds me of how Helen used to be when she took pride in her appearance. A diamond necklace sparkles as she approaches me.

'Hi. It's Emily, isn't it?'

I can smell expensive perfume as she stands beside me. 'Yes,' I respond, unsure who this glamorous stranger is.

She holds her hand out. 'I'm Sandie Jackson. I believe you used to live in my house.' She looks nervously behind her.

'Oh, yes, that's right.' I reach my hand out, shaking hers firmly. I note there's no wedding ring on her slim fingers. 'Very pleased to meet you, Miss Jackson.'

'I've been meaning to introduce myself for a few days, but the weather's been so terrible, I've barely ventured out of the house.' She smiles. Her teeth are impossibly white.

'Yes, I was starting to think the only weather you get here is wet, and wetter.'

The woman laughs, far too loudly, too forced. It sounds fake.

'I just wanted to say if you want to come and have a nosey around your old house, for nostalgia's sake, then you're more than welcome. I've not done anything to the place since I bought it, but the people before me had terrible taste, I'm afraid to say, hence the ghastly fake leaded lights on the windows, and I'm afraid it doesn't get much better when you get inside either. Nothing to do with me,' she states firmly.

I glance towards the old house, then back to the lady standing in front of me. It is difficult to think of any happy memories from that place, although there must have been some, before Alice disappeared.

I have no desire to go into the house, but I don't say this. 'Thank you. That's very kind of you. I might take you up on that when I have a bit more time.'

'What brings you back to Palmerston?' she asks breezily. 'Catching up with friends and family?'

And the penny drops.

I'm surprised it took her so long to cut to the chase. I had expected a little interest in my return to the neighbourhood, once people realised who I am, so I can't blame her for fishing.

Knowing that she is more than likely just looking for gossip, my barriers instantly go up.

The smile doesn't leave my face, although it doesn't reach my eyes. 'I'm a journalist working on a story in the area, and needed to do some research. I thought I'd catch up with Mrs Abbott while I was here. I was very good friends with her daughter, Alice.'

Sandie Jackson looks embarrassed. This is the usual response when you mention knowing Alice Abbott. I'm totally used to it, and in fact have grown to expect it.

'So, a story?' she says with feigned intrigue. 'About what?'

I feel uncomfortable, as if I am being interrogated by this glamorous stranger.

I see with relief that Adam's electric-blue Audi TT is heading down the street towards me. 'Oh just this and that. It was very nice to meet you, Miss Jackson, but I'm afraid I have to go. My brother is here to pick me up.' I hurry towards the car, opening the passenger side door and climbing into the seat beside him.

'Who's that?' he asks, cocking an eyebrow.

'Just a neighbour introducing herself. Lives in our old house actually.'

'Ah, yeah, I knew I recognised her. I've never seen her close up though. Definitely looks better from a distance.'

I shoot him a withering look.

'You hungry?' he enquires, changing the subject quickly with a cocky smile.

'Yeah, I could eat.' I slept late and haven't had breakfast, so lunch would be good.

'Great. I know this cool little place.'

He pulls the car away from the curb, proceeding to drive far too fast towards town.

21

H is driving is erratic and far from exemplary. I find myself gripping the seat on more than one occasion as he pulls out in front of other vehicles, turns without indicating and fails to give way at roundabouts. I'm looking at him nervously but he doesn't seem to notice my discomfort. I'm not used to being driven by other people, and I realise I don't like it at all.

'I wanted to apologise again about last night. How are you?' He seems genuinely concerned.

'It was a bit of a shock but I'm fine. Tom was upset though.'

'Lily has a twisted sense of humour and she struggles sometimes with knowing what is acceptable behaviour.'

'How were things with you two after we left? It sounded… heated.'

He turns his head towards me, revealing scratches all over the left side of his face.

'Yeah, you could say that.' He smiles, but looks embarrassed.

'Oh my God, Adam! Did she do that to you?'

'Yeah, but you should see the state of her face.' He notices my shocked expression then backtracks. 'That was a joke. I didn't touch her. She has a fiery temper. We both do, I suppose.

She doesn't like it when people tell her what to do. I guess she hasn't had that for a great deal of her life, so she's used to doing whatever she wants.'

'That's no excuse. You shouldn't be letting her get away with that. She could have had your eye out!' I realise I'm sounding more than a little like our neurotic mother.

'It's fine, really. Looks a lot worse than it is. Lily's not usually violent. She was a little drunk. I'm not making excuses. What she did was awful, but she hasn't had it easy. I told her what she did was bang out of order, and she accepts that now. I think she'd like to try to make it up to you.'

'It's not me she needs to make it up to. Tom was pretty shaken last night. I heard him crying in his room for ages after we got home.'

Adam looks irritated. 'That lad needs to sort himself out. I get that he's had more than his fair share of shit, but it's been a long fucking time. A grown man shouldn't be crying like a baby.'

I am shocked by his lack of empathy. 'Adam, Tom lost his sister. She was abducted from their house while he was asleep in the next room.'

'Yes, I'm familiar with the story,' he replies sarcastically.

'That's harsh. He's really messed up about what happened. He desperately wants to remember the events of that night. I'm trying to help him, but I'm not sure those memories are even in there anymore. He's done a sterling job of blocking them out.'

'You're trying to help him remember? Do you really think that's a good idea?'

'I think it's a *great* idea. He needs to move on, and I think once he realises there was nothing he could have done, then he might be able to. And if he can tell me anything that might help with my story, then that is an added bonus too.'

'I think he's fucked-up enough without actually remembering what happened that night. You should leave well enough alone.'

'He's supposed to be your friend. A little understanding wouldn't go amiss.'

'Hey, I'm his friend! His only friend in fact. I don't mean to sound callous, but you've not been around here for a while. You don't know what I've done for him.'

'I'm just say–'

'Don't.'

22

We drive the rest of the way into town in silence. I hope I haven't screwed things up with Adam already, but my heart lifts when he parks up outside a little café, turns and smiles at me, saying, 'Let's eat. I'm starving.'

Could my brother finally have grown up?

A very pretty slim teenaged waitress takes our jackets then leads us to a table by the window. I glance at the menu, ordering a chicken salad when she returns. Her eyes linger on Adam a second longer than is professional while she takes his order. He winks at her and she blushes, then leaves for the kitchen.

'So, Emily, what *exactly* are you doing back here?'

'I'm working on a story for the magazine.'

'Let me guess what it might be about. Alice Abbott?' He feigns a yawn, raising an eyebrow.

'Yes, kind of, but I'm also looking into this new kid, Becky Clarke, from down the road.'

'Surely you don't think they can be connected.'

'I know it's unlikely, but nobody knows that for sure.'

'It's been twenty-five years. They're not connected.'

'Look, Sherlock, if whoever took Alice was, say, thirty at the time, he would still only be fifty-five now. And anyway, even if they aren't connected, it's my job. I just do what I'm told by my boss. I think this'll be cathartic for me. I haven't really thought about Alice much recently, but this new case has brought it all back and it's made me realise that I never really came to terms with what happened.'

A few minutes after giving us our drinks, the waitress returns, placing my salad in front of me, and a burger with fries next to Adam. He shovels a few chips into his mouth, takes a huge bite from his burger, and washes it down with a mouthful of Coke. When he speaks, he still has food in his mouth.

He doesn't look at me.

'Do you think you might unearth what actually happened to her?'

I fork some salad leaves into my mouth before answering. 'I don't know. Probably not. But that's not what this is about. This is just about telling the story and seeing if there are any connections. My boss was extremely excited when I told him about my past. The other reporters, the other stories... it's mostly been speculation. But I want to tell the facts. I was there. I knew her. She was my best friend.'

Adam's eyes dart up to mine, then back to his plate of food. 'But you don't really know any facts. Nobody does. You were just a kid. So, surely anything you can offer is speculation too.'

I swallow a piece of chicken and take a sip of water to wash it down. 'I don't think so. I know what went on in the days leading up to Alice going missing. I was with her every day. I have my diary that tells me exactly what we were doing, and detailed descriptions of conversations. I think I'm in a better position that anyone else to give some insight into events surrounding Alice's disappearance. I'm not going to speculate on anything. I'm not even going to make any suggestions as to what happened to her. I'm going to tell the story as I know it, and leave the readers to draw their own conclusions. I'm also hoping Helen Abbott will give me some new information. My boss thinks, given our history, she might be more inclined to open up to me than other reporters. She might tell me something that she wouldn't tell anyone else.'

'What like? "Oh by the way, I killed her"?'

'No. Not at all. Don't be ridiculous. Small facts that she might have omitted in the past. The Abbotts were notoriously tight-lipped with the press, so for me to be able to interview her is amazing.'

'And has she actually agreed to an interview?'

'More or less, yes. I haven't really found the opportunity to talk to her properly yet. But I will.'

We eat a few more mouthfuls of food. Then Adam continues, 'So, do you actually think you could help Tom to remember something?'

'I don't know. He was very young. I'm not even sure how much *I* remember, or how much of it is ingrained in me from reading my diary. But I'd definitely like to try. I feel I owe it to Alice to try to help her little brother.'

'So, what theories have you got? What do you think actually happened to her?'

I think about this for a while before I answer. 'I don't know. My rational educated brain tells me that she's probably dead. But I can't help wondering if she's still out there somewhere. That's the trouble with not having an answer. You'll always wonder. What about you? What do you think?'

Adam looks uncomfortable. 'What do I know? I was eleven. Nobody told me anything. Mum and Dad moved away so quickly after it all happened. I hardly even remember her.'

'Really? That's odd. She was at our house a lot. I think you actually had a crush on her.'

Adam's face flushes and he looks angry. 'Like I said, I don't really remember. Anyway, I sometimes think it's best if everyone moves on. No good comes from dwelling on the past. And it certainly won't bring her back. I think everyone should get the fuck over it.'

'Yes, well if I can get this story written, then I'm hoping that I will, and maybe some other people might benefit from it also. I was actually wondering if you would mind helping me with something this afternoon.'

'Sure, I'm not busy. What do you need?'

'I've got a name of a guy I need to pay a visit to. He might have some information. But I don't really want to go on my own.'

'Who's the guy?' Adam seems interested, which is a bonus.

I consider not telling him who I want to visit, but decide it's best to be honest with him. 'I think he's possibly a paedophile.'

Adam places his knife and fork down beside his plate calmly. 'Excuse me?'

'You heard. I've been doing some digging around, and I've been given this guy's name. I want to ask him a few questions.'

'What the fuck? Are you serious?'

'It'll be fine, especially if you're there with me.'

He shakes his head. 'No way, this is utter madness. If you've got information, you should be handing it to the police. This isn't a game.'

'Handing it to the police will not help me with my story,' I reply. 'I know this isn't a game. But I don't see the harm in going to check him out. See if he knows anything. If it looks like he's dodgy, *then* we can go to the police.'

'Emily, nothing about this sounds like a good idea to me. It sounds bonkers. Are you actually listening to yourself?'

'Adam. Be a man!' I joke.

He looks angrily at me.

'All I'm asking you to do is come along with me to meet this guy. I'll ask him a few questions, and then we leave. It's simple.'

'And why would he talk to you?'

'He probably won't. But if I don't try, I'll never know.' I pull my sad little girl face. 'Please?'

Adam shakes his head. 'Fine. But the first sign of trouble, we leave.'

'Of course!'

'I can't believe we're actually going to do this.'

'Believe it, little brother. This is exciting, isn't it? Me and you... together, after all these years. Who'd have thought it? Come on, eat up and let's get out of here.'

23

W e rush down the rest of our food. Adam pays the bill and we head back to his car. I describe the old warehouse, and he knows where it is. He drives through town and parks next to a children's playground. We cut through a small wooded area. When we come out the other side, a dirty old wall is in front of us. Graffiti covers most of the brickwork.

The few windows and doors I can see have metal grates over them to stop people getting in. As we walk around the perimeter of the building, we come to a window at the back, partially covered by a huge old bramble bush. Adam pushes some of the branches aside to reveal a small window with the cover broken away. The glass is smashed and there's enough space to climb through.

Adam looks at me. I glance around nervously.

'You sure about this?' he asks.

'Not really. But I'm doing it anyway.'

'Go on then. Before I change my mind. Here, I'll give you a bunk-up.'

Adam cups his hands together to form a step and I climb up and through the broken window. The drop on the other side is lower than the ground outside, and I fall clumsily down into the darkness.

I hear Adam pulling himself up the wall as my eyes adjust to the dingy light.

As I take in the surroundings, Adam falls to the floor beside me. I look around.

The place is littered with rubbish.

There are used condoms strewn around the floor. Beer cans and cigarette butts adorn the rest of the ground.

There's a disgusting smell of damp and shit and piss, and the building is freezing.

I feel as if we shouldn't be here. Part of me wants to turn round and leave immediately, but I tell myself I need to do this. Adam will protect me.

There's a filthy mattress on the floor up against the wall beside me, with a dirty old blanket on top of it. On the floor beside it is a child's rag doll, with one eye missing.

Its clothes are also missing.

Adam joins me, looking around. 'This place is all sorts of wrong,' he whispers.

I nod, swallowing down my fear.

In front of us is a door jammed open with rubbish. The doorway opens out to a long corridor. The little light that's getting in through the windows barely reaches ten feet down the corridor.

Drip. Drip. Drip. Like a metronome.

The sound echoes from somewhere off in the darkness. I head to the door, pulling it open as wide as I can. It's stiff, and as it moves, it makes a loud scraping noise.

I step into the corridor, pulling out my phone to get some light.

The beam lights up various doorways off to each side. There are still some old factory signs hanging on the walls, directing to the canteen, the main office and reception. We walk slowly down the corridor.

The smell is almost unbearable.

I pull my jumper up over my nose and mouth to try to help, but it does little to alleviate the unpleasantness. At the end of the corridor, I swing my phone around me. There is a large red arrow spray painted on the wall, pointing to the door on our left. I look at Adam. I can barely make out his expression in the dim light, but he nods in the direction of the arrow, motioning me to continue.

I open the door with a creek and step into another dark corridor. Someone has lit some candles which are placed sporadically along the corridor, casting enough light to see where we're going. I put my phone away. The red arrows are sprayed at irregular intervals down the hallway. At the end of this corridor are large double doors and a sign that says 'canteen'. The word has been sprayed out, and 'RAB' has been spray painted crudely across the two doors.

'That's who we're after,' I whisper to Adam.

He nods. I push the doors and enter the canteen. There are upturned tables and trays all over the place. On the floor to my left is a bedraggled teddy bear, its stuffing poking out from holes on its body.

In the centre of the room lies a filthy double mattress with a sleeping bag.

Children's toys litter the floor around the mattress.

Drip. Drip. Drip.

'I don't like this,' Adam whispers.

I put my fingers to my lips, telling him to keep quiet.

A sound.

Footsteps?

I can't see any movement.

I take a few tentative steps towards the mattress. It reeks.

There are beer cans and food wrappers scattered everywhere.

I shudder.

A small filthy pair of Disney knickers lie on top of the sleeping bag.

There are empty cartons of juice and sweet packets piled around the makeshift bed. More used condoms are on the floor beside the mattress.

I take a few steps further into the room and Adam grabs my arm. 'Emily, I think we should leave. Now. Call the police and tell *them* about this place.'

'No, we're here. I don't like this any more than you, but what if that little girl is in here somewhere and we leave without helping her?'

'What good can we do if some psycho jumps out on us with a machete?'

I look Adam up and down. 'I'm quite sure you can handle yourself in a fight.'

He pulls an irritated face but follows after me. As we move towards the kitchen area of the canteen, a voice echoes around the room.

'Who the fuck are you, and what the fuck do you want?' enquires the thick Scottish accent.

It's raspy and deep. It sounds like the voice of someone who has smoked far too much for far too long.

I look around but can't see anyone. 'I'm looking for Rab,' I reply.

The room fills with loud laughter, which turns into a raspy cough. 'Nobody's looking for Rab.'

Adam's looking nervously around the room, frantically trying to figure out where the sickening voice is coming from.

'I want to ask you a few questions!' I shout into the void.

'Fuck off!' comes the reply.

Then a few more coughs and splutters.

The sound of someone hacking up, then spitting.

The voice sounds as if it's coming from the corner of the room, by the kitchen area.

Adam leans close to my face, whispering slowly, 'Keep him talking.' He edges away towards the counter.

I frown, holding up my hands questioningly, but he simply gestures for me to keep talking.

'Come on, Rab,' I continue, 'I only want to talk to you.'

The sound of a bottle rattling across concrete comes from behind the counter.

'Nobody wants to talk to Rab!' he shouts back.

Adam approaches the counter. He stealthily reaches over in a grabbing motion, pulling a filthy-looking tramp up from behind the worktop by his long greasy grey hair.

'Get the fuck off me!' the man shouts as Adam pulls him over the counter, slamming him hard onto the floor and holding him down under his right foot. Adam leans across and slaps the man in the face. 'Shut the fuck up!'

I run over to the kitchen, grabbing Adam's hand before he hits the man again. 'That's enough!'

24

The man's wriggling about underneath Adam's boot, which is pressed firmly on top of his chest. He's cursing and swearing, and there's blood on his face.

'Are you Rab?'

'Who the hell wants to know?'

'I have some questions for you, and then we'll leave you in peace.'

'Get to fuck,' the man growls. He opens his mouth to reveal missing teeth and rotting gums. A rank smell wafts from within.

'Adam, take your foot off him.'

Adam looks at me in disgust. 'Are you mad?'

'I said let him go.' I reach out and pull Adam away. The man sits up but makes no attempt to stand or run.

'I'm looking for some answers, and I really hope you can give me what I want,' I tell him calmly.

The man laughs quietly. 'Sorry, darling. You're a little old for me.' He looks from me, to Adam, then back again. 'Your boy here would have been more my type anyway. A few years ago, granted.'

Adam grimaces. 'You sick fuck!' He kicks Rab hard in the gut.

Rab recoils in pain, coughing and spluttering. He leans over and spits a globule of blood and snot and God knows what else on the ground beside my foot.

'Show my sister some fucking respect, you piece of shit, or there's more of that coming your way.'

Rab laughs and looks up again. 'Hmm, brother and sister, huh? Now that would have been sexy. I bet you were a couple of cuties.' He winks and blows a kiss at Adam, who moves towards him, preparing to kick him again.

I step in front of him, holding up my hands.

'Adam, stop!' I look back down at the pathetic creature on the floor. 'What do you know about the disappearance of Becky Clarke?'

He laughs.

'What's so funny?'

'Have you seen her? I've seen her picture on the front page of the paper, and I tell you, no fucker would touch her.' He laughs again.

I detest this man immensely, but something tells me he's not lying about this. There's something about his reaction. 'So, you and your friends haven't got her hidden away somewhere in here then, I take it.'

'Fuck no. This place is disgusting enough as it is.' He chuckles. 'Mind you, put a paper bag over her head and I'm sure someone might give her a go.'

Adam goes for him again, but I grab him and push him away.

'I'm sure you wouldn't want the police coming sniffing round here, would you?' I hiss at Rab.

The smile disappears from his face.

'I don't know nothing about her.' He hocks up and spits again.

This time it lands on my shoe. I'm almost sick. 'What about Alice Abbott?'

His eyes shoot up to my face. 'Now there's a name I've not heard in a while. The little girl lost.' A smile spreads across his face.

'Do you know what happened to her?'

'Sorry, love, I only arrived here about fifteen years ago. That girl was long before my time. But I've never met anyone who knows anything about her. And believe you me, a sweet little thing like that, they would have been bragging if they did. I know I would. She was perfect.' He licks his lips. I shiver uncontrollably.

'So, you expect me to believe that a girl like that vanishes and none of your lot know anything about it?' I can't hide the disdain from my voice.

'I don't give a fuck what you believe, sugar tits. Who the fuck are you anyway, coming into my place, roughing me up and asking me questions? I ought to fuck you up. If I was ten years younger, you'd be sorry.' He picks up an old beer can from the ground next to him, gives it a shake, then drains the dregs from it.

He belches. 'All I know is if that cute little thing had been here, I'd know about it. Mind you... there have been so many little girls here over the years, it's hard to keep track.' He looks at Adam. 'Little boys too.' Rab licks his lips again.

Before I know what's happening, Adam is on him.

He reaches down, pulling Rab up from the ground, then slams him hard onto the kitchen counter. Adam lifts him and slams him back down again.

'You sick fucking fuck!' he shouts as he pulls him up again. 'Prison's too good for a waster like you. You deserve to be castrated then burned alive.' He punches Rab in the face, a stream of blood splatters out of his mouth, hitting the wall behind us.

He falls backwards, banging his head on the corner of the worktop, landing in a heap on the floor.

He's gurgling.

Adam spits on him, then kicks him repeatedly: his stomach, his chest, his head. Adam's boot keeps connecting with Rab's face, which is becoming a bloodied mess.

I try to pull Adam away, but he lashes out, hitting me in the face. I fall to the floor.

As I look up, all I can see is a frenzied mess of flailing limbs and blood.

Rab's sputtering and shouting but Adam doesn't stop.

I get to my feet and I run.

I run as fast as I can back down the corridor, to the small window.

I pull a chair against the wall, climbing out.

As I fall to the wet ground, I take deep gulps of fresh air.

I can't breathe.

Everything is a blur. I want to be sick.

I pull myself up using a bramble bush, tearing my hands on thorns, but I don't care.

I can't see. Tears distort my vision.

I run through the woods, branches slapping at my face, scratching me.

I finally find my way back to the car, but it's locked.

I slump down to the floor and struggle to get my breath.

I'm sick all over the pavement beside me.

25

Sandie feels frustrated. She tried to be nice to Emily, but feels distinctly like she was fobbed off. Perhaps she came on too strong with the offer for her to come into her old house. Sandie didn't like the way Emily's brother had looked at her either. Eyes filled with lust. Sandie knew the type of man he was. Would probably try to bed her so he could brag to his mates that he has slept with an older woman. But not Sandie. She would never allow that to happen.

She had class. She had taste.

Sure, he was handsome, and she couldn't help but notice his muscles bulging through his tight leather jacket, but it took more than muscles and a handsome face to impress her. She liked a man with some substance. Jim Abbott had intrigued her from the start. She knew who he was, of course. Everybody did. She was kind to him at first because she felt he deserved it. But on talking to him, she soon discovered a real person. Not just the man from the news. There was more to him than a missing daughter. He was sweet, and caring, and funny. And he was intelligent too. It didn't take long for Sandie and Jim to fall for each other.

Sandie shakes her head and looks at her watch. It's been roughly forty-five minutes since Emily left the house. As Sandie glances out of the window, she sees something rare. Helen Abbott is leaving the house. She pulls the door shut behind her but does not lock it. She shuffles down the path, glances nervously up and down the street, as if she is making sure there is nobody around, then heads down the road towards town. She stops briefly outside Alan Gillespie's house, staring up the path towards the front door, before continuing on her journey.

The Abbott house is empty. This does not happen often. Sandie can only recall a couple of times since she has lived here. She decides to take her chance. She exits her house and moves stealthily across the street. She pauses at Helen Abbott's gate, making sure nobody is watching, then creeps down the path towards the front door. She turns the handle and the door opens. One final glance over her shoulder, and she slips inside.

Sandie stands inside the front door, in the dingy hallway. She is breathing heavily. Nervous. She glances around, listening for any signs of life from outside. She creeps down the hallway and into the front room. Piles of papers and clippings are littered around the floor. A dirty coffee mug sits on the arm of an old armchair. The room smells stale and musty. The windows have not been opened in years. Sandie resists the overwhelming urge to open the window and tidy up. She picks up some of the papers, leafing through them. Nothing of interest. Bills and final demands for arrears. This woman is up to her eyeballs in debt. It hardly surprises Sandie.

She smiles to herself in the knowledge that Helen Abbott is struggling, then tells herself this is unkind.

She hears a car outside and freezes. It drives slowly past then continues down the street, and Sandie lets out her breath. She crosses the room to a small dresser opposite the window, opening a drawer stuffed with photographs. Sandie picks up a handful and flicks through them.

They are *all* of Alice.

Alice as a baby, sitting on Helen's knee. The contrast of the woman then and how she is now is unbelievable. There is a picture of Alice and another young girl, who Sandie assumes must be Emily. They are wearing net curtains as if they are dresses, and Alice has one draped over her head. Both girls are smiling widely. Two boys sit in the background looking sulky. One she recognises as Alice's brother Tom. The other boy stares at Alice and Emily from the corner of the room, smiling with them.

The next photo is of Jim Abbott. Alice is about eight and sitting on his knee. It is Christmas, and she wears a pretty red velvet dress. Her hair is in pigtails, tied with gold tinsel, and they fall loosely onto her shoulders. She throws her head back mid laugh as Jim stares at her adoringly. It strikes Sandie that if Alice was around today, she would be devastatingly beautiful, and a pang of jealousy flows through her. She sees the smile on Jim's face and wishes she had known Alice.

Sandie carefully places the photos back in the drawer and closes it.

She freezes.

Was that a noise from within the house?

Sandie stands, statue still, afraid to breathe.

A few seconds pass like hours, but there is no further sound. Satisfied that she is alone in the house, she turns and heads back out into the hallway. Glancing down the hall, she sees the kitchen, much like the layout of her own house. To her left are the stairs. If the house is similar in layout to her own, then the basement is entered through the kitchen. She follows the gloomy hallway into the kitchen at the end. Sandie passes through without paying much attention. There is little of interest there. Some dirty dishes in the sink and a mousetrap against a skirting board.

The key to the basement is in the door. Sandie turns the key, hearing the satisfying click of the lock. She opens the door and stands at the top of the narrow stairs. A black chasm extends below her. The light from the kitchen window falls onto the top few steps, but after that, only darkness. A musty stale smell drifts into her nostrils. Like mothballs, and mould. And death, Sandie thinks, then chides herself for being so melodramatic. It's a basement, the same as hers. Nothing sinister. Just a room. She fights the urge to turn and run out of the front door, back to the safety of her own house.

There is a light switch beside her. She flicks it on. A dull bulb flickers a few times somewhere round the corner at the foot of the steps, but does little to illuminate the staircase. She reaches into her pocket, retrieving her phone, using it to light the floor ahead of her, and slowly descends into the musty basement. As she places her weight on the wooden steps, they creak loudly beneath her.

When she reaches the foot of the steps, she sees the basement is in fact nothing like her own. Boxes are piled everywhere. Although the room is relatively tidy, in comparison to the rest of what Sandie has seen of the house, it is still chaos compared to hers. The large cardboard boxes are piled almost to the ceiling. A thick layer of dust covers the tops of them, and cobwebs hang from the corners of some. There is a pile to her left that looks as if it has been recently disturbed. The dust has been wiped from the tops and one of them is loosely open.

She pulls the box from the top of the pile, placing it on the floor in front of her. 'ALICE' is written on it in neat black letters. She opens the flaps, looking inside. Soft toys and neatly folded child's dresses and sweaters are piled tidily in the box. Sandie places her hand on top of the dresses and strokes them. She closes her eyes and sees her own daughters as young girls. She tries to imagine the pain she would have felt if anything had happened to either of them. She shakes the thought from her mind and closes the box. She pushes it to one side and pulls another from the pile onto the floor. The word 'JIM' is scrawled on this one. Not so neat. Angry, scratchy letters.

She opens the flaps. A red and blue chequered flannel shirt is screwed up in the top of the box.

She lifts the garment to her face and inhales deeply, but no trace of Jim's smell remains. It's old and musty. No care has gone into packing this box. She clearly pictures Jim wearing this shirt, and recalls the last conversation she had with him, five years earlier.

He had told her that he had decided it was time for them to be together. He was leaving Helen. He didn't care anymore. They were going to leave and start a new life abroad. He said there were a few things he had to take care of, and had arranged to meet her the following day at the train station at noon.

Sandie had waited at the station in the pouring rain. She shivered in the cold, avoiding the curious glances of passers-by, who must have wondered what this poor sad pathetic woman was doing standing in the rain with a suitcase. Mascara running down her face and dripping onto her blouse.

She waited for three hours, afraid to leave in case Jim arrived. But he didn't. Sandie never saw or heard from him again.

Sandie rifles through the box. More clothes she recognises. Jim's favourite Rolling Stones T-shirt. Sandie smiles as she pictures him in it, walking towards her with a grin. She rifles further, reaching down to the very bottom of the large box. Her hand brushes over something smooth and cold. She grasps it and lifts it out from under the dusty old clothes.

She stares in disbelief at what she holds in front of her.

All of a sudden, she is dizzy.

This does not make any sense.

A sickening feeling spreads through Sandie's body as the realisation of what she is looking at sinks in, and she finally understands. She places it in her pocket and carefully closes the box, putting it back where she found it. She looks around the dingy basement and then heads back up the stairs into the kitchen. She locks the cellar door and returns to the hallway, to the foot of the stairs.

Placing her foot onto the bottom step, a loud creak resonates through the house. In the silence, it sounds almost deafening. She looks up the stairs into the darkness, then continues up into the gloom. At the top of the stairs, she looks around. The landing is much the same as her own. She sees a bathroom opposite with the door open. The blind is halfway down at the window, allowing a small amount of light into the space. All the other doors are closed. She takes a few tentative steps forward, and again, the floorboards creak. She pauses. Another sound comes from a room at the end of the landing. Was it a cough?

She freezes, but remains calm.

Someone is moving around in the room.

She looks around for somewhere to hide, but it's too late. The door opens and Tom Abbott stands in front of her. He doesn't see Sandie at first, but as he steps towards her, he looks up, and she is caught like a deer in the headlights. Tom looks confused, then afraid.

'What are you doing in our house?' he asks shakily.

Sandie holds out both hands in front of her, keeping her eyes fixed on his.

'I'm a friend of your mother's. She asked me to stop by and pick something up for her.'

'Bullshit. I know you. You're the lady from over the road.

Mum doesn't like you. I'm calling the police.' He turns to go back into his room.

Sandie takes a few steps along the carpet towards Tom. 'Tom, wait,' she says calmly.

He turns round. 'How do you know my name?' He looks terrified.

'I'll level with you, Tom. You don't know me, but I know you. I am a very good friend of your father's.'

Tom looks away. 'Dad's gone,' he says sadly.

'I know he is. I'm trying to find him. You want to find him too, don't you?'

He looks at Sandie but doesn't say anything, although the fear seems to have gone from his eyes.

'Why don't you and I go downstairs and put the kettle on,' Sandie says calmly. 'I think it would be good for us to have a little chat, don't you?'

Tom still looks sceptical, but Sandie smiles at him. She knows the effect her smile has on men, and Tom begins to relax. He shuffles past her and heads down the stairs. Sandie follows closely behind him.

Sandie Jackson has a plan.

26

I sit on the floor resting against Adam's car. He's still inside the building. The sky darkens and it starts to rain. I'm getting soaked. Lightning flashes. There's a loud crash of thunder almost immediately. The rain's torrential. My hair's plastered to my face which is sore from Adam's strike. He eventually arrives back at the car, unlocks it and gets in, waiting for me to join him. I climb into the passenger seat and sit staring at him, with water dripping from me. He has blood on his T-shirt and splattered across his face, and his knuckles are bruised.

We're both sodden. He doesn't say a word.

'Adam, what the hell was that?'

He doesn't look at me. 'You heard him. He admitted to messing about with kids.'

'He was trying to wind you up. Couldn't you see that?'

'He was a sicko. A fucking child rapist. He deserved it.'

'And what about me? What about this?' I point to my throbbing cheek.

'I'm sorry about that. I didn't mean to.'

'Adam, we're not the police. We don't decide who is guilty

and innocent. We don't dish out punishment.' Adam's shaking his head. I continue, 'Is he... is he dead?'

'No! Don't be ridiculous. Do you honestly think I'm a killer?'

'I don't know. After what I just witnessed, I don't think I know who you are at all.'

'And whose fault is that?' he spits back at me, the venom in his words blatantly obvious.

'What do you mean by that?'

'You never wanted to know me. You never tried. You left home as soon as you could get out of there. You left me.'

'Adam, I went to university. I went away to study. By the time I came back, you were long gone.'

'You cared more about Alice Abbott than you did about me. You were never a sister to me.' The hatred in his voice is alarming.

'I'm sorry if you feel like that, I really am. But that's rubbish. You weren't exactly the easiest person to get along with. You were always so angry.'

'What did you expect? Mum and Dad dragged me away from here, away from my friends. They moved us to a city where I didn't know anyone. I didn't fit in, but they didn't care. They didn't ask me what *I* wanted to do. Then they sent me away to boarding school. They didn't want me. You were always the golden child, but me, I was the consolation prize.'

'They loved you, Adam, but they didn't know how to handle you. None of us did. You were... very hard work.'

'That fucking girl, she ruined everything.'

'Alice?'

'Yeah, fucking Alice. Who else?'

'It was hardly her fault. She didn't ask for any of this.'

'It was. It was her fucking fault. All of it!'

. . .

We sit in silence for a few minutes. Adam puts his head in his hands. I put my hand on his shoulder.

'Adam, I might not have been there when we were younger, but I'm here now. And I'm not planning on going anywhere. Whatever you need, I'm here for you.'

He looks at me. 'Did I hurt you?' he asks sheepishly, and for a moment I see a flash of the little boy I remember.

'I'll survive.'

He leans towards me and hugs me tightly.

My phone rings. I pull it from my damp jeans and answer it. 'Hello?'

There's silence on the line, but I can hear breathing. 'Is there anybody there?'

'Emily. It's Tom.'

'Hi, Tom. What's up?'

Adam's eyes shoot towards me.

'Where are you?' Tom sounds upset.

'I'm in town. What's wrong?'

'Can you come home please. Right away.'

'Yes, sure. What's going on? Is your mum all right?'

'I remember,' he says coldly.

It takes a few seconds to register.

'What?'

'I know what happened to Alice.'

The line goes dead.

I sit staring at my phone.

'What's going on?' Adam asks.

'It was Tom. He says he remembers what happened the night Alice disappeared.'

Adam looks shocked. 'What? After all these years, he suddenly remembers?'

'We were talking last night. I gave him Alice's old teddy bear.

I don't know if that's got anything to do with it, but he wants me to come back. Right now. Can you get us home quickly?'

Adam starts the engine, speeding us back to Pear Tree Close.

Outside the house, I place my hand on Adam's shoulder as he starts to climb out of his car.

'Perhaps you should wait out here,' I tell him.

'He's my mate,' Adam protests.

'I know that, but he's upset. I don't think it's a good idea to crowd him. I'll come out and get you in a minute. I want to see how he is first.'

'I'm coming in!'

'Adam, no! I think you've done enough damage for one day, don't you?'

Adam doesn't look happy, but he gets back into the car, leaving the door open. I rush up the path, finding the front door ajar.

As I enter the house, Helen's in the kitchen.

She's hysterical. 'Emily, thank goodness you're here. I don't know what to do.'

'Where's Tom?'

'He's down in the cellar. I went to see what he was doing, and he has Jim's hunting rifle. He screamed at me to get out. He seems very agitated, so I did what he said. I don't know what to do.' She's in tears.

'Does he have ammunition down there?'

'Yes, I think so. I don't know.'

'Call the police and stay up here, right?'

She nods and shuffles towards the phone.

I hurry to the cellar door, which is wide open.

The light's off down below.

I try the switch but nothing happens. The storm rages outside. The occasional flash of lightning floods bright light through the tiny downstairs windows, illuminating the space below, and casting eerie shadows around the room.

'Tom, it's Emily. I'm coming down.' I call down the stairs. There is no reply. I edge forward onto the steps, the now-familiar creak beneath my weight sounds as I descend into darkness.

Another flash of lightning helps me to see my way down.

At the bottom, I turn the corner.

Tom's sitting on an old wooden chair in the middle of the room.

The boxes of Alice's belongings are open, the contents strewn around the floor. I can't see Tom clearly, but in the dim light cast from the tiny street-level windows, I can see his silhouette.

He has the gun propped up against the chair.

He's holding Alice's bear in his lap. His other hand rests on the shotgun.

'Tom, what's going on?' I ask slowly.

I see the dark shape of his head lift up in my direction. He doesn't reply.

'Tom?'

'I wanted to remember.' His voice is quiet but steadier than usual. 'So, I started looking through Alice's things. Mum has never let me even look at this stuff. I wasn't allowed. She used to get angry if I asked.' His voice trails off.

'And what have you remembered?'

A sudden flash of lightning, accompanied by a deafening crash of thunder.

His face is illuminated, ghostly. He's expressionless. 'Everything,' he says calmly.

I edge towards him. 'Tom, why don't you let me take that gun and we can talk about it, okay?'

'No!' he screams, saliva trailing from the corners of his mouth. 'Don't come any closer. You shouldn't come near me.'

I stop and hold up my hands. 'Fine, Tom, I've stopped, all right? Why don't you tell me what's wrong?'

He picks up the bear from his lap, looking at it sadly. 'You know, my mum thought I had taken this. When she realised it was gone, she came into my room one night; I was sleeping. She was screaming at me, "What have you done with it? Where is it?" I didn't know what she was talking about of course. She dragged me out of bed and hit me around the head. Kept slapping me. I didn't know what was happening. Dad came in and pulled her away. I had to take a couple of weeks off school, because they didn't want them to see the cuts and bruises. I was eight,' he says flatly.

He draws the back of his hand over his mouth, wiping away the trails of spit and mucus.

'Tom, I'm so sorry. Your mother was devastated; she didn't know what she was doing.'

'Oh, she did, Emily. She knew exactly what she was doing. And you know what? I deserved it. I deserved worse.' Tears are streaming down his face.

'No, you didn't. You were a little boy. You must have been just as upset as they were. She was your sister. None of this was your fault.'

Tom gives a humourless laugh. 'That's where you're wrong. You couldn't be more wrong. It was all my fault. All of it.'

'What do you mean?' I'm edging closer, slowly.

'It was me,' he says calmly.

'I don't understand, Tom. What was you?' I ask, but I'm sick with fear that I already know the answer.

He shakes his head slowly and tosses the bear onto the floor. He lifts the shotgun up in front of him.

'I killed her. I killed Alice.'

27

A cold shiver runs down my spine.
I hear a creak as someone puts a foot onto the steps at the entrance to the cellar.

Tom positions the barrel of the gun under his chin, resting his head down on it, his hands around the trigger.

'Tom, don't!' I shout. 'Please, this must be a mistake. Of course you didn't kill her. Listen, put the gun down and let's talk about this. Adam's outside, why don't I get him to come in and talk to you. We can all sit down and talk about what you think you remember. Would you like that?'

'No! I don't want him!'

I take a few steps towards him but he shouts for me to stay where I am. 'I'm sorry,' he says sadly.

There's a deafening blast as the gun goes off.

My ears are ringing.

I can't hear.

Everything then seems to happen all at once.

Tom's body slumps forward, then falls to the floor.

I hear a scream behind me, but I'm not aware of who it is.

A hand on my shoulder.

A flash of lightning illuminates the room.

Everything's red.

Blood.

Everywhere.

On the ceiling, on the walls and across the glass of the window.

Alice's clothes and toys are splattered with blood and brain matter.

Tom's body spasms.

Blood pours from what's left of his head. There's a smell like a butcher's shop around me, and a metallic taste in my mouth.

My ears are still ringing.

Something thick and warm oozes down my face.

I run my hand through my hair and look at it. Wet, and red.

I see Adam's face in front of me.

He's shouting at me, but I can't make out what he is saying.

Red and blue lights flash through the window from the road outside.

I can't hear anything. I don't understand what's happening.

Adam spins me round towards the stairs.

Another flash of lightning reveals Helen Abbott lying in a heap on the floor. Her body is convulsing. Adam leads me up the stairs. There are policemen in the kitchen. People are rushing past us, down into the cellar.

Adam ushers me out of the house.

My knees are weak. I see Sandie Jackson staring at me from one of the windows of my old house across the street, a look of terror on her face.

I collapse, and everything goes black.

28

S andie stands at the window behind her net curtain, red and blue lights flashing through the glass, illuminating her living room, distorting her furniture, making the room look even worse than it is. She has seen the Blake girl leave the Abbott house with her brother. He led her away with his arm around her. She looked shaken and not entirely with it. Somebody was wheeled out on a gurney. She thought it could have been Helen Abbott.

Nobody seems to know what has happened, and the police won't tell her anything. All anyone would say was that there had been an incident and that she should return to her house, that there was nothing to worry about. One thing was for sure, she had heard a gunshot. And now there were a lot of police and paramedics over the road at the Abbott house. Jim Abbott used to have an old shotgun. He had told Sandie about it once when they were in bed. He joked that maybe he should just shoot his wife in the face and be done with her that way. Sandie had scolded him, telling him it was not funny to joke about killing people. 'Who's joking?' he had replied, deadpan.

At the time it scared her, but in hindsight, she wished that she had taken that gun herself and blown the bitch's head off.

She looks across the road and sees Alan Gillespie standing at his living room window, staring over in the direction of her house. Although the lights are off and she is in darkness apart from the reds and blues, she can't help thinking that he is staring straight at her.

She shivers and steps away from the window.

She crosses the room to a dresser against the far wall. Opening a drawer, she pulls out a dusty cardboard box. She carries it to her kitchen. Switching on the light and sitting down at the table, she gently removes the lid, placing it beside her. Jim Abbott's face stares up at her from an old Polaroid picture on the top of the pile of papers in the box. He's smiling and has his arm around Sandie's bare shoulder. In the picture she looks embarrassed and is trying to turn her face away from the camera. She blushes as she recalls the moment the photograph was taken.

They had just made love for the second time that day.

Jim was preparing to leave and head back home to his wife, and Sandie had been upset. She didn't want to be 'the other woman' in Jim's life anymore. She wanted to be the only woman. 'Soon, Sandie, soon. But it's not the right time at the moment,' he had told her as he stroked her hair, kissing her gently on the cheek.

'I don't think it'll ever be the right time for you,' she replied. He picked up her Polaroid camera from the dressing table and turned it around, snapping a picture of the two of them.

He handed her the photograph, shaking it. 'Look how happy you make me.'

Sandie glanced at the picture as Jim continued, 'There was a time in my life when I was absolutely sure I'd never be happy again. And that feeling has stuck with me for many years. I'd just about given up hope. And then I met *you*, and all that changed.'

He had put his arm around Sandie again and hugged her close to his hairy chest. His smell had filled her nostrils and she had not been able to stop herself from smiling. He had taken her chin in his hand, softly turning her face up towards his. 'I have been numb for so long, I will not let my happiness get away. I promise you that. I love you, Sandie, but I need you to be patient. Helen's still in a very bad way, and Tom is not doing well either. As much as I want to, I don't feel that I can leave them yet. I don't know what she would do to herself, or to Tom. I don't know how Tom would cope with being left alone with her. There are too many things I would worry about. So, all I'm asking is for you to bear with me and give me a little time to sort out my current situation, and when that is done, we can be together. I can't wait to introduce you to Tom. He could really benefit from having a caring woman like you in his life.'

Sandie had blushed. 'Do you think he would like me?'

'How could he not? You're the kindest, most genuine, beautiful person I've ever met.'

Sandie had brushed a strand of loose hair self-consciously behind her ear. She had never been good with compliments... not back then at least. 'But won't he think I've split up his family?'

A sad look crept onto Jim's face. 'Oh baby. Our family was broken way beyond repair a long time before you showed up. You just made me realise that I had to do something about it. You know, before I met you, there were times when I thought about taking that gun and ending my life. I could see no other way out of my despair. You can't know the guilt I've had to live with for so many years.'

'You have nothing to feel guilty about. What happened to Alice, it wasn't your fault.'

A look flashed onto Jim's face, only for a split second, and then it was gone. 'We left our little girl alone. We were supposed to protect her, and we weren't there. But although that'll never leave me, I finally feel like I can move on, that I have a chance of living again. And that is all because of you. And of course, I can't wait to meet your daughters. Have you told them about me yet?'

'They know I'm seeing someone. They've noticed a change in my demeanour. But they don't know any of the details. You know…'

'That I'm married.'

'Exactly. I don't think they would care too much, but it's more me. I'm embarrassed. I've never wanted to be "that woman". When I found out my husband had cheated on me, it broke me. I remember wondering how any woman could do that… knowingly sleep with another woman's husband. I hated her more than I hated him. Of course I forgave him, and we had many happy years together before he died, but that hatred for her never went away. And now… I'm the woman who is knowingly sleeping with a married man. *In love* with a married man.'

'My situation is completely different. Any feelings other than resentment and blame were gone between Helen and me many years ago. We only stayed together for Tom's sake. And I think in hindsight it probably did him more harm than good. Now, my love, I have to go. But I promise you, we'll be together soon.' He picked up a pen, scrawling something on the back of the Polaroid, then tossed it onto the bed beside Sandie before heading out of the door.

Sandie picks the photograph up out of the box on the table. As she examines it in the dim light of her kitchen, all these years later, she still remembers it as if it were yesterday, and she blushes again. Turning the photo over in her hand, she reads the message on the back. *Just a few more weeks, darling, I promise. X*

A tear rolls down Sandie's cheek and drips onto the photograph. She has lost count of the times she has sat crying, looking at this picture. She kisses the photo, then places it back into the box and carefully replaces the lid.

'I'll find out what happened to you, Jim,' she says to herself. 'I swore it all those years ago, and I swear it again now. I'll find out what happened. And I'll make her pay.'

Sandie carries the box back to her lounge, slipping it back into her dresser drawer. Taking one last curious glance at the circus outside her window, and wondering what the hell has happened, she heads up the stairs to bed.

29

T he next few days are a blur.

Because of the gun, the Abbott house is classed as a crime scene and there are forensic investigations taking place.

I stay with Adam and Lily down the road.

I spend most of it in bed, drifting in and out of consciousness.

Helen's suffering from severe shock and is staying in the hospital until her condition improves. The police have been to question me a few times. They want to know if Tom said anything to me before he pulled the trigger.

Something tells me I should keep this to myself, so I tell them that all he said was that he can't bear to go on anymore, and that he's sorry.

I remember what Cathy told me about not always being able to trust returned memories in cases of psychogenic amnesia, and I'm fairly sure that what Tom told me he remembers before he shot himself is not the truth.

It can't possibly be. I *refuse* to believe it.

It doesn't make any sense.

Adam comes in to check on me from time to time. He brings

me food that I do not eat, and water that I gulp down greedily, but he does not ask me any questions.

And I love him for that.

I check my phone. I've got about twenty missed calls and a few voicemails from Dave at the office. I hold the phone to my ear to listen to them. His first message is calm, asking what the hell is happening. Tom's suicide has been in the news. Of course it has. The Abbotts sell papers, even now. The second is a screaming tirade of expletives, but the gist of the message is that he wants an update as soon as possible, and is wondering why I haven't checked in after what's happened. He doesn't even ask me how I am. Dave's not exactly the epitome of a caring boss. I dial his number. He answers on the first ring.

'Blake, what the fuck's going on? Where have you been?'

'I've been sleeping mostly.'

'What the fuck happened with Alice's little brother?'

'He shot himself.'

'Yeah, I know that. Everybody in the country knows that by now. Why, Blake? Why the fuck did he shoot himself?'

I think for a moment... but not so long that it looks like I'm lying.

'Haven't a clue, Dave, I'm sorry. I've hardly seen him since I've been here. I can only imagine that my presence here awoke some deep, buried memory... or maybe it's just brought every-thing back, the sadness, the sorrow of losing his sister... being asleep in the next room when she was taken. I don't know. I can only guess.' The lies roll off my tongue all too easily.

'Did he speak to anyone before he did it?'

'No. I found him in the basement with the gun. I'd been out for lunch with my brother, and Helen Abbott called me and asked me to get home quickly. When I arrived home, Tom Abbott was down in the basement with his father's gun. I tried to talk to him, but he just said he couldn't go on any longer, and pulled the trigger.'

'Right. Perfect. This is good, I think. Great work!'

'Excuse me?' I can't believe what I'm hearing.

'People don't shoot themselves for no reason. Must have had something to do with Alice's disappearance.'

'I don't think so. He was eight.'

I can hear Dave thinking at the end of the line. He's breathing heavily. Trying to work this into a story.

'Dave, he was a very troubled young man. I spoke to him briefly the night I arrived. He was very, very messed up. I don't think he ever recovered from what happened to his sister. I don't think anyone here has. It's extremely sad. As I said before, me being here has clearly brought it all back, the pain... the trauma of losing her. They were very close. I must have opened old wounds, and it was too much for him.'

'Right. What about the mother?'

'What about her?'

'How is she reacting to it all?'

'Her son just blew his brains out... How do you think she's reacting? She's devastated. Understandably.'

'Fine. As soon as she's ready to talk, find out what she's got to say about it all.'

'Got it.'

'And, Blake...'

'Yes?'

'Don't fucking leave it so long before checking in next time. Especially if something kicks off. You should have called me straight away. You're not off on a trip down memory lane there, remember that. You're working. I'm paying you to be there.'

'Right.'

He hangs up before I can say anything else.

I try to sleep. Every time I close my eyes, I see Tom's brains splattered all over the Abbotts' cellar.

I feel his warm blood on my face.

And I know his death is most probably my fault.

I try to make sense of what he told me.

Could it be true?

He was eight. I know that there have been cases of children that young killing their siblings, but it never crossed my mind that Tom could be behind Alice's disappearance. He doted on her and she lavished him with all the attention an older sister should. Two siblings could not have been closer than Alice and Tom. He was a soft boy, he wasn't angry, or aggressive. I couldn't ever have imagined him hurting a fly, let alone a hair on Alice's head.

Then of course come the questions about Helen and Jim Abbott's involvement.

If he was telling the truth, if he had killed Alice in her house that night, then why did the Abbotts not tell the police?

They must have known. Surely it had been some sort of accident? A game gone wrong?

Were they covering up for their son?

No jury would convict an eight-year-old boy of killing his sister by mistake?

Something about this doesn't feel right, and I know I need to make sense of it in my own head before I discuss it with anyone else.

I don't believe Tom killed Alice.

This must have been a false memory, somehow triggered by something I said to him.

I sleep.

I wake.

I sleep again.

I wake again. I assume it's morning, but in truth I have no idea.

As my eyes open, I see a figure sitting in the corner of the room.

At first I think it must be Adam, but as they adjust, I see a shock of blue hair, and I realise it's Lily.

She's sitting in her knickers, braless, watching me with a smile on her face.

She's even thinner than she looks with her clothes on. She looks like a pre-pubescent boy. Her breasts are small and pointy, and her skin is stretched tightly over her skeletal figure.

She sits with her legs crossed in front of her, her arms spread out over the arm rests of the chair.

Small red marks are dotted around the underside of her elbows, and there are marks and bruises on her thin abdomen.

She realises I'm awake but doesn't seem embarrassed by her nudity.

I pull myself up into a sitting position on the bed. Her eyes remain on me the whole time.

She's still smiling.

I look around the room, feeling embarrassed to look at her directly. 'Lily, hi.'

'You're finally awake!' she shrieks, sounding like an excited child. 'I thought you were going to be asleep, like *fur-ever*.'

'Where's Adam?' I'm groggy.

'Not here. Had to pop out, so I'm keeping an eye on you. Damn, Emily, you certainly worked a number on Thomas! What the fuck did you say to him?'

'I... I didn't say anything to him.'

'Yeah you did. Adam told me you were trying to help him remember what happened to his sister.' Lily raises her eyebrows. 'So, did he?'

'Did he what?' I'm confused and want her to go away.

'Did he remember anything? What did he tell you before he, you know, blew his fucking brains out?' She stares at me. The smile is gone from her face. Her eyes stare directly into mine.

I feel uncomfortable. 'No, he didn't say anything.'

She cocks her head as if she doesn't believe me, and pouts. 'You can tell me. We're almost like sisters, aren't we?'

'If you say so.'

'There you go then. Sisters shouldn't lie to each other. That's not very nice, is it?' She sounds like a little girl.

'I'm not lying.'

'But Adam said Tom phoned you, while you were out visiting that kiddy fiddler in the old factory in town, and that he told you he remembered what had happened the night his sister disappeared. *No?*'

I have to think quickly. 'Yes, but when I got there he was just sitting with the gun in his lap. I asked him what was going on and he said he couldn't go on, knowing that he had been in the house when Alice was taken. Then he pulled the trigger.'

My mouth is dry. I reach for the glass of water next to the bed and drink it down, taking my time, hoping the conversation is over. She watches my every move, looking unconvinced.

'Come on, Emily. He must have said *something*?'

30

There's the sound of a door closing from downstairs. I hear Adam call up to Lily, then bound up the stairs.

He bursts into the room and Lily springs up from the chair.

'What are you doing in here?' He then notices me sitting up in bed. 'Emily, you're awake, that's great. How are you feeling?'

He looks nervously at Lily, who hurries out of the room, glancing back at me before she is gone.

'Not bad. I feel like I've been sleeping for ages. What time is it?' I stretch and yawn. My body aches a little.

'It's almost midday. You were wiped out. The doctor gave you quite a strong sedative to help calm you down, and I thought it was best to let you sleep as long as you needed. The police are finished over the road, so you can go back there whenever you want. Of course, you're welcome to stay here as long as you need to. I totally understand if you don't want to go back there.'

'Thanks, that's very kind,' I reply, but in truth, I would rather be there than where I am, with his weird girlfriend questioning me.

Adam approaches the bed, sitting on the edge of the mattress. 'Are you all right, sis?' He places a hand on my leg.

'I... I don't really know.' I don't know what to tell him. I don't
want to repeat what Tom told me. I don't know if I am all right.
'How's Mrs Abbott? Have you seen her?'

'I went to the hospital, but she was asleep. She's pretty upset,
understandably. Look, was Lily bothering you just then?'

'I wasn't expecting to see your girlfriend sitting in front of me
half naked when I woke up, but I guess she wasn't doing any
harm. It *is* her house after all.'

'Did she say anything to you?' Adam seems angry.

I shake my head. 'Not really. She wanted to know if Tom had
said anything before he... you know...' I don't want to say it.
Saying it will make it real.

'Right.'

'I guess she's just interested. She was around when Alice was
taken. I suppose it's easy to forget that because she was a baby.'

'She has a very morbid sense of curiosity. I'll speak to her
and tell her to leave you alone.'

'It's fine, Adam. Don't worry.'

'It's not fine. It's out of order. She'll not be bothering you
again, I promise you.'

He stands up from the bed, looking down at me sadly. 'Are
you hungry?'

'Not at all.'

'I'll give you some peace. Come on down whenever you're
ready. I'll make you some food if you like.'

I tell him again that I'm not hungry. He gives me a sad smile
and leaves the room. I hear him go next door. I hear raised
voices. His, and then Lily's.

Something smashes.

Adam shouts, and Lily screams back.

Something else breaks.

A scream and a heavy thud against the wall, then everything
is quiet.

I decide that I'll go back to the Abbott house as soon as I'm dressed. I'd rather stay in a house where my best friend was probably murdered, and her brother recently shot himself, than stay here and listen to Adam and Lily tearing pieces off each other.

Adam knocks on the door and comes in. He's carrying some clothes. He clears his throat. 'Your clothes were covered in blood, and stuff. I've got some of Lily's things for you. I hope they fit.'

I doubt very much if they will, but I smile and thank him.

He leaves me to dress.

Surprisingly, the clothes do fit, just about. Some ripped black jeans and a black jumper with skulls on it. Nothing too extreme, thank God. I wouldn't choose these clothes, but they'll do to get home in. I make my way downstairs and find Adam in the kitchen.

He doesn't see me at first. He's leaning on the kitchen worktop with his head hung low.

It looks as if he is talking to himself.

When he finally notices me, he looks embarrassed.

'I think I'm going to head back to the Abbotts,' I tell him.

'You don't have to. I promise Lily won't bother you again.'

'It's not her. I feel that's where I should be. Helen will probably need some company. God knows how this is going to affect her. Besides, I need to write up all my notes from the last couple of days. While it's still fresh in my mind. If I don't start actually writing some of this story, I won't have a job to go back to.'

'All right then. If you're sure. I'll walk you down the road. I don't want you going over there alone, and Mrs Abbott probably won't be home for a few days.'

31

We walk to the house in silence. When we get there, I unlock the door and we make our way inside.

The place is a mess. It looks as if it's been burgled. It's eerily quiet, and as I walk down the hallway, an overwhelming sense of foreboding overcomes me. I realise I don't want to be here, but I feel my options are limited.

Adam must sense something's wrong. 'You okay?' He places a reassuring hand on my shoulder.

I nod and continue down the dark hallway.

We go into the kitchen. The cellar door is wide open. We both look nervously in its direction. The house feels cold. I flip on the kettle, pushing the basement door shut.

I hold up a mug. Adam shakes his head.

'I'll be off. But if you need anything, just shout. If I'm not down the road at Lily's, I won't be far away.'

I thank him and see him to the front door.

As he leaves he turns to me nervously and asks, '*Did* Tom tell you anything?'

I shake my head. 'Nothing,' I lie.

Adam frowns and nods, then turns to go. I watch as he walks

down the road. He's skulking, like he doesn't want to leave, but when he turns and realises I'm still watching, he picks up his pace a little. He's at Lily's front door, and turns one last time to look over his shoulder. He gives a little wave and disappears inside the house.

I close the Abbotts' front door and make my way into the living room, but before I can sit down, there's a knock. I head back into the hallway.

Alan Gillespie is standing on the doorstep. He looks concerned.

'Alan, hi,' I say.

'How are you?' he asks, looking around the whole time, as if he's being watched.

'Not great. I'm still a little groggy, and pretty shaken.'

I hear a door open somewhere out in the street.

He steps nervously from one foot to the other. 'Do you mind if I come in?'

I stand aside and motion for him to enter. Before I close the door, I glance around the street.

There's nobody outside.

I tell Alan I'm making coffee and he follows me through to the kitchen. I get out a second mug.

He's hovering in the doorway. He looks towards the cellar. 'Is that where it happened?' he asks cautiously, tilting his head in the direction of the door.

I nod in response, pouring two cups of coffee. I hand one to him, then turn the key in the cellar door. It locks with a loud click and I feel suddenly more at ease.

We sit down at the kitchen table. I'm looking out at the birds on the bird feeder.

'What the hell happened?' Alan snaps. 'This might have just pushed poor Helen over the edge. I'm not sure how she'll come back from this.'

I shake my head. I don't know what to tell him. 'I'm not really sure myself. I got a phone call telling me to come home. When I got here, Tom was down in the cellar with Jim's old shotgun.'

Gillespie shakes his head. 'Did Tom say anything? You know, before he did it?'

I consider the question. He's staring straight into my eyes. I decide not to tell him. 'Not really. He was waffling. Not making any sense.'

'I heard what sounded like a gunshot... saw all the police cars outside. I didn't know what the heck was happening. I told Helen she should have got rid of that gun a long time ago.'

'Alan, over the years, it would be fair to say you have developed a friendship with Helen Abbott, right?'

He looks at me and his brow furrows as he frowns. 'Yes, I suppose you could say that. Strange as it seems. People round here, they can't believe it. But she knows what's what.'

I take a sip of my coffee. 'And how long did it take you to win her over? Surely she must have been wary of you at first, given the allegations.'

Gillespie puts his cup down on the table in front of him, shaking his head.

'No. Bizarrely, Helen was always on my side. Even when the police and everyone else were convinced I had something to do with it, she never accused me. She even came to see me at home one night, and apologised. Can you imagine that? Her going through all that with her daughter, and she comes to apologise to *me*. I think that's when I realised what a good person she was.'

I take a few moments to process this. I get up, take a packet of biscuits from the cupboard, offering one to Gillespie. He shakes his head.

'Do you not think that's a little odd?' I ask him.

'What do you mean?'

'Her daughter had gone missing, and you were the prime

suspect. Yet she comes and apologises to you. She doesn't think it's you. Not for one minute? Do you think that's how most parents would react?'

Gillespie considers the question. 'No. I suppose now you come to mention it, it was very kind of her. Very trusting.'

'And what about Jim? Did he ever come to see you?'

'No. I saw very little of Jim, but he would say hello to me in the street, or wave if he saw me.'

'So, neither of Alice's parents seemed to think that you had anything to do with her disappearance right from the get-go?'

'No. That was how it seemed to me.' Gillespie narrows his eyes, tilting his head slightly to one side. 'Where are you going with this, Miss Blake? Did Tom say something to you?'

'No. I'm just curious, that's all.'

Gillespie finishes his coffee, then tells me he should be getting home. I see him out, close the door and walk back to the kitchen.

32

As I'm clearing up, I drop a coffee mug, which shatters into pieces on the hard kitchen floor. I swear under my breath, then look around for a broom.

I realise with a sickening feeling that I'll have to go down into the cellar.

I open the door and try the light switch with no result. I walk slowly down into the basement, which seems brighter with the autumn sunlight that flows through the small windows.

I get to the bottom and quickly turn to where the cleaning apparatus live, avoiding looking in the direction of the mass of red towards the middle of the room.

I grab a broom then run quickly back up to the kitchen, realising I've been holding my breath the whole time.

I close the door behind me and proceed to clear up the broken mug. I wrap it up in some newspaper from the work-top, placing it in the kitchen bin. The bin is almost over-flowing with rubbish so I take the bag out. I unlock the back door and toss the bag out into the garden with the rest of the rubbish. I catch sight of my reflection in the window and realise how ridiculous I look, and I suddenly feel a strong desire to be in my own clothes, so I head up the stairs to my room.

I pull on a pair of loose jogging bottoms and a sweatshirt, folding Lily's clothes neatly and placing them next to my laptop on the dresser. I consider making a few notes on my computer about the events of the last few days, but can't find the inclination to open it up. Despite having slept for the most part of the last few days, I feel exhausted.

I consider what Alan Gillespie has told me.

The Abbotts treated him with kindness during the time he was being investigated. They never accused him, and even went as far as to befriend him.

Is this because they knew he was innocent?

The Abbotts could only have known for sure that Gillespie was not guilty if they knew what had actually happened to Alice. If Tom had indeed killed her, the Abbotts would have known about it.

A child could not have covered something like that up on his own.

He would have had help. From adults.

I sit on my bed and picture the scene when Jim Abbott came home from the party to check on his children. I imagine the look of horror on his face when he discovered his daughter's lifeless body, and his son responsible for her death. I imagine the panic he must have felt. I imagine him returning to the party, to explain to his wife what he had found.

Did they behave as if everything was fine, only to return home and cover up for their son?

I think of Tom as a child. He was a sweet little boy. He was always so quiet and polite. A stark contrast to my loud, boisterous, pain in the arse of a brother. Tom always seemed to be living in Adam's shadow. Suddenly, I'm remembering a scene from our childhood. It's a few days before Alice disappeared. I'm in the park with her. She's wearing denim dungarees and a pink T-shirt. Her blonde hair in a plait down her back. I'm wearing a tracksuit. We're playing on the swings and we see our brothers coming out of the woods. Adam walks a few steps ahead of Tom. They see us and turn to go. Alice calls out to them. I tell her to leave it, I don't want the boys to come and spoil our game, but she calls them over regardless. Tom's nervous and avoids looking at me. Adam's muddy, they have been building a den somewhere in the woods.

I don't want to talk to Adam. I can't remember why, maybe we have had a fight, but I feel annoyed with him. Alice is chatting to him about his den. He tells her that when it's finished, it'll be really cool. He says he needs to find some carpet to go in it.

'My dad's got some old carpet at home. Why don't you and Tom go and ask him if you can have it?' she tells Adam.

He can't keep the smile from his face. 'No way? You serious?'

'Yes. My dad's got loads of stuff down there you might be able to use.' She looks at Tom who's drawing pictures in the dirt with a twig. 'Tom, go home with Adam and ask Daddy if you two can have that old roll of carpet down in the cellar. I'm sure he won't mind.'

Tom drops his twig and follows her instructions, like a doting brother.

As they leave, Adam turns back to Alice, a huge smile on his face. 'Thanks, Alice. You're amazing,' he shouts, and as they run off towards the house, he turns and waves bashfully at her.

Tom following, looking back with a grin over his shoulder, gives me a little wave.

33

As I drift out of my reverie, I look around Alice's room. Could that little boy I knew back then be a killer?

I don't want to believe it, but I think I might have to. And the thing that shocks me even more is the realisation that the Abbotts must have known about it. Not only has Helen Abbott had to live with the loss of a child, she has had to carry a secret. A secret so devastating that she's not been able to talk to anyone about it. I imagine that since her husband left, she has felt very alone.

For a moment I wonder if Alan Gillespie knows.

Has she trusted him enough to tell him the grisly truth?

Everything I know about Alice and the Abbotts is shattered. I realise I've known very little about what actually happened. And suddenly the full horror hits me.

Alice never left this house. At least, not alive. Maybe she died in the room I'm sitting in.

All these years I've wondered where she is. I've researched to find any trace of her online. Any shred of evidence that she's still alive. She's been dead all along. I feel a sudden pang of anger towards Helen. She's let me suffer. She's let me wonder. How can she have kept quiet all these years? It makes sense of her behaviour towards Tom when he was in my room, and her anger at him for touching Alice's things down in the basement. I don't know how I'll be able to look her in the face when she comes home, but something tells me I should keep this newfound knowledge to myself.

For now.

I feel a little lost for the rest of the day. As I'm preparing some food in the evening, the weather deteriorates once again. I'm not hungry, but I know I need to eat. I'll need my strength.

Helen Abbott has a secret, and I fear that she'll want to find out if I know what it is.

How much did she overhear before Tom shot himself?

I remember hearing someone coming down the stairs, but I don't know how much she'd have heard before the gunshot. I can't imagine she'd be much of a threat, but she might want to find out how much I know.

I'll have to be very careful.

I head downstairs and throw together some food from what little Helen has in the fridge. I throw most of the meal I prepare in the bin.

Just after eight o'clock, I turn off the lights in the house and head back upstairs to my room.

As I undress, I get a text from Adam.

Wot you doing? Want some company?

I can't bear the thought of seeing Adam or Lily right now. I don't want to see anyone. I just want to sleep, so I send a reply telling him I changed my mind and am staying in a hotel for the night, and that I'll probably return tomorrow.

He simply replies, *Ok, no worries. Sleep tight.*

I brush my teeth and crawl into bed.

Every time I close my eyes, I see the flash of the gun. I hear the deafening sounds of the shot, and my ears are ringing again.

I see Tom's head exploding across the walls and over my face.

The wind howls outside. Debris and detritus from the garden blow against my window, and it sounds as if skeletal fingers are tapping on the glass.

I've never felt so alone.

For the first time since I got back to Palmerston, I wish I hadn't come.

I close my eyes and fall asleep to the tapping at the window.

34

A noise wakes me.

I don't know how long I've been asleep. I feel groggy. I find my phone on the bedside table and check the time. It's just after midnight. The wind's still raging outside, and heavy rain batters against the windows.

I hear something banging in the garden. I go through to the back bedroom and look out of the window to investigate.

The gate's open.

It blows violently open and shut in the wind. I must have left it open when I went out the first day I was here. It's making a hell of a racket, so I decide I'll have to go out and close it. I don't want it to disturb the neighbours, and doubt I'll sleep much with that noise anyway.

As I look down into the garden, I see something move and I freeze.

A figure creeps across the lawn in the shadows. It stops by the swings. I see the shape of a head look around in the dark before it continues to move towards the house.

Panic spreads through me like a fever. My heart beats heavily in my chest. I think back to earlier this afternoon.

Did I lock the kitchen door after putting the rubbish out?

I go slowly to the top of the stairs, holding my breath, and try to be as silent as I can.

I wait and listen.

The kitchen door creaks slowly open and then clicks closed, softly.

Somebody is in the house.

A shadow falls across the hallway carpet at the bottom of the stairs, from the direction of the kitchen. The panic is surging through me, but I realise I must try to remain calm.

Keep calm, think straight.

I head back into my bedroom, closing the door quietly behind me. I pick up my phone and turn it off, looking around the room for any sign that I've been there. The bed is crumpled and looks slept in. I make it as quickly as I can.

I hear the creak of footsteps on the stairs.

I throw myself silently to the floor, pushing my chest down hard into the carpet as much as I can, and crawl uncomfortably under the bed. There's not much room, but I can just about fit.

I hold my breath, and time seems to slow. Blood pulses through my ears, and I feel my heart is pounding so loudly that whoever it is will be able to hear it.

The door slowly creaks open and dark boots step into my room. I see the arc of light from a torch sweep slowly and purposefully around. The person comes closer to the bed. Their feet are almost directly in front of my face. They step away, moving across to the other side of the room. I hear drawers being opened. Whoever it is, they're looking for something. The feet come back over towards me, and the person sits on the bed. Springs creak down above me as the slats come closer to my face.

I gently let out my breath, trying to be as quiet as I can. I hope the bed isn't warm from my body heat. I hope whoever it is doesn't feel it.

The fear is crippling, but my survival instinct tells me to keep as still as I can.

I hear rummaging above me. The sound of pages being turned. He has my diary, and he's reading it. I can hear him breathing heavily.

I lie for what feels like hours as a stranger reads my childhood diary. I feel sick. Angry. I somehow resist the urge to come out fighting. I surmise that if I have the element of surprise, I might be able to get in a few blows to his head before he has the ability to fight back. But I decide to stay where I am. I don't know who it is, or how strong they are.

Suddenly, the person stands up from my bed and walks back towards the dresser. I hear the sound of things being moved around. He's picking things up and examining them.

He's taking his time.

He's not afraid.

After what seems like a lifetime, the intruder leaves the room and walks slowly down the stairs. I hear the back door open and close again. I allow myself to let out a breath, then gulp down air greedily, but I remain hidden under the bed.

I'm too scared to come out. I fall asleep there, hiding and terrified.

35

I wake with the sunrise. I have no idea what time it is, and for a minute or so I don't know where I am.

I'm still under the bed and it takes a while for my brain to process the events of the night before. I crawl out from under the bed.

I'm stiff and sore.

At first glance, everything looks as it should, but when I look towards the dresser, my laptop isn't there.

Whoever came into the house last night has taken it. I rush back to the bed, slipping my hand under the pillow.

My diary has also gone.

I sit on the edge of the bed, head in my hands. I want to cry, but I feel too angry. I think about calling Adam, but I don't want him to worry. I consider the police, but I know it will be pointless. Whoever it was will not have left any trace, of that I'm sure. My things are gone, and I doubt I'll ever see them again.

I dress quickly and head next door to see Alan Gillespie. I don't really know where else to go. He takes a while to answer the door. He looks weary. I think Tom's suicide is taking its toll on everyone in its own way. Gillespie invites me in.

'Are you all right?' he asks, looking me up and down. I realise I must look a state, and I haven't showered, but I don't really care.

'Someone came into the house last night.'

Gillespie looks confused at first. 'What do you mean?'

'Somebody came in through the back gate in the middle of the night. They came into Helen Abbott's house, and into my room, and stole my computer and my diary.'

'Jesus! Why would someone do that?'

'No idea.'

'Have you called the police?'

I shake my head.

'Why the hell not? This is serious. Where were you?'

'I hid under the bed.'

He opens the fridge and pours two glasses of orange juice from a carton, offering one to me. I take it and gulp down the sweet liquid. He pours another.

'Emily, you have to tell the police. I'm off to the hospital today to bring Helen home. She'll be devastated to hear about this.'

'I didn't know she was coming home. Is she definitely ready?'

'She's insisting. I did offer her a bed at mine, but she won't hear of it. She says she needs to be in her own house. She was asking after you.'

'That's kind. How is she?'

Gillespie pauses to take a sip from his drink. 'She's doing remarkably well. Far better than I expected. But I guess she has trained herself to deal with tragedy.'

'Please don't tell her about this, Alan. I don't want her to worry. I think she has enough going on already.'

'But Emily, if it's not safe—' he begins, but I cut in.

'It's safe. Whoever it was, they got what they were looking for. I don't think they'll be back.'

Alan Gillespie pauses and looks intently at me before speaking. 'When Jim left, I thought that was it for her. I didn't know how she was going to make it through. Don't get me wrong, I don't think their relationship was ever that great after Alice disappeared. They used to fight. I'm fairly sure he hit Helen, but she would never admit it. But somehow, they were support for each other. They both shared their own private hell, and after he walked out I think she felt totally alone.'

Gillespie makes his way to a chair and slowly slumps his weight into it. 'It infuriated me when I heard he had gone. I saw him just a few days before and he was telling me how things were going to change, how he was going to put right some things that were wrong in his life, and change his and Helen's lives for the better. He had a real spark in his eye, and the silly old fool that I am, I believed him. I actually thought he was going to get her away from here or something, a fresh start. It can't be good for her, still being in that house. But then I saw Helen, not a week later, and she told me he had left her. She was calm as anything. She didn't cry, didn't get angry. Just told me, very matter of fact, that Jim was gone.'

I finish my second glass of juice and place the cup down on the table. 'Did you think it was odd that he left, after all that time?'

'At first I didn't believe it. I was sure he'd be back. Thought maybe he was drunk in a pub somewhere. But as the weeks went on, it became apparent he wasn't coming home. But no, I don't think it was odd. That family suffered a lot. Their world was turned upside down, and that takes its toll on people. He tried to support Helen as much as he could, but eventually it got too much for him. The Abbotts, they always blamed themselves, I think. They had to live with the guilt that they had gone out and left those kids alone in the house.'

I stand up, crossing to the back door, looking out to Gillespie's garden. 'It was an irresponsible thing to do,' I shake my head, 'What sort of parent–'

Gillespie interrupts me. 'They all did back then round here. It was a safe neighbourhood. Your parents left you and your brother in the house also. It could have just as easily been you, if whoever took her had wandered into *your* house instead.'

I don't know what to say. He has a point. 'I suppose.'

'How's your brother?'

'Adam?' I don't know how to answer this, because truthfully I don't really know. He seems messed up. 'He's doing all right,' I lie. 'It seems he's dating Lily from over the road.'

Gillespie's eyes flicker, and then he nods. 'I thought I recognised that chap from somewhere, but I couldn't put my finger on it. Now, that is *interesting*.' Gillespie's voice trails off slightly. He seems to be thinking, staring into space.

'Are you okay?' I ask him.

He looks at me, and for a second looks as though he doesn't know who I am. 'Yes, I'm fine. Still a bit of a shock what happened to Tom, you know. I still find it difficult to comprehend people who can take their own lives. It's such a selfish thing to do. Don't you think?'

I consider the question before answering. 'I think for someone to take a shotgun and blow their own head off, they must be feeling pretty desperate. I'm not sure we should really be judging anyone. Especially not Tom.'

Gillespie smiles. 'Very wise words, Miss Blake. Forgive me, I sometimes say the first thing that comes into my head without thinking it through. A by-product of living by myself for so long.'

'No worries, Mr Gillespie. You're entitled to your opinions, as much as anyone else.'

He glances at his watch. 'I'm afraid you'll have to excuse me. I'm going to have to go and collect Helen from the hospital. Unless you would like to join me?'

I can't think of anything I'd like to do less, so I make an excuse and head home.

36

As I walk down Gillespie's path, I see Adam watching me from the bedroom window of Lily's house. When he sees me looking, he backs away, without waving.

I frown and return to the Abbott house.

I search the house, feeling slightly uneasy. When I'm satisfied there are no intruders, I relax a little. I find the key to the cellar is still in the lock. I take the key, slipping it into my pocket. I don't think it will be a good idea for Helen to see the basement.

It's a mess. It'll need to be cleaned thoroughly.

Helen shouldn't have to do it, but I don't want to either. I'll talk to Gillespie when he is back, and see if he can recommend anyone local. He has lived here long enough; he must know a cleaner.

I go upstairs to my room, hiding the cellar key in the top drawer of my dresser under some clothes.

After about forty minutes or so, I hear the sound of a car outside. I look out of the window and see Gillespie's Volvo pulling up.

I see Helen sitting in the passenger seat. She is looking at the house, sadly.

Gillespie gets out, opening the door for her. He helps her out and escorts her down the path at the front of the house. Helen Abbott looks even older. She's walking with a stick and taking small unsteady footsteps. Gillespie's supporting her weight, and she looks frail.

About halfway down the path, she stops, then stumbles. Gillespie catches her.

He is tender towards her. Gentle, and almost loving. I wonder if anything has happened between them since Jim Abbott left five years ago.

I go to let them in, and Helen's cold eyes settle on my own as I open the door. She stands there, staring at me, without saying a word. I step towards her and embrace her.

I whisper into her ear, 'I'm so, so sorry.'

She does not respond, nor does she return the hug. She simply walks past me down the hallway and into the living room. I hear the television click on and the sound of daytime telly fills the house once again. I hear Gillespie telling her he'll make her a cup of tea, then he heads out into the hallway, down towards the kitchen, beckoning me to follow him.

'You'll need to give her time. It'll be difficult for her being here for a while.'

'Has she said anything since you picked her up?'

Gillespie shakes his head slowly, biting his lip. 'Very little.'

I tell Gillespie I'm going for a walk. I don't know what to say to Helen, and I don't want to be in the house with her. I leave Gillespie busying himself in the kitchen.

As I pass the living room, I pop my head round the door. Helen's sitting in her chair, still in her coat. The TV's on, but she's looking in the opposite direction, just staring at the wall.

She doesn't acknowledge me in the slightest, so I leave without saying a word.

I walk away from Pear Tree Close without looking back. I want to be far away from this house.

The reality of what has happened is slowly sinking in.

Somebody has broken into the house. They have taken two very specific items relating to Alice Abbott. Who would want to steal these items? I honestly don't know. But I intend to try to find out. I think of poor Tom and his shocking confession, but I know there's something more to this. It's not as simple as he made it seem. The fact that somebody has stolen my things confirms this in my mind.

The mystery is far from solved.

I cannot... *will* not believe that Tom killed his sister, my best friend.

Without realising it, I find I've walked to the old park behind the woods. It all looks the same as it did the last time I was here. The swings are a little rustier, the grass a little less well kept, but it remains largely unchanged.

I sit on a swing and rock back and forth.

As I look to my right, I see Alice sitting on the swing next to me.

She's laughing, and Adam pushes her, making her swing higher and higher. Tom's sitting on the floor next to the swings, laughing as Alice complains that she is frightened. But she's not frightened. She loves the feeling as she plummets downwards. I can tell from the expression on her face. She's beaming. I see four happy children playing on the swings in a quiet safe neighbourhood, and I wonder how that changed.

We were each robbed of our childhoods.

Alice in the most definite way, with the loss of her life it would seem. Tom with a secret so horrific that ultimately it ended his life. Adam and I lost our innocence when Alice

Abbott disappeared. Our whole family disintegrated, and we were never those happy children ever again.

I wonder if Alice and Tom have got off easy.

We're the ones who are left to deal with all the shit.

They don't have to worry about anything anymore.

I feel guilty for such a callous thought. I still can't process what Tom told me about Alice.

I need to find out the whole truth, and my educated guess would be that there's only one person left around here who can give me that.

Helen Abbott.

I'll need to broach this subject with great caution, but I need to get some answers.

I head home, but as I approach the house, I see Adam at the Abbotts' front door. It looks like he's arguing with Helen Abbott.

I duck behind a tree and watch from out of sight.

Adam is gesticulating. His arms are flailing about all over the place. He looks furious. Helen also looks angry. She's poking his chest with her index finger, jabbing angrily at him. Her expression is wild.

I can't hear what they're saying, but he leans right into her ear, saying something with his head close to hers. Helen pulls away and slaps Adam hard in the face.

For a moment I think he's going to hit her back, but she slams the door before he has the chance.

He stands on the doorstep for a few moments, rocking back and forth. He reaches his hand up, rubbing his cheek where he was slapped, and then he punches the wall next to the front door. He looks around nervously, then thrusts his hands into the pockets of his leather jacket and turns briskly, hurrying back towards Lily's house.

37

Sandie is not afraid to admit when she is wrong, and given the events that have unfolded in the last few days, since her chat with Tom, she concedes that telling him about her relationship with his father was not the brightest idea she has ever had. Tom had taken some convincing, but when she took him back to her house and showed him the photographs, he could not really argue the case anymore. He had not taken it well.

After bombarding him with questions about his father, Sandie had walked him back across the road, satisfied that he knew nothing about what had happened to Jim. She had heard that Tom was... unhinged, but she had never imagined that he would kill himself. A pang of guilt creeps over Sandie and she remembers how fond Jim was of his son, but she quickly swats it away. There are often innocent casualties for the greater good. Sandie reminded herself of the bigger picture.

The frenzy had been intense since young Tom had shot himself. Sandie had had to lie low for a while. The police were around for a few days, investigating the crime scene, she supposed. But after it became apparent that he had killed himself using Jim Abbott's licensed rifle, which had laid abandoned in the basement for years, there was not much left to investigate and the scene was released.

Emily had spent a few days recovering at that terrible girl's house with her brother. The poor thing looked extremely unwell when they dragged her out of the house. Sandie imagined it must be unpleasant for someone to blow their brains out right in front of you. She shakes her head and smooths the pleats in her skirt with both hands. Helen Abbott was home from the hospital, looking even more bedraggled. You could say she had let herself go a bit before the incident with Tom, but now she was gone, right down the drain.

Of course, Sandie was not proud that her actions may have had such disastrous consequences, but she has had her own fair share of damage through this process. Her relationship with her own daughters has been irreparably destroyed through her pursuit of the truth about Jim Abbott. And of course, that's assuming that the suicide had anything to do with Sandie having spoken with Tom earlier on that day. It could just be one of life's great coincidences. Perhaps he'd been planning it for ages. He could even have been on his way to do it when he found her creeping round the house. For all she knew, thanks to her, he may have stayed alive a few hours longer than planned.

A noise from outside draws Sandie's attention to the window, and she sees Emily coming out of the Abbott house and hurrying off towards the park. She looks troubled. Sandie can't imagine that sharing a house with a mad woman who has just lost the last of her two children can be much fun for a young woman. Although from Sandie's observations, this woman does not seem to be a fun kind of girl. In fact, come to think of it, Sandie can't recall having seen her smile once. She doesn't know what's wrong with young women these days. Her own daughters are the same. They walk around being morose, and then wonder why they are single. What man would want such a joyless woman?

When Sandie was young, she was fun. She laughed. She loved, and she enjoyed her life. Nursing your cheating husband through bowel cancer, then finding real love, only to have it snatched away again, can take the wind from a person's sails. At least Sandie can blame many years of life for making her miserable. What excuse do these girls have? These youngsters nowadays don't know how good they have it. She's always telling her daughters to enjoy life while they can.

A thought crosses Sandie's mind. Helen Abbott is in her house alone. She is just out of hospital. She is weak, and her defences are down. Perhaps now would be the ideal time for Sandie to speak to her, confront her. Demand to know the truth.

She strides to the mirror, surveying herself. Her hair is immaculate, as always, and her houndstooth woollen skirt accentuates her firm thighs. She undoes a button on her blush pink blouse, showing a little more of her cleavage. Pursing her lips, Sandie applies a fresh coat of lipstick. She smiles at herself in the mirror, picks up the item she found in the box in Helen Abbott's basement, and grabs a jacket from a hook in the hall.

Sandie marches across the street, pounding on Helen Abbott's front door. Her endgame is in play.

She hears the shuffle of the woman as she approaches. The door opens slowly and Sandie is standing face to face with Helen Abbott. She holds a paring knife in one hand, and an apple in the other. The old-looking hag eyes her up and down, and then a flicker of recognition shows on her face, which quickly turns to a sneer.

'What do *you* want?' she spits.

'I think it's time you and I had a little chat, don't you?' Sandie replies, her stare not moving from Helen's eyes. Helen Abbott tries to close the front door, but she is too slow. Sandie jams her foot in the frame, preventing it from shutting. 'Oh no you don't. I want some answers.' She pushes the door inwards, almost knocking Helen off her feet. She steps into the disgusting hallway, closing the door firmly behind her.

Helen Abbott turns and walks away. 'I know exactly who you are, you homewrecker, and I have nothing to say to you!' she shouts as she walks towards the kitchen.

Sandie follows her, a wave of anger spreading over her. 'Oh no? Really?' She pulls the object from her pocket, throwing it at the back of Helen Abbott's head as hard as she can. The woman stops and spins round, a look of sheer disbelief and bewilderment on her face. 'How about now?' Sandie screams, pointing at the floor where the object has landed.

Helen Abbott's eyes drift down towards the floor, and she freezes. She looks into Sandie Jackson's eyes, a knowing expression on her face, then back down at the old leather wallet lying on her hall floor. Her husband's wallet.

'This changes things,' Helen says, a pensive look on her furrowed face. 'I think you had better come in then.' She turns and hobbles down the hall into the kitchen, and Sandie follows close behind.

Checkmate, Mrs Abbott, she thinks.

38

After my parents moved away from Palmerston, I found it very difficult to build new friendships in the city. I was greatly affected by the loss of Alice, and I did not want any more friends. I had come to learn that friendship ended in pain and sorrow, and for many years I kept myself isolated.

Nobody could ever have replaced Alice in my world anyway.

As I was approaching my fourteenth birthday, my parents decided they wanted to do something special for me. They asked me if I would like to invite any friends round for a birthday party after school. I had nobody to invite. I was not close to anyone at school. I was a loner, as much as I hated to admit it. My parents wouldn't let it go and insisted that we do something as a family, so I said that I would be happy just to go for a burger, and maybe bowling in town.

Adam seemed excited by this idea also. My parents agreed that this is what would happen, and it would be 'the best birthday ever'.

And despite everything, I actually believed it.

Before we moved away from Palmerston, our parents always made a big deal of our birthdays, but not so much afterwards.

With all the fuss and talk of celebrations, I actually started to feel like it would be a proper birthday, like it had been before. I was even a little excited about it.

The week of my birthday, my mother came home from work one evening and sat me down, very seriously, telling me that she was so sorry, but something had come up at work and that she would not be able to get away in time to make it to dinner and bowling, but that my father would still take us. I told her that I could wait until she was less busy, but she insisted we didn't change the plans. So on the Friday, Adam and I waited outside the school gates for my father to pick us up.

Nobody came.

After a few hours, it was obvious he had forgotten, and we walked home. We didn't live too far from the school, about a half hour walk or so, and I knew that my parents kept a spare key under a pretend rock in the front garden.

While we were walking home, Adam asked me if I was upset.

'Why would I be upset?'

'Your birthday's ruined.'

'It's just another day, isn't it?' I said matter-of-factly.

We walked on in silence for a while, then Adam took my hand. I looked at him, and he smiled. He told me not to be upset, and that when we got home we could play some games. It's one of the few times I can remember Adam being nice to me.

We arrived home, letting ourselves in. It made no odds to me that we were home without our parents. A lot of the other kids in my class at school quite often went home to an empty house. I was fourteen, and I didn't need looking after anymore. I knew that my mother would probably be upset when she found out, but there was nothing I could do about it. It was my stupid dad's fault, and if he ended up in trouble then it served him right as far as I was concerned.

I remember telling Adam that I didn't care that the night had not gone to plan, but inside I was so angry. I hated my parents for getting my hopes up, and then letting me down, yet again. They let me believe that things could be normal again. That *we* could be normal.

But I couldn't tell Adam that.

I made us some food, just beans on toast I think, it was all we had in the kitchen. We went into the hall cupboard and rifled through the games.

They were dusty. They didn't get much use anymore.

We pulled everything out. Right at the bottom was 'Twister'. We had always played that on our birthdays. It used to be a family tradition. I had forgotten we had it.

Adam held it up, a huge smile on his face. 'Can we play this?'

Seeing the joy on his face, I couldn't let him down. So we carefully opened up the box, setting the game up in the middle of the living room. As there were only two of us, we didn't use the spinner, which kind of defeated the object, but we took it in turns to shout out the next move for each other.

It's one of the few times I can remember being happy after we left Palmerston. We played for hours. And for that short while, we were two normal kids having fun. We weren't the neighbours of a tragic girl who went missing in the middle of a hot summer night. We were just us. Stupid kids, playing a stupid game.

And we loved it.

We were in a complicated human knot, Adam snaking through my legs and twisted around in front of me. We were giggling and larking about.

We didn't hear my mother arriving home.

The first we realised of her presence was when the music we were playing was switched off.

I turned to see my mother standing by the stereo, a look of horror on her face.

'Where's your father? What are you doing here?'

'I think Dad forgot,' I replied, innocently.

My mother stormed over to us, grabbing at my arm. 'Get up!' Her nails dug into my flesh.

Adam fell onto the floor, he looked so scared. She pulled me up to my feet, then pushed me towards the living room door.

'I want you both to go to your rooms, now!'

'Mum, calm down,' I said. 'It's fine.'

'It's not fine! Your father knows never to leave you two alone. How could he?'

'It's okay, Mum,' I replied. 'We're fine, we're both all right.'

Her eyes darted to my face, filled with anger.

'I said go to your room!'

'But it's my birthday, Mum, I don't want to go to my room. We're having fun.'

My mother spun round, her eyes bulging. 'How dare you talk back to me! Everything I do, I do for you, Emily, don't you understand that? I do it to keep you safe. It's not safe. And your father knows that. I should have thought better than to leave him in charge.'

'Mum you're not making any sense–' I start to say.

'Be quiet! Shut up and go to your room.'

We heard the click of the door as my father came in. He appeared in the doorway, swaying slightly.

My mother took one look at him and exploded. 'You're drunk!'

'I went for a few drinks with the guys from work.'

'You were supposed to pick the kids up from school and take Emily out for her birthday.'

'Oh shit.'

'Is that all you have to say? You know it's not safe, and that's all you can say?'

I remember looking at Adam, and he was staring at my mother with a look of such hatred on his face. My mother was in front of my father, slapping his face, hitting his chest, pounding him over and over again.

He tried to grab her wrists to stop her from hitting him, but her hands somehow made it through to his face. Over and over.

'Stop it, Mum, what are you doing?' I cried, but my mother was going mad, and my dad was trying to restrain her, trying to protect himself.

'I hate you!' I screamed at my mother. 'I didn't even want a birthday party. It was your stupid fucking idea.'

I remember running past her and up the stairs to my room, slamming the door.

My parents argued for hours, and then I heard the front door close loudly. I remember looking out of my bedroom window to see my father getting in his car, fumbling with his keys before driving away.

He was drunk.

He didn't come home for a few days. I actually thought he might be dead. I convinced myself he'd crashed his car.

I didn't speak to my mother at all. I kept expecting her to apologise, but she didn't.

After my father eventually came home, it was not mentioned.

They acted as if it hadn't happened and everything was totally normal.

39

It wasn't until a few weeks later that my father got me alone. Adam was out playing football and my mother was working late, as usual.

She spent more time at work than she did at home.

Dad sat me down in my room and told me he was sorry.

'It's fine,' I told him.

'It's not. It's really not, Ems. I let you down, and I let your mother down, and I'm truly sorry.'

'It's Mum who should be apologising. I hate her. When she's like that, she's like a crazy person. She's mental,' I said stubbornly.

'Emily, your mother loves you very, very much. She only wants to protect you. It will be hard for you to appreciate it right now, but one day, when you're older, you will understand.'

'No I won't. I'm not a kid anymore. I wish you would stop treating me like a little baby. I'm fourteen. Loads of kids at school with younger brothers and sisters are trusted to look after them for a short while, but Mum won't even go to the shops and leave me to look after Adam. It's so embarrassing.'

My dad shook his head. 'Ems, I wish I could explain it to you, but you're too young to understand her reasons just now.'

'It's because of what happened to Alice, isn't it?' I snapped.

My father looked at me sadly. 'Yes. In a way.'

He put his arm around my shoulder and pulled me closer to him. 'You can think what you like about your mother, but please, don't ever hate her. She only wants what's best for you, I can assure you.'

'But she was awful to you that night. How can you defend her after the way she behaved?'

'Because I deserved it. What I did was inexcusable. Your mother is a wonderful woman, and she would do anything to protect you. We both would. And everything we have done is to keep you safe.'

I don't think my relationship with my mother was ever the same after that night. I tried, but I'd seen something in her that was unhinged and terrifying.

She had hurt my father and I felt that was unforgivable, despite what he said.

Looking back, I suppose I can see that Alice's disappearance hurt my family a great deal, just as it hurt her own family.

My mother and father were always fun-loving carefree people. They lavished us with love and affection, or at least they had before Alice was gone.

Afterwards they were far less affectionate.

I was older and able to handle it more, but I think Adam saw it as rejection. It damaged him. I wonder how much my parents treated him as a child has determined the way he's turned out as an adult. He clearly has anger issues. He believes he was unloved and abandoned. He still seems to blame Alice for everything that's gone wrong in his life, and to some extent he's right. If she hadn't disappeared, then we might have had some semblance of a normal family life.

I guess we'll never know.

Just as Helen Abbott will never know what it's like to grow old with any of her family around her.

40

Helen Abbott stands at the kitchen worktop. She doesn't offer Sandie a drink. She makes no attempt at friendliness. It has been established where the two women stand with each other, after years of it being unsaid, and this is where their relationship shall remain. Helen calmly slices the apple she is holding, without looking. Her eyes are fixed on Sandie's own.

'So, what do you want, Mrs Jackson?' she asks coldly.

Sandie slams her hands down on the kitchen worktop so loudly she almost makes herself jump. The palms of her hands sting from the impact. 'I want to know why your husband supposedly upped and left all those years ago, standing me up, and didn't think to take his wallet with him!'

Helen Abbott smiles. 'Perhaps he was in such a rush to get away from *you*, he forgot to take it.'

'That's bullshit and you know it.' Sandie picks up the wallet from the hall floor and opens the folds. It is still full of money, but this is not what she is after. She slips her fingers into the folds of the leather, pulling out the old creased photograph. She carefully opens it up and puts it down on the counter in front of Helen.

Helen stares at it.

'Jim loved Alice, and that was his favourite picture of the two of them. He would *never* have left without it. He loved me too, and we were leaving, together.' Sandie is calmer, composed.

'You think I don't know that?' Helen spits at her from where she stands. 'I'm not fucking stupid. I knew exactly what the two of you were up to. For Christ's sake, half the street knew. You weren't exactly *discreet*.'

Perhaps for the first time in her life, Sandie Jackson does not know what to say. She had not been expecting this. They always thought they had been so careful.

Helen looks her up and down and sneers. 'You think you're better than me. You swan around here in your fancy clothes and your expensive shoes, with your hair all done pretty and a face full of designer make-up trowelled on, and you think your shit doesn't stink? You had an affair with *my* husband!' Helen Abbott comes round the counter so she's standing right in front of Sandie, and leans in so Sandie can smell her rancid breath. She turns her face away from the putrid smell. God knows when this woman last bothered to clean her teeth.

'I used to be attractive too, you know,' she whispers bitterly. 'I used to wear nice clothes, and make-up, and jewellery. And you know what, people looked at me, the same way they look at you. Men wanted me. Women wanted to be me. We were happy, and you stole Jim from me. You tempted him away and you fucked him in our bed! How do you think that made me feel, on top of everything else that happened? I'll tell you... it was the final straw!'

Sandie shakes her head. 'No, Helen, you're wrong. I didn't steal anything from you. Your relationship with Jim was over long before I met him. You made sure of that. What happened to Alice was terrible, and nobody deserves that, and I feel for you, I truly do, but you stopped living. The night she disappeared, you disappeared too, and that wasn't fair on Jim. And God knows he tried to stand by you, but you made it so fucking hard. But he tried to do the right thing, he really did.'

Helen Abbott actually laughs at this. 'The right thing? Jim wouldn't know the right thing if it slapped him in the face. Nothing about that man was right. He was poison. You think it was *me* that killed our relationship? Is that what he told you? I can hear it now... "Oh, Helen has withdrawn since we lost our little girl... Helen doesn't understand me... she doesn't give me what I need, blah blah fucking blah", and you fell for it hook, line and sinker, you stupid little tart. Let me tell you, it was him. It was all him. It was the decisions he made. It was the lies he told. It was the choices he made, and he killed this family. Every single one of us. He was a useless pathetic old bastard, and you know what, I think you were made for each other. You certainly deserve each other.'

Sandie slaps Helen Abbott hard across the cheek. Her hand stings again, but this time it feels good. Helen puts the apple she has been slowly slicing down on the kitchen side, and raises her hand to her face.

'Tell me what happened to Jim. Tell me where he is!' Sandie screams.

'You really want to know?'

'Yes! Yes, I do.' Sandie tries to regain some composure. Dignity is everything. She doesn't want to lose the upper hand.

Helen Abbott flashes a wicked smile. 'Fine. I'll tell you.'

41

I arrive home to find Helen in the kitchen, gazing out of the window, glassy-eyed. She looks at me vacantly, then back out the window. Bizarrely, she's been cleaning. I can smell bleach, and she's wearing rubber gloves. An apple sits, half sliced, on the worktop next to her, uneaten.

'Helen, I wanted to say–'

'Don't.' She interrupts me with an assertiveness I've not seen since I arrived. 'Don't say anything, please.' She snaps off her rubber gloves, rolls them into a ball and slings them casually in the sink. Turning towards me, she opens her mouth as if she's going to say something, then thinks better of it. She turns and heads towards the cellar door.

'I can't find the key to the basement,' she says. 'Do you know where it is?'

'No,' I lie. 'Perhaps the police have it.'

'I'll have to ask them. I need to get down there. It'll need clearing up. And most of my cleaning stuff for the house is down there. You know, the hoover and stuff.'

I can't help but glance around the house as she says this. I shouldn't think it'll make a whole lot of difference to her life if she can't get access to her vacuum cleaner for a few more days. The key is safe in my dresser drawer for now, until I can find someone to clean up the mess downstairs.

'I'm not cooking tonight, so you'll have to get your own dinner,' she says.

'That's okay. I'm not very hungry anyway.'

She looks at me again and shakes her head. 'He was all I had left, you know.'

I don't know what to say, so I keep quiet.

'He didn't need you messing with his head the way you did. He was trying to get on with his life. We both were.'

'Helen, I don't think what happened was because of anything I said to Tom.'

'Of course it was,' she spits. 'Trying to get him to remember things from that terrible night. Some things are best forgotten.'

'I'm sure,' I reply without thinking.

She shoots me a look, and I decide to leave this here.

I feel annoyed and don't really want to be in the house with her. 'I'm going to go out for a walk.'

'Suit yourself.'

As I turn to go, I think of Adam arguing with Helen on the doorstep, so I turn back.

'Why was my brother here?'

She looks at me blankly but does not say anything. Her eyes shift from my face. She looks uncomfortable.

I try again. 'Earlier, when I was coming home, I saw him out the front, talking to you.'

'He came to pay his respects.'

She's lying. They were arguing about something, most definitely, and it ended with her slapping him in the face.

'That was kind of him,' I say.

She doesn't reply. She just turns away and hobbles back towards the kitchen as I let myself out.

42

I walk back to Alan Gillespie's house and knock on the door. He seems surprised to see me again.

'Emily, did you forget something?'

'No. I need to talk to you. Please can I come in?'

'Of course.' He steps aside, letting me past him into the hallway.

He closes the door, sliding on the security chain. 'It's a pretty safe neighbourhood, but with my history, I like to make sure,' he says, as if he's embarrassed to be securing his home.

I walk into his living room and stand waiting for him. He slowly lowers himself down into his armchair, gesturing for me to sit on the sofa opposite him. I take a seat and stare at him for a few seconds. He has a puzzled expression on his face.

'Is everything okay, Emily? Is it Helen? Has something happened?'

'I don't know.' I fidget in my seat, not knowing where to start. 'There's something odd going on.'

'How do you mean?' Alan's staring me directly in the eyes.

'When I returned home, I saw my brother at Helen's door. They were talking. It actually looked like they were arguing.'

Gillespie waits for me to continue.

'She slapped him in the face.'

'I see...'

'But then she totally denied it. I asked her why he was there, and she panicked and said he had come to pay his respects. Why would she lie about it?'

'Maybe she feels awkward and doesn't want you to feel stuck in the middle of whatever's going on with them.'

'But why would anything be going on with them? I don't understand.'

'Who knows. I'm sure she had her reasons. Perhaps she thought he hadn't supported Tom enough. I wouldn't worry too much about it if I were you. Remember, she's suffered a terrible loss. She's not herself. Perhaps your brother said something about Tom that upset her.'

'It's not only that though.' I look down at the floor.

'What is it then? Is there something you're not telling me?'

I want to tell him about Tom. I need to tell someone, but there's nobody. I don't even feel like I can talk to Adam about it.

'Emily?' Alan pushes.

'It's nothing. Everything's really messed up. Nothing's making a whole lot of sense, and I need to rationalise this whole situation.'

'I think that is perfectly understandable given all that's happened to you since you arrived back here. You know you can talk to me whenever you like, don't you.'

Gillespie seems so warm and amicable. If I tell him about Tom's confession, then that's another person involved. He might even insist that I go to the police, and I definitely do not feel ready for that at the moment.

'Thanks, Alan.' I smile. 'Can I ask you something about Alice?'

'Anything you like.'

'Did you ever suspect that Helen and Jim Abbott had something to do with her disappearance?'

Gillespie looks at me, his grey eyes serious and questioning, like he's trying to figure something out. He lets out a long breath through his nose, shaking his head. 'No.'

'Never?'

'When the press ran that story accusing the Abbotts of being involved, I saw the fallout from it. I saw a family ripped apart at the seams. There was no guilt there as far as I could see. Just sadness. And the courts obviously didn't think they were involved because they awarded them all that money from the papers.'

'Yeah, I suppose.'

'Why do you ask?'

'No reason. I just wondered, after what happened with Tom, you know.'

'That boy was screwed up from the day Alice was taken... with him being in the house, you know. He felt guilty. Anybody would. I don't think there was ever any coming back from that for him. As much as he tried, he was damaged goods. Unfixable. And sadly, it culminated in the events of the other night. I don't think that had anything to do with any guilt on the Abbotts' part, other than Tom's own sense of guilt for not having been able to help his sister.'

'So, you can't think of any reason you know of that Helen Abbott would be arguing with my brother?'

Gillespie shakes his head. 'I don't think so.'

I stand up from my chair. 'Right then. I guess I should be going. I think I need my bed.'

I walk to the mantelpiece, picking up a pen and a scrap of paper. I scribble my number on it. 'If you think of anything, please let me know.'

'Of course.' He takes the paper and slips it into his pocket before showing me to the front door.

I return to Helen's house and let myself quietly inside.

I can still hear the TV blaring from the front room, the neon blues illuminating the dark hallway.

I creep past the living room, tiptoeing up the stairs. I don't have the energy to make awkward small talk with her tonight.

As I take my mobile out of my pocket and place it down, it vibrates on the bedside table. It's a text message from Alan Gillespie.

Can you pop back in the morning? There's something I need to talk to you about.

I reply, telling him I will be there first thing, then switch off the lamp.

The room is plunged into darkness, and as the wind howls outside my window, I drift off to sleep.

43

I have terrible nightmares.

      I see Tom's face, covered in blood.

He's laughing at me, but then his face turns into Adam's, and he reaches out, grabbing me by my hair. He's furious, he's punching me in the face, and Helen Abbott is standing beside us, laughing the whole time.

Alice is dancing around the room, humming a childish tune and giggling.

I know this is a dream, but I can't wake up.

It seems to be on a loop. Once I manage to struggle free from Adam's grip, he's Tom again, and it all starts from the beginning. I know exactly what's coming, but I can't seem to do anything about it. Each time, I see Helen's face contorted with laughter.

Alice skips around in a circle, her face is aging. She's turning into an old lady, but she still has the body of a little girl. When she hums and giggles, it's still a child's voice. The whole scene is absolutely terrifying.

A noise wakes me from the hellish nightmare in a cold sweat.

The bedclothes are drenched and my hair is plastered to my head. As my eyes adjust to the darkness, I see a figure in the corner of the room. I lie still, petrified, staring at the shape in the corner.

It does not move. I *cannot* move.

My eyes adjust to the dark some more and I realise it's just a shadow of a pile of clothes. I feel stupid for being so afraid.

As I lie in the dark room staring up at the ceiling, I hear more noises from outside. Muffled voices and some dull thuds.

I climb out of bed, creeping to the window, peeking carefully through the blinds, but can't see anyone outside. I hear the noise of pans clattering from the kitchen below me and then something smashes. I go to the back bedroom and look out to the garden. There's a shaft of light shining across the garden from the kitchen window. I see the gate is firmly shut and bolted.

Helen is still up. I pull on a nightie and make my way down the stairs. She doesn't hear me. She's in the kitchen, rifling through cupboards. She's down on her hands and knees in a filthy nighty, pulling things from shelves.

The kitchen drawers all hang open, the contents strewn about the floor. It looks like a crime scene again. She mutters and mumbles to herself. I can't make out much of it, but every now and then I hear the odd word.

'Must be here somewhere,' she says, then more muttering.

I watch her for a good five minutes before she notices me. She looks at me blankly, then returns to what she's doing, without offering any sort of explanation, as if what she's doing is perfectly normal.

'Mrs Abbott... Helen, are you okay?'

'Go back to bed, Emily.'

'Can I help you with something?'

'I think you've done enough,' she hisses across the room.

A glass topples from a shelf and smashes on the floor. She doesn't even flinch. As she scuttles around the floor, she cuts her hand on the splinters but doesn't stop her manic search. Blood drips onto the tiled floor and falls in large irregular spots, further spoiling her nightdress.

'It was definitely here. I just need to find it.'

I suspect she is looking for the key to the cellar, but have no intention of telling her that I know where it is. 'Would you like me to help you up to your bed?'

She glares at me. 'I don't want to go to fucking bed,' she tells me through gritted teeth.

I feel that anything else I say will only anger her more, so I return to my room.

I lie in bed listening to the sound of things breaking. Eventually, after an hour or so, the noise stops. All I can hear is the sound of Helen Abbott sobbing. After some time, this noise stops also. I hear her footsteps on the stairs, then the creak of floorboards as she walks down the landing.

I see a shadow under my door.

She stands there for a few minutes. My heart is thumping, and for some reason I feel afraid. I don't know why, but I creep to the door and turn the key in the lock as quietly as I can.

I see the door handle turn.

She's trying to get in.

She realises the door's locked and retreats. The light goes out on the landing and the house is quiet. Outside a fox screams. An owl hoots, and I feel very alone. I think I'm in way over my head. I need to make sure that Helen Abbott does not suspect that Tom told me anything before he shot himself. I think my life may depend on it. In the morning I will talk to Alan Gillespie again to find out what he knows. Something's not right, and I need to find out the whole story.

I decide I'll speak to Adam and find out exactly what was going on with him and Helen on the doorstep. I struggle to get back to sleep. Every noise from outside is a predator trying to get into the house. Every creak in the house is a killer creeping into my room. I'm paranoid and scared, and I'm living in the spare bedroom of somebody who has lied and covered up the murder of her daughter for twenty-five years.

I don't know what else this woman is capable of, but I suspect she's not the confused old lady I thought she was when I first arrived.

I look at my phone for the last time before I doze off. It's 4.30am. It's raining outside again. I'm starting to think it must always rain here. I don't remember it being like that.

I wonder if the events in a place can help to influence its personality, but then I decide that's just stupid. A place is nothing but a location. Nothing can make a place bad, only people.

The wrong people make a bad place.

I'm starting to suspect that Palmerston, or at least Pear Tree Close, is rotten to the core.

44

I don't sleep well at all. I'm awake most of the night. In the morning, the house is silent. I'm grateful that Helen's not awake yet. I throw on a pair of jeans and a jumper, then unlock my bedroom door quietly. I creep down the landing, stopping outside her bedroom door as the floor creaks loudly underneath my weight. I stand for a moment, holding my breath, but hearing the sound of Helen Abbott snoring heavily from within her room, I continue to the top of the stairs.

I make my way downstairs, heading to the kitchen for coffee. Broken glass litters the floor. The cupboards are all still open, the contents mostly on the floor. It looks like the aftermath of a police drugs raid, but of course this was all Helen's doing last night. I give up on the idea of coffee and decide to have one with Alan Gillespie instead. I leave the Abbott house and head next door to number twenty-four.

Pressing the doorbell, I wait impatiently for a few minutes. There's no answer and no sound of movement inside, so I ring the bell again. He must have overslept. I take a few steps over to the front window, peering inside. There's no movement within, no lights on. Nothing. Walking back to the front door, I knock loudly with my bare knuckles. The door swings inwards.

Instinct makes me afraid. I reach out, pushing the door to the wall, calling into the hallway.

'Mr Gillespie? Are you here?'

There's no reply.

'Your front door's open... I'm coming in.'

I step over the threshold, into the dark hallway.

Nothing looks out of place as I head into the living room. Everything is neat and tidy, as it was the previous day. There are no signs of an intruder, no overturned lamps, nothing broken on the floor. In stark contrast to the house I have just left, this house is spick and span, but something feels wrong. I make my way up the stairs.

'Mr Gillespie, it's Emily. Are you in bed?'

I continue to call out as I make my way into the bedrooms. Each one is pristine. No drawers with the contents pulled out, no obvious signs of an intruder or a burglary. I arrive at the master bedroom at the end of the hall. The door is wide open. The bed is neatly made. I approach the bed. Pulling back the covers, I run my hand over the sheet. It's cold to the touch.

There is a glass of water and a book next to the bed. Again, nothing in the room is out of place, but I can't shake the feeling that something's not right. I return downstairs and out the back to the kitchen. The kettle's cold, there's no coffee cup in the sink. I walk to the back door, surveying the garden which is tidy and well looked after. Glancing around the kitchen, I notice a piece of paper on the worktop, folded neatly beside the cooker. A weight from a set of kitchen scales has been set on top of it to stop it blowing away. My name is written on it, so I move the weight and pick up the folded paper. As I do, something slides out from inside it, landing on the floor.

I look down and see something glinting in the light. And I recognise it instantly.

45

A lice's necklace.

The other half of my heart-shaped pendant is lying on the floor by my feet. I bend down and pick it up. I turn it over in my hand and see the inscription of Alice's name on the back. I pull mine out from inside the neck of my jumper, holding the two halves together.

They are a perfect match.

I unfold the paper, reading the note that's written on the other side.

Emily, I know you will be disappointed to read this, but I cannot live this lie any longer. I have kept the devastating truth to myself for twenty-five years, and had thought that I would take this secret to my grave, but your recent return to Palmerston, and apparent investigation into the circumstances of your friend's disappearance, have reopened old wounds and made me realise that this will never go away.

I know you wanted to believe that I was innocent, but the truth is I am not.

I took Alice from her bed all those years ago, and when I realised the gravity of what I had done, I killed her and disposed of her body.

I cannot live with this guilt any longer, I have to end it. Please do not try to find me. By the time you read this note, if indeed you even find it, I will already be dead.

Tell Helen that I am sorry.

But at least now she will have closure, and will hopefully be able to lay this story to rest.

You can give this confession to the police.

I am guilty, and I deserve what is coming to me. Goodbye.

Alan Gillespie.

I read the note again, then fold it up and put it in my jacket pocket, along with the necklace.

I don't know what to make of this note.

I don't believe it.

It doesn't make any sense.

I now have two confessions to Alice's murder, and I don't believe either of them.

I pull my mobile phone from my jeans and call Adam. He answers on the second ring.

'Yo, sis!'

I tell him I'm across the road and coming over to Lily's house.

I'm walking down the path as he comes out of the house, closing the door behind him, pulling on his leather jacket.

He looks tired.

Large dark rings hang under his eyes and he looks ten years older than the last time I saw him. I used to suspect that he was into drugs when he was younger, and the thought returns to me now.

He does not look healthy, and Lily certainly fits the bill of a drug addict, with her waif-like figure. I can't help thinking this girl is bad for my brother. A bad influence would be the wrong choice of words as I know first-hand that Adam is far from a saint, but I think maybe she brings out the worst in him, encourages his bad side in a way.

I shake the thought from my head, wanting to believe he's changed from the angry boy I used to know.

'Adam, can I come inside?'

'Lily and I were up pretty late last night in town. She's still sleeping, let's go down the road and grab a coffee.'

He puts his hand behind my shoulder and steers me back down the path towards the street. As we come out of the gate, he turns left and walks to the end of Pear Tree Close. He cuts down an alley which opens out onto a small parade of shops. We enter a coffee shop called 'Joey's'. He orders a double espresso. I order a large Americano, then we slump down into two oversized brown leather armchairs in the window.

'What's up?' he asks.

I glance nervously around the coffee shop.

There's a skinny girl with freckles and glasses on a laptop, sitting alone in the middle of the room. An old couple with a west highland terrier are sitting at a table for two by the counter. The man sips coffee as he reads the newspaper, and his wife feeds pieces of her muffin to the dog. Nobody's paying any attention to us. The barista is making our drinks, so I pull the note out of my jacket and hand it to Adam. He gives me a quizzical look.

'Just read it,' I tell him.

His eyes scan the page and they widen as he reads. He folds it in half and hands it back to me. 'Shit, Ems. What the fuck?'

I pull the necklace out of my pocket and give it to him. He's turning it over in his hand. The full gravity hasn't hit him. I don't know if he would even remember the necklace, so I pull mine out to show him.

'It's hers. It belonged to Alice. We got them together. Friends forever and all that rubbish. After she disappeared I tried to find it in her bedroom, but it wasn't there, so I always assumed she had been wearing it when she went missing. We never took them off. I still wear mine all the time.'

Adam has a sad expression on his face. His eyes glaze over as if he's reminiscing, but then he's back with me.

'I was supposed to meet Mr Gillespie at his house this morning. He said he had something to tell me. But when I got there the door was open, and no sign of him. Just this note with the necklace in the kitchen.'

Adam's eyes do not move from mine. He holds me with a cold stare. 'It sounds like he's lost his nerve and left you this instead. This would certainly be something to tell you. You need to give this note to the police. Fuck telling Mrs Abbott. Just go straight to the police.'

'I'm not so sure.'

46

The waitress brings over our drinks and I wait for her to walk away before I continue.

'I've spoken to Alan Gillespie a lot since I got here, and not once have I got the impression that he knew anything about Alice.'

'No offence, Ems, but he's been lying about it for twenty-five years. I would imagine that he's gotten pretty good at telling his story.'

Adam's flippancy irritates me.

'No, I don't think so.'

He screws up his face.

'Something doesn't ring true here. I don't think it was him.'

'Emily, you have the man's signed confession in your pocket, and the necklace Alice was wearing when she was taken. I'd say that's fairly conclusive evidence, wouldn't you?'

Although I know how this must look to Adam, this 'confession' doesn't make any sense, especially when I consider Tom's pre-suicide confession. After twenty-five years of wondering what had happened to my best friend, I now have two men wanting to confess to her murder in almost as many days. Of course I can't tell Adam about what Tom said. This is a nugget of information that my gut tells me I must keep to myself. I pick up my mug, sipping the hot coffee. Adam throws his espresso down his throat, placing the empty cup on the table.

'Adam, I don't buy it.' I shake my head.

'But why would he confess to killing Alice Abbott if he didn't do it?' Adam whispers. 'And how would he have this?'

He hands the necklace back to me and I put it gently in my pocket. I shake my head again.

'I don't know, but something feels wrong.'

Adam slams his hand onto the table.

'Emily, stop messing about and trying to play detective. People are dead. My friend shot himself, for fuck's sake. Please take the note to the police and pack your bags and go.'

'You want me to leave?'

'That's what you do, isn't it? You only came back to find out what happened all those years ago, and now you have your answer. The dirty old man next door did it, like everybody always said. Fuck, and to think he's been living next door to her mother all these years. That's fucked-up. Anyway, case closed. Now we can all move on with our lives, right? Go and write that in your trashy magazine and get back to living your life. Forget all this bullshit.'

Adam's tone frightens me slightly. I know he's trying to protect me, but I'm the older one. I can look after myself. I don't need him telling me what to do.

'Adam, I don't understand. Why lie about it for all this time and then all of a sudden change your mind. "Oh yes, by the way, it was me". It doesn't make sense.'

'He explains it all in that note, Emily. You digging around has opened up the old wounds, and he realises he's never going to be free from this guilt. He killed a little girl, probably raped her too. God knows how long he kept her alive in there before getting rid of her.'

'I'm not sure, Adam. My gut tells me not to believe this.'

Adam looks at me. His eyes are pleading. 'Emily, please. You have the answers you've always wanted. What more do you need? You don't know anything about his man, so I suggest that when he hands you a note confessing to the murder, you take it and go straight to the police. I'm worried about you, Emily. I don't think you will *ever* accept what happened to Alice. You have the answer right there. You have the explanation, and the mystery is over.'

'What about the girl who's disappeared down the road?'

He shakes his head. 'What about her? Kids go missing all the time. Gillespie doesn't mention her in the letter, so like I told you before, they're probably unconnected. It's just another little girl gone missing. Another set of fucked-up lives set in motion.'

He sounds so matter of fact about it all, as if he's talking about a lost pet rather than somebody's child.

I change the subject. 'So, what's the deal with you and Lily?'

He eyes me suspiciously, not used to me showing an interest in his personal life. 'What do you mean?'

I choose my words carefully. 'She's... interesting.'

'She passes the time,' he says without emotion.

'Charming.'

'It's difficult, Ems. I've been with a few girls over the years, but I seem to be really good at picking the fucked-up ones. They always seem to have issues, or whatever.'

I can't help but smile sarcastically. 'No offence, but is it any surprise the stick-thin girl with blue hair has issues?'

'I know. I didn't really pick Lily. I had no intention of getting into a relationship with her. It kind of... happened. I have this tendency of meeting girls and before I know it, it's a full-blown relationship and I'm like "whoa, how the heck did this happen?"

and they're planning weddings and talking about babies and stuff. This one girl, Jenny, I met at work, she was lovely. I told everyone she was the one. She seemed perfect. We went on a few dates and then she got pregnant. She wanted to keep it. She said we should get married. We had literally been seeing each other for about three weeks. That's hardly the firm foundation for a stable family.'

'Shit, Adam. What happened?' I'm genuinely interested. If I have a niece or nephew out there somewhere, I'd like to know.

'I made her get rid of it. It took some doing. She was determined she wanted to keep it, but in the end she saw sense. She quit her job because she hated me for it. I see her around town from time to time. Last time I saw her she was with this guy, poor sod. I wanted to warn him.... "run, while you still can".'

Again, I am surprised by Adam's lack of compassion when talking about a sensitive subject. He is telling me about the abortion of his child with a casual flick of a wrist, as if it means nothing.

'After that, I kind of stayed away from girls for a while. It scared the shit out of me. I'm not ready to be a dad. Shit, I can barely look after myself, let alone a kid. I really dodged a bullet there. I had this really long period where I was unsure about a lot of things. I thought maybe I might be gay. Maybe that's why I can't seem to find the right girl.'

I raise a questioning eyebrow in his direction.

'Thought, past tense. I'm not,' he says casually. 'I went to a gay bar in Brighton. This guy hit on me and it freaked me out. I'm totally fine with gays, but it's definitely not for me.'

Adam fidgets uncomfortably in his seat.

'And then there was Lily. I went with Tom to a party at her house, and she threw herself at me. Would not take no for an answer. And here we are.'

'I've not seen her about for a few days. I hope she's not

avoiding me after what happened at her house. You know, when she was questioning me about Tom.'

'She's fine. She can just be... kind of intense, I suppose.'

'Is it serious with you two? It must be fairly serious if you're living together.'

'We're not. I have my own place in town, but my flatmate is a total dick. We were shit-faced and got into a huge fight and ended up smashing a window. He cut himself pretty badly. We're not really talking at the moment, so I'm staying at Lily's on and off until things calm down. When he's out I stay there, but if he's around, I find it easier to be out of the way. I wouldn't want a repeat performance. I might end up killing him next time.' He shoots me a grin.

'That's not funny. Especially after seeing you with that old guy in the warehouse the other day. I really thought you were going to kill him.'

Adam looks embarrassed.

'Why are you so... angry?' I ask him.

Adam picks up a napkin and twists it tightly in his hands. He doesn't answer for a while. He just looks at me with empty eyes. His face is devoid of any emotion. 'Do you really need to ask me that?'

I pick up my coffee and take a mouthful, considering my next words. 'You said the other day you blame Alice for every-thing. You think I abandoned you... you think Mum and Dad abandoned you. But eventually you have to stop blaming your own bad choices on things that happened when we were kids.'

He frowns and seems annoyed, but doesn't say anything.

'You need to take responsibility for your own life. If Lily isn't the girl you want to be with, then don't.'

He laughs at this, a dark look in his eye.

I continue. 'Don't be scared. Yes, it might hurt her, and yes, she'll more than likely get angry, but that's no excuse to waste time in a relationship that isn't right. You're not getting any younger. You're going to have to sort things out eventually.'

'You're wrong. Lily cares about me. She loves me. When nobody else gave a shit, she was there for me, which is more than can be said for you. And yeah, she might not be "the one", whatever that means, but she's better than being lonely and spending my life on my own.'

He's getting worked up, I can tell from his voice. He's getting louder, more animated. The old couple across the room are looking at us nervously. They probably aren't used to raised voices in here. The girl with the laptop tuts and plugs her head-phones into her ears, shooting us an irritated look.

'I'm sorry, Adam, but that's bullshit. Being with the wrong person is not better than being with nobody. You don't need to be with somebody. How can you expect to be happy with someone when you can't be happy with yourself?'

'That's easy for you to say. You had Mum and Dad. You haven't spent your whole life feeling... unwanted.'

'That's rubbish!' It's my turn to get angry.

The old couple with the dog stand up and shuffle out of the café, looking at us disapprovingly as they pass by.

'You had the same parents as I did. They wanted to be there for you. You left. You didn't stay in touch. You never spoke to them. You didn't return their calls. I remember on the morning they...'

I'm getting worked up and emotional.

'The morning of the accident. Dad was trying desperately to get hold of you on the phone before they set off in the car on holiday. He called you about twenty times. He left you messages. You just didn't care. You passed up the last opportunity you had to speak to our parents. You'll never get that back. That was your choice. Nobody else's.'

Adam gives me a strange look, then shakes his head.

We sit in silence for a few minutes, neither of us wanting to look at the other. We've both said too much. We've both let our emotions get the better of us. I feel guilty. Adam seems vulnerable.

I should try to comfort him, but I still feel annoyed. It's amazing that two people who grew up in the same house can have such opposing views of each of their childhoods.

He looks at his watch, then stands abruptly. 'I'm meeting a mate. Promise me you're going to take that note to the police. Please?'

He looks at me pleadingly again, and against my better judgement, I agree. 'I'll finish my coffee and then drive to the police station.'

'Good.' He bends down and kisses me on the cheek. 'Give me a ring later, perhaps we can go get some dinner or something.'

I tell him sure, and he rushes out of the shop and around the corner out of sight.

I sit sipping my coffee and my phone beeps in my pocket. I pull it out and a scrap of paper falls out. I don't recognise the number on the screen, so I open the message.

'Hi Emily. It's Lily. I just wanted to apologise for my behaviour the other day. I know you were probably in shock after Tom, and I was insensitive. I hope there are no hard feelings.' I type a quick reply telling her it's fine, then pick up the scrap of paper from the floor. It's the name of the guy that Alan Gillespie gave me when I first arrived in Palmerston. As I go to screw it up, something occurs to me. I pull the confession out of my jacket and unfold it, placing it on the table in front of me, next to the scrap of paper. I look from one to the other, then back again.

The handwriting is totally different.

Whereas the first one, definitely written by Alan Gillespie, is a neat and tidy cursive, the note I found this morning is scrawled in scratchy capital letters. There's no way that these two things were written by the same person. No way at all. I don't know who's written the confession, but one thing is for certain, it wasn't Alan Gillespie. I stand up and dial Adam's number. He doesn't answer.

Swearing under my breath, I shove my phone back in my jeans pocket. I fold the two notes up together and carefully place them in my jacket pocket, leaving the coffee shop to walk back towards Pear Tree Close, cutting back down the alley. Whoever wrote the note wants me to believe that Alan Gillespie killed Alice all those years ago, and they've gone as far as to plant a piece of Alice's jewellery in his house.

47

I head back to the Abbott house. Helen is up and busying herself tidying up the mess she made last night in the kitchen. She looks embarrassed when I enter the room, but she doesn't say anything. She's kneeling on the floor, putting pieces of broken glass and china onto some sheets of newspaper she has spread out on the floor in front of her. She's cut her hand again and there's blood on the paper and the floor, but she makes no effort to stem the flow. I kneel down beside her and she glances at me, reaching her hand up to brush her hair out of her face, leaving a smudge of red over her cheek. Her hair is a mess and full of tangles. She's wearing a dirty pair of linen trousers with dried blood wiped over them. Her drab grey cardigan is buttoned up all wrong, and her shoes don't match.

She looks completely and utterly mad.

If you had to conjure up the image of an insane old women in your mind, the woman kneeling beside me would be pretty close to what you imagined. She smells bad too. I'm sure she hasn't had a wash for days. I reach out and take her hand. Pulling some tissues from my pocket, I wrap them around it and squeeze to try to stop the bleeding. She looks at me and gives a weak smile. I take her other hand and place it around the tissue, then pull my own away.

I retrieve my necklace out from inside my jumper and hold it towards her.

'Mrs Abbott... Helen... do you remember this necklace?'

She glances at the necklace and her eyes fix on it.

'Yes, of course I do. Alice had one the same.'

'Not the same. The other half of this one. Mine has my name on it, and hers had her name.'

Helen smiles to herself. 'That's right, yes. I remember taking you girls to get them. You were so excited when you were allowed to get your names engraved on them. You told her that it meant you were friends forever. Neither of you would ever take them off.' She shakes her head.

'Mrs Abbott, I need to ask you something about Alice's necklace.'

She looks up into my eyes and holds my gaze. She frowns, trying to anticipate what I'm about to say.

'Do you have Alice's half of the necklace? Do you know where it is?'

Helen shakes her head and then continues to lift the broken kitchenware from the floor, placing the pieces onto the newspaper.

'Alice never took it off, just like you. She was wearing it when she...' Helen stops, a tear in her eye. 'The night she went away.'

'Are you absolutely sure of that?'

'One hundred per cent.'

She folds the newspaper around the broken glasses and plates, then stands up. She takes a roll of tape out from a drawer and wraps it around the parcel a few times, then drops the whole thing into the bin before shuffling to a tall cupboard in the corner. She takes out a broom and sweeps the floor. A coldness runs through me as I realise I needn't have gone down into the cellar for one after all.

There's no system to what she's doing, and she just ends up spreading the splinters around the floor and into the grouting between the dirty tiles. She places the broom back inside the cupboard then shuffles towards the door. She stops in the door-way, but doesn't turn round to face me.

'Careful if you're wandering round without any shoes on. I can't get down to the hoover in the basement, so there might still be some splinters of glass on the floor.'

She waits in the doorway for a moment, then heads into the living room. I hear the television click on, then the familiar sound of the daytime programmes that she spends her life watching drifts through the house. I stand up and I notice that Helen's half-eaten breakfast is on the table. She's set a place for Tom, and prepared breakfast for him. It sits, looking sad and lonely on the table beside hers. I glance towards the cellar door and notice that the door has been hacked at with a screwdriver or some other tool. There are deep gouges and stab marks in the wood around the handle.

She's desperate to get back down into that room, but I can't for the life of me understand why. It will be a stark and brutal reminder of what happened to her son. I'm not sure I can even face the mess down there. I shake the image of the red-soaked basement from my mind and make myself a cup of coffee. I sit by the counter, mulling over the events of the last twenty-four hours. Helen has confirmed that Alice was wearing her necklace when she disappeared.

The necklace that I have in my jacket pocket.

But Helen Abbott is not the most trustworthy of people, if Tom's confession is anything to go by. As much as I could not or did not want to believe what Tom had told me about Alice's death before shooting himself, I know that Alan Gillespie's confession note is a fake. Somebody wants me to believe that Gillespie is guilty. Whoever wrote the note was somehow involved in Alice's death. Tom is dead, I know that for a fact as I saw it far too closely with my own eyes, which leaves Helen Abbott. But I also know for a fact that Helen was in the house last night. I was here with her. Plus, she is a frail-looking old mad woman.

Alan Gillespie is a big-built tall man. There's no way Helen Abbott could have overpowered him in his own home.

And even if she had, where was Alan now? She can't have him imprisoned down in the cellar because I'm the only person who knows where the key is. No, Helen is not the culprit in this instance, which would only leave one person.

Jim Abbott.

He would be the only other person who knew the truth about Alice's death, that his own son had killed his daughter. I can only theorise that Helen has been lying about not knowing Jim's whereabouts for the last five years. She must have contacted her husband to let him know what's been happening, and he's returned to clean up the mess and keep the family in the clear. But where is he? Is he in the house somewhere? Possibly hiding up in Helen's bedroom? Suddenly I feel afraid again and I look around the room.

There's nobody there, but the darkness and gloom of the Abbott house feels hugely oppressive. I stand up and rush to the hall, grabbing my jacket from the coat hook, I head out the door without saying a word to Helen. I don't know where I'm going, I just know I have to get out of this house.

Briefly stopping on the doorstep, I reach up and take hold of my heart pendant in my hand. I turn it over between my fingers, caressing it, and close my eyes.

48

Six Years Earlier

It's a warm summer's day in early August and I'm sitting in my parents' kitchen in Highgate, North London. I turn my heart-shaped pendant over and over in between my fingers, miles away in a daydream. Thinking about lost friendships and a time when things seemed so different.

'Emily!' my mother barks. 'Are you listening to me?'

I look blankly at her. I haven't heard a word she's said for the last five minutes. Something about feeding the dog, I think. 'Yes, Mum.'

'Are you sure you'll be okay staying here on your own while we're away? It's not too late for us to put Barney into the kennels. I know your job keeps you very busy. I don't want to be an inconvenience.' She crosses the kitchen and sits next to me at the table, glancing at the pendant in my hand, giving me a weak smile.

'It's absolutely fine, Mum. I'm looking forward to it. You and

Dad go and enjoy your holiday. Barney and I will be just fine.'
The old schnauzer hears his name and one ear pricks up, but he
doesn't have the energy to get up from his bed. I smile at him.
The French doors are open and I can see my dad down the end
of the garden, pacing with his phone to his ear. He looks
annoyed. He comes in through the door.

'Any luck?' I ask.

He shakes his head. 'Nope. I've tried five times. And left two
messages. I honestly don't know why you kids bother having
mobile phones if you never bloody answer them.'

I catch my mother's eye and mouth 'kids' to her, raising one
eyebrow. She swats her hand at me in the air.

'I wouldn't worry, Dad,' I reassure him. 'You know what he's
like. He only ever gets in touch if he wants something... usually
money. I don't think I've heard from him in about a year.'

My mother gets up from her chair and busies herself over by
the sink. My dad sits down in the seat she's just vacated. There's
something up with him. I can't quite put my finger on it. He
seems nervous. I pull my phone out and dial Adam's number. It
rings a couple of times and is then diverted to voicemail.

'Adam, it's Emily. Dad really wants to talk to you before he
and Mum head off to Cornwall. He's tried calling and left you
some messages. Can you please give him a ring? They're setting
off in about an hour. Okay.' I hang up. Dad stares at me and
shakes his head. I see Mum glancing at me nervously, but she
looks away when she sees me return her gaze. She pulls a tin of
dog food out of the cupboard and opens it, transferring it into a
small bowl which she places on the floor by her feet. Barney
slowly raises himself from his bed in the corner and trots over.
He sniffs at it, walks round it, sniffs again, then trots back to
his bed.

'He doesn't eat a lot these days,' Dad says, as he eyes me
watching the dog. 'He doesn't really *do* much anymore either.

He'll only need a little walking, but he'll let you know if he wants to go out.' Dad has a sad expression on his face. The dog has been their faithful friend for fifteen years. I think my mother loves him more than she loves my brother. The dog lowers himself stiffly onto his bed, letting out a long slow sigh as he does so.

'I'm telling you now, if that dog dies while you're away, it's *not* my fault, okay? That's my one condition.'

My mother shushes me. 'Don't say things like that. He understands every word, you know.'

Barney lifts his head from the bed, looking in my direction. He tilts it to one side, then lays it down again. I let out a small laugh and my dad joins me.

'He'll be fine. There's plenty of life left in the old boy yet,' my dad tells me, rather unconvincingly.

My mother approaches Barney's bed, crouching down beside it. She ruffles his ears and top of his head, and he closes his eyes pleasantly. It almost looks as if he is smiling. She looks over to me. 'You will look after him, won't you?' she asks me, a worried edge to her voice.

'Of course I will, Mum. It's only a week. He'll be fine. I'm sure I'll be okay too; in case you are worried,' I say with a little too much sarcasm.

She stands up and comes over to me, placing her hand on my shoulder, giving it a gentle squeeze. Dad walks out to the garden again with his phone. My mum gets some plates out from the cupboard then crosses to the fridge, taking out a selection of groceries. She busies herself making some sandwiches. 'There's plenty of food,' she tells me. 'But if you need anything, your dad's left twenty quid under the black lamp on the mantelpiece in the living room.'

'Gosh, I'll be sure and hit the shops then,' I joke. She smiles.

She joins me again at the table, placing the plate of sandwiches in the middle. She gets a bottle of cold lemonade from the fridge and pours three glasses. Dad joins us. I can tell from his demeanour that he still hasn't managed to get hold of Adam. Dad picks up a couple of the sandwiches, dropping them onto his plate.

'So, Cornwall should be lovely at this time of year. We're having a great summer so far, so hopefully the weather will hold out for you,' I say cheerfully. 'What's on your itinerary?'

Mum looks at Dad but doesn't say anything.

'We're just going to take it easy for a week, I think,' Dad says. 'Nothing too raucous at our age.'

'I still don't understand why you're not taking poor Barney. I'm sure the owner of the cottage will let you if you give them a ring.'

'The drive's too long for him. I don't think it would be great for him to be in the car that long in this heat. To be honest, I'm not sure how your mother's going to cope with the journey.' He winks at me. She smiles again.

'I'm glad you decided to go away. It'll do you some good to have a little break from here. It can be so oppressive in London in the summer. A nice bit of sea air will do wonders for you both.' I see Dad looking at his phone. 'Please try not to worry too much about Adam. Don't let him ruin your holiday. Promise me?' I've got quite good at ordering my parents around over the years. My dad nods. 'I don't know why you're so desperate to talk to him. It's not like you'll get much from him aside from a few grunts and some surly comments.'

'You know I always like to talk to you both before we go off on a trip, and we haven't been on holiday for a while, so...' he trails off.

'It's only Cornwall, Dad. You're not going far, and you'll be back next weekend. I'm sure he can cope. You go and enjoy your holiday.'

49

After lunch, I help Mum clear up the plates while Dad busies himself out by the car, making sure the roof rack is secure. Barney senses something is up and drags himself out of his bed to investigate. I pick him up and cuddle him close to my chest, kissing the top of his head.

'Right, buster! I'm not taking any nonsense from you. You can consider this week a boot camp for badly behaved lazy dogs. I'll sort you out.'

'I heard that!' my dad shouts in through the front door.

Barney licks my ear and I smile. We walk out into the garden and I sit in an old wooden chair on the lawn, with Barney on my lap. He makes no effort to escape as I stroke him gently, playing with his thick wiry coat between my hands. He licks my fingers. The sun beats down on my face and a blue tit swoops past me, landing on the branches of a small tree to my right. I feel extremely content and am looking forward to my own 'holiday' dog-sitting. I've squared it with my boss so I can work from home for the most part of it. I have my laptop with me and a few stories to write up for the magazine, but apart from that Barney has me all to himself for seven glorious days.

Dad finishes packing the car and my parents stand by the front door. They both hug me tightly and tell me they love me, like they always do, every day. I hug them back, but I don't say I love them. I always feel too embarrassed.

I will regret this forever.

They get into the car and as they drive away, slowly my mum turns to wave. I'm holding Barney, and I waggle his paw at them. The car disappears down the road, and Barney and I go back into the house. I try Adam again, to no avail.

Two days later, the house phone rings in the middle of the night. Barney's sleeping at the end of the bed and sits up grumpily at the disturbance. I'm groggy and don't quite understand what the noise is at first. I realise after a moment, and glance at the clock. It's 1.30am. Who would be calling my parents' house at this time of night. Then I realise it can only be Adam. I pick up the phone ready to give him a piece of my mind.

'Hello?' a crackly voice at the end of the line says.

'Who's this?'

'Hi, this is Officer Dobson with the Devon and Cornwall police.'

My heart thumps and the room spins around me. Everything seems to slow down.

'Yes?' My voice is shaky.

'We found this phone at the sight of an accident. This number is listed as the home number, so we thought we would give it a try.'

I feel sick as I try to process the information. The police officer has my dad's phone. 'It's my parents' house. I'm dog-sitting... They're away. Are they okay?' I ask hurriedly. Officer Dobson takes a split second too long to respond and I know that something is wrong.

'What's happened?' I scream down the phone.

I hear bits of the next stream of words, but it doesn't seem to compute in my head. 'Heavy rain... car accident... off a cliff... no survivors.' I drop the phone and scream.

Barney looks alarmed and jumps off the bed. He's licking my ankles.

I fall to the floor in floods of tears. The officer must be wrong. My parents can't be dead. That's ridiculous. It's not possible. I was sitting with them in this house two days earlier, eating ham and cucumber sandwiches. There must be some mistake.

I have to go and make a positive identification. This will be the last image I have of my parents, and I have to do it alone. I hate Adam for that at the time.

The next few days are a blur. I don't sleep much. I try to phone Adam again, but he doesn't answer. I leave him messages, telling him to call me and that it is urgent.

Mum's sister, Aunt Janet, comes to stay. She's sympathetic and her kindness makes me cry. I feel like my whole world has fallen apart. I don't know how I'll cope without my parents.

I look at Barney lying patiently in his bed waiting for my parents to return, and it breaks my heart.

Janet sets to work arranging the funeral. I don't have to do a thing, which is for the best because I'm incapable. I can just about muster the energy to drag myself out of bed at noon every day.

I try Adam again. He doesn't answer, doesn't return my phone calls.

Eventually, after a week, I get annoyed and leave him a message telling him what's happened. I give him the details of the funeral the following week, and hang up.

I throw my phone across the room and the screen smashes, but I don't care.

It's just another broken thing in my life.

50

The funeral comes and goes. I don't feel much. I'm surprised. I don't cry. I feel like I can't. I'm numb. Some of my colleagues stand dutifully beside me, trying to comfort me, but it does little to help. I feel empty. But more than this, I'm angry at Adam. The day that I should be grieving, and all I can feel is pissed off at my little brother.

After the church, a few friends and family return to my parents' house for the wake. I'm carrying a plate of egg sandwiches to the table when I see Adam walk into the living room. He's holding a near-empty bottle of vodka and he's unsteady on his feet. As I see him, I drop the platter and it smashes loudly on the floor. Egg and bread and tomato are all over the carpet. Barney trots over and sniffs it. He licks a bit of the egg, then retreats to his bed in the kitchen.

Adam smiles at me. 'Have I missed the party?' he slurs. His greasy bleached-blond hair hangs limply in front of his eyes. He's wearing black skinny jeans and a black jumper with holes in the elbows. He's thin and looks tired. I take a few steps towards him. I stand, staring into his face, and then I hit him, hard across the cheek. He just stands looking at me, so I slap him again, then again.

Aunt Janet rushes over and pulls me back from him. She tells him to go upstairs and sober up.

'Screw this. I'm outta here,' he says, then saunters out of the house.

The next morning I'm woken by noises from downstairs. I make my way down the stairs to find Adam in the kitchen. He's making coffee. He holds up a cup towards me and I shake my head. I can barely stand to look at him.

'I only came back to get some stuff. I assume the house is going to be sold, and I wanted to make sure none of my stuff was here,' he says casually.

I can barely believe what I'm hearing, but nothing will surprise me with Adam. 'Is that all you have to say?'

'What do you want me to say?'

'Mum and Dad are dead, Adam. You didn't call. You didn't even make it back for the funeral. What's wrong with you?' My voice is getting louder. I try to get a grip on my emotions, but it's difficult.

'Nothing wrong with me, Ems. I'm absolutely fine. Am I supposed to pretend I had some sort of relationship with our parents just because they drove their car off a cliff?'

'You're an arsehole. A total fucking arsehole. I can't fathom why Mum and Dad bothered with you at all.'

Adam picks up his coffee taking a big gulp, raises his eyes and looks directly into mine. 'They didn't. None of you did. And then you wonder why I don't rush back for the funeral?'

'Excuse me?'

'What, because Princess Emily summons me, I have to drop everything and come home? Is that it?' He gives a quiet laugh.

'Our parents *died*, Adam. This isn't a game, or a joke, or some way to get at you. They're dead. And you stand there, talking about selling the house?'

'It'll have to be sold. I'll expect half of the cash too.'

'Dad tried to call you. Where have you been?'

Adam pulls a chair from under the table and slumps down into it. 'I've been busy.'

'You didn't have five minutes to return any of our calls?'

Adam gives me a strange look. I can't read it, I don't know what he's thinking, or if he is indeed thinking anything at all. He cocks his head to one side, opens his mouth as if to speak, then changes his mind. He just smirks. 'If you're finished lecturing me, I'm gonna head off. I've got a train to catch. I don't suppose you can give me a lift to the station, can you?' He raises an eyebrow cockily.

I don't respond. I turn around and walk back up the stairs.

'I take it that's a no?' he shouts after me. From upstairs, I hear the front door slam. I don't bother going to the window.

When I go back downstairs later on in the day, I find that some of my parents' things are gone. I can only assume that Adam has taken them. Probably to sell.

A few days later, I wake to find Barney dead at the foot of the bed. As I sit on the floor and cradle his lifeless body in my lap, my half-heart pendant falls out of the neck of my nightdress, in front of my chest. I turn it over between my fingers, caressing it, and close my eyes as the tears stream down my cheeks.

51

Present Day

As I walk through old familiar streets that seem so alien to me now, thoughts race through my mind at light speed. I need a plan of action. I can't speak to Adam because he's made it quite clear how he feels about the situation. He thinks it's all clear-cut. But he doesn't know what I know. I decide against explaining about the two notes to him. He'll just be angry.

I need to do this on my own. I need to speak to Helen Abbott. But how? She's angry with me. I think she blames me for Tom. And I don't know what she is capable of. I don't want to put myself in a situation that I may regret. When I talk to her, it needs to be on neutral ground, and there need to be people around. I need to be safe.

I pass a sign tied to a lamppost. 'Clothing sale on today only. Many designer brands, amazing prices' it says in bold red letters. 'Miss it, miss out!' it declares. I take out my phone and snap a picture of the address of the shop. It's in town.

I have an idea. I turn around and head back to Helen's house. When I get home, she's sitting in her chair, staring blankly at the television, even though it's not switched on. As I enter the room, she glances at me, then back to the blank TV screen.

'Helen...' I start. This needs to be tactful. 'Why don't you let me take you out today? There's a sale on in one of the clothes shops in town. I hear there are some great bargains to be had. I'll help you choose some new clothes. Shopping always makes me feel better when I'm feeling down,' I say breezily.

She laughs. 'I don't think a new pair of shoes is going to fix *this*, Emily.'

I cross the room and perch myself on the arm of her chair, placing my hand on her shoulder. 'Helen, I really want to take you out. I think it might help. Even just getting out of this house for a few hours might make you feel a bit better.' I rush to the hall and pick up her shoes and coat, piling them into her lap. 'Come on, get yourself dressed.'

'Emily, I really don't want to–' she begins, but I don't let her finish.

'I won't take no for an answer. Now, come on.' I pull her up from the chair and slip the coat over her shoulder. She smells like old sweat and cigarettes. I look at her stringy limp hair and throw in for good measure, 'I'll take you to get your hair done too. My treat.'

She protests but I bully her out the door and into my car. I feel like an abuser, forcing an old lady out of her house with brute strength, and hope that nobody witnesses the bizarre spectacle.

As I drive, Helen sits in silence, staring out of the passenger window. As we pass by places, I comment on how Alice and I used to play there, or walk here, or eat chips there. Helen doesn't respond much, aside from a few 'Mmm-hmms'.

I make the salon on the high street our first stop. I need time to think about what to say, so I sit her in the chair and wait patiently while the hairdresser transforms Helen's greasy hair into a finely coiffed shoulder-length do. A touch of colour takes years off of her, and I can almost see the Helen Abbott I once knew. As she catches a glimpse of her former self, I notice a smile flicker briefly across her lips, but then it is gone, as if she is punishing herself for being happy.

The stylist finishes and I tell Helen how amazing she looks. She blushes, but she knows it's not true. Her hair is an improvement, but she still looks like a bag lady, just with better hair. I pay the horrendously expensive bill and we head across the street to the clothing store. The shop is full of women all searching for bargains. As we enter, a few of them turn and stare. They obviously recognise Helen. I wonder if they recognise me. I remember a few of them. My picture will no doubt have been in the paper over the last few days, after what happened with Tom, so maybe they are staring at me. Who knows. I feel uncomfortable, but I pretend I'm fine.

I drag Helen further into the shop and go to the nearest rail.

'What colours do you like?' I ask her casually.

'I don't really...' She holds the bottom of her grubby cardigan, as if by explanation.

'I remember you used to wear a lot of green.'

'Yes, Jim always liked me in green. He said it brought out my eyes.'

'There you go, that's a start.' I pull a green dress from the rails and hold it up to her. 'How about this?'

She shakes her head, trying to push the dress away from her. 'Oh no, I'm far too old for that.'

'Nonsense.' I hold it up to her again. 'Try it on.'

'I don't want to. What am I even doing here? This is wrong. I shouldn't be here. I'd like to go home, Emily,' she says, like a petulant child, but I ignore her. I walk down the aisle, pulling random items off the rails and handing them to her with no care if they will suit her at all. I just need to form a bond. I need to get her to trust me.

When she has a pile of clothing in her arms, I steer her towards the dressing room.

The first few things she tries on, she seems awkward and embarrassed, but as she tries on more, and sees that she looks better, she starts to relax. *Bingo*, I think.

She steps out of the changing room in a pair of dark grey flared trousers and a long-sleeved blue silk blouse. She looks nervously towards me, too shy to pose, but I can tell she wants to. 'I like this,' she says quietly, looking down towards the ground. I have to admit, it's a vast improvement.

With the new hair-do, she could almost pass for the old Helen Abbott. Almost. Apart from the twinkle that used to be in her eyes. I suspect that may be gone forever.

52

After much encouragement, and pushing from me, Helen leaves the shop with a few new items. She also leaves wearing a new outfit. I asked the young shop assistant if she could remove the tags so the clothes could be worn straight away. She looked Helen up and down and smirked, before doing as I asked. Much as I tried, Helen refused to let the girl throw her old clothes in the bin. So, Helen strides from the shop in a glamorous white silk blouse and a long flowery skirt, with her tatty old clothes folded neatly with the rest of her purchases in a paper bag.

As we leave, I suggest we grab a coffee, and maybe something to eat. She looks at her watch as if she has somewhere else to be, but we both know she doesn't have an excuse, so she reluctantly agrees. I choose a quiet-looking bistro, just off the high street. Aside from one other couple in the corner, we have the place to ourselves. We order some food and the waitress totters off on her high heels. Helen tuts as she walks away and shakes her head disapprovingly.

'Why these young girls have to make such a spectacle of

themselves, I don't know. It's possible to look nice, without look-ing... well, you know...' she trails off.

'Cheap?' I suggest. Helen smiles and nods. 'So that was nice, right?'

Helen throws me a confused look.

'Shopping. I know you've been through a lot, and I'm not saying this will fix anything, but a little retail therapy never hurt anyone.'

Helen shifts nervously in her seat, averting my look.

I decide to go for it. 'It must have been hard for you, these last few years. Without Jim.'

Her eyes dart up to mine and she immediately looks away. 'I've managed fine without him. Tom and I didn't need him.'

'I know, you're doing really well. But still, you shared a very difficult experience together. He must have been there for you when you needed to talk about Alice?'

'We shared nothing. Anything that we might have shared was gone a long time before Jim left. He never wanted to talk about Alice. He thought we should move on. Forget the whole thing.' There's a bitterness in her words.

'Surely not. Nobody could ever expect you to forget what happened. Especially Jim.'

Helen laughs and shakes her head. 'You wouldn't believe half the things Jim expected me to do.' She stares off into the distance; a sad look falls over her face.

'Such as?'

She shakes her head in response.

'After he left, you've never had any contact from him at all?' I ask.

'Nope,' she shoots back.

'And you have no idea where he might be now?'

She smiles. 'No idea at all. I don't care anymore. Good riddance.'

'So, if he was back in Palmerston, you wouldn't know about it, I guess?'

Helen fixes me with a cold stare. 'I'd be the last person he would contact. Why all these questions?'

The awkward silence that ensues is broken by the clip-clopping of the waitresses high-heeled shoes on the hard wooden floor. She stops in front of the table, dropping a plate of pasta in front of Helen. The red sauce slops over the edge, dripping onto the table and splashing onto her new blouse. The waitress doesn't notice. She plonks my cobb salad in front of me and turns away without saying a word.

Helen sighs and takes a tissue from her handbag. She spits on it and wipes at the red stain on her blouse, making a messy pink mark. 'I knew I should have thought better of buying white silk.'

'I'm sure it'll all come out in the wash.'

I stare at her but feel she's not really listening, until she looks up at me and says coldly, 'Things usually do in the end, dear.'

We eat mostly in silence. Helen's eyes dart around the restaurant, as if she's expecting to be caught doing something she shouldn't. My phone rings a few times. It's Adam, but I can't speak to him. I press the divert button each time, but he doesn't give up. I switch it to vibrate, but for a good ten minutes he bombards my phone.

Eventually he tires and the buzz of the phone is replaced with silence. From time to time, we hear the waitress crossing the room. She picks things up from tables, folds them, and places them back. She is trying her hardest to look busy without actually having to do anything, and at the same time, ignoring the only four customers in the establishment. It's a skill, and she has it down to an art.

I feel I've failed in my mission to find out any information about Jim Abbott. Helen's reluctant to talk about him and has offered very little in answer to my questions. I decide I'll have one last attempt.

'Did you know Mr Gillespie has just upped and left?' I ask casually, as if I am commenting on the weather.

Helen freezes and her eyes dart up to my face. She looks scared. She swallows a mouthful of food then places her knife and fork down beside her plate, then knits her fingers together. 'What do you mean?' she asks, almost whispering.

'Just that. I went round to see him yesterday, and his front door was on the latch. He wasn't there, and he hadn't slept in his bed as far as I could tell. The house was neat and tidy, doesn't look like anyone's broken in or anything. He's just... gone.'

'Have you told the police?' she asks, a strange quiver in her voice.

'No. It didn't seem suspicious,' I lie. 'I don't think the police would be interested.'

Helen shifts in her seat. She picks up her napkin and dabs at the corners of her mouth. She looks at me. I feel she's considering her next move, but the whole time her eyes do not shift from mine.

'Alan Gillespie is very much a creature of habit. I've lived so near to him most of my adult life, and he rarely leaves the house. He certainly wouldn't go anywhere without making sure all the doors were locked. Not with the sort of trouble he's had. The last thing he'd want is someone getting inside his house. What's more, he'd tell me if he was going away. He'd want me to water his plants. No, I think this is *very* odd.'

I have her attention. This is the most engaged she has been all day, so I press on.

'You know, I was round at his house the night before, for coffee and a chat. He does seem like a lovely man. And he thinks the world of you.'

Helen's cheeks flush a little. Her eyes dart around the room again, as if I'm saying something scandalous and people might overhear, which is ridiculous. The only other people are far enough away that they can't hear a word.

I continue, 'He mentioned that he thought he might have seen Jim hanging around in the street the other day.'

Helen Abbott's eyes are still fixed on my own. A doubting expression flickers across her face, but it's gone in a split second. '*Alan* said that?' she asks, but something in her voice tells me she doesn't believe me. 'Are you quite sure about that?'

'Oh yes. He told me that he'd seen a man from his window, standing at the end of the path, staring at your house. When he had turned to walk back down the street, he was sure it was Jim.'

Helen picks up her knife and fork, spiking a few pieces of pasta and holding them in front of her face. 'I'm afraid he was mistaken,' she says, popping the food into her mouth.

'But why? Surely it's a possibility. Mr Gillespie knew Jim for years. He'd know him if he saw him, wouldn't he?'

Helen places her cutlery down again. 'Jim would never come back here, Emily. He knows there's nothing left for him here. Why would he return?' she asks with a slight smile.

'Perhaps he has seen the news and found out about Tom. He loved Tom, didn't he? I'm sure he'd be devastated if he heard what happened. Especially given that it was *his* rifle.'

'Emily, I really am rather bored of this conversation. In fact, I'm rather bored of your company.' She pushes out her chair and stands. 'I'm going home. Don't worry about driving me, I think I'd like to walk.'

I look out of the window at the rain that's falling outside. 'Are you sure, Helen? You'll get soaked.'

'Quite sure,' she replies, turning her back on me. She strides out of the restaurant more purposefully than I have seen her move since I arrived, and the door slams shut behind her. I see her disappear round the corner as the white silk becomes see-through, clinging to her skin. Her new bra is visible underneath. She makes no attempt to shield herself from the rain and walks at a leisurely pace.

I'm beginning to think this woman really is stark raving mad.

53

Helen Abbott turns her back to Sandie and places both her palms on the kitchen worktop. Her head falls forward, her greasy lank hair tumbles in front of her face as she lets out a long drawn-out heavy breath. She has the demeanour of a woman defeated, and Sandie feels elated. This is the moment she has always imagined. This is what victory feels like. Standing proud over Helen Abbott as she reveals the truth about what happened to Jim, and apologises for the years of heartache she's caused Sandie.

'You just couldn't keep away, could you?' Helen growls.

'I'm sorry?'

'It wasn't enough that you stole Jim from me... that you lured him away with your high heels and short skirts, and your low-cut tops. Oh no, you had to come back and keep pushing after he was gone. Move into the fucking street. Why would you do that? Right across the road from me, so I had to see you every goddamned day of my life.'

Sandie laughs. 'That was the plan, you stupid bitch. I wanted you to see me. I wanted you to know. Every day. I wanted you to be reminded of what I'd done. I took the house across the road from you absolutely on purpose. I made the owner an extremely generous offer. One she couldn't refuse, you see. Much higher than the market value.'

Mrs Abbott snorts. 'More fool you.' She laughs.

'No, more fool YOU!' Sandie prods Helen Abbott hard in the back of her shoulder with a pointed finger. 'More fool you for not appreciating what you had. More fool you for letting yourself go, for turning into a withered old hag, long before you should have. More fool you for not making the slightest effort to try to fix your marriage when it was blatantly obvious to everyone that it needed fixing. More fool you for driving your husband, the only man who ever loved you, to despise you! Because you drove him straight out of that front door and into my arms. And I have to thank you for that, Helen Abbott.'

Helen does not turn round. She stays in her position, leaning on the counter, her shoulders heaving up and down.

Sandie continues. 'You think I wanted to live in this shithole of a street, in a run-down old house across the road from the wife of my lover? A house that smells of damp and mould, no matter how much I scrub and clean. Of course I didn't. There was one reason and one reason alone that I moved in across the road from you, and that was so I could keep an eye on you.'

'And you certainly did that, didn't you, Mrs Jackson? Do you think I couldn't see you, twitching at the curtains every five minutes? Everybody can see you. Everybody in this street thinks you are a nosey old tart. We all see you parading around in your fancy clothes, thinking you're better than all of us...'

'I *am* better than you!'

'Shut up. Just shut the fuck up! You've said your piece and now I'll say mine. You're an idiot, Sandie Jackson. You should have stayed away. If you'd stayed away then things might have been different. I know you came and spoke to my Tom the day he killed himself. I know you told him about you and Jim. He told me. He tells me... told me everything. You came into my house when I wasn't here, and you spoke to my son, telling him your filthy little secrets. How dare you?' Mrs Abbott's voice is getting louder as she gets angrier.

'Oh, give up the *woman wronged* act, Helen. You said you would tell me where Jim was...'

But Mrs Abbott ignores her and continues. 'If you'd stayed away, then Tom might still be here now, and I wouldn't be left alone in this shitty world. And maybe I deserve it. I guess I do. I know after everything, I don't really deserve a happy ending, but you, Sandie Jackson, you absolutely deserve this.'

'Deserve what–' But the words don't have time to finish forming in Sandie's mouth, as Helen Abbott spins round, much faster than Sandie would have imagined she was capable of.

It happens so quickly that Sandie barely has time to comprehend it. Something warm and wet spills down her front. She sees the paring knife in Mrs Abbott's right hand, covered in blood from having sliced through Sandie's windpipe. The blood comes faster, spraying out in front of her. Sandie raises her hands to her neck, trying to stem the flow, but it's pointless. She tries to speak but all that comes out is a pitiful, sickening gurgling noise.

She looks down and sees her entire front is soaked in blood, and bizarrely she thinks, *That'll never come out.*

And that is the last thought that Sandie Jackson ever thinks.

She is dead before she hits the ground.

54

I arrive home in the dark. The rain is still pouring down, making deep puddles on the road and the pavement. I pull in next to the curb outside the Abbott house, noticing the lights are off. Maybe she didn't come home. Maybe she took shelter from the rain somewhere along the way. I step out of the car, putting my foot straight into a deep puddle at the side of the road. My sock is soaked, and as I run down the path to the house, my trainer squelches.

My hair is plastered to my head, and as I unlock the front door, I run a hand through my wet fringe, trying to disperse some moisture before going into the house. I step into the darkness, closing the front door behind me. I stand with my back to the door, looking into pitch black. The house is silent. I flick the light switch and the bright bulb hurts my eyes as they adjust to the light. I see a train of wet footprints in front of me, leading down the hall and into the kitchen.

Helen is home. So why are all the lights off?

I walk slowly down the hall and into the kitchen. On the middle of the floor, sit Helen's soaking wet clothes. Her new silk blouse is thrown in a heap onto the dirty tiled floor, the flowery skirt on top of it, a puddle of water surrounds them both.

I notice a shaft of light falls across the kitchen floor, the only light within the house. I turn to its source. It falls through from the door to the cellar, which stands open. I walk to it and peer down the stairs.

Silence.

I place my foot on the top step and it creaks as I lower my full weight onto it.

Something tells me to turn round and leave the house, run as far away as I can, but I continue to make my way down into the basement.

I reach the bottom and the cold air rushes onto my face. The smell of musty air. The dust fills my lungs. As I turn the corner, I freeze. In a heap on the floor lies the lady from across the road. She's covered in blood. And very definitely dead. I know this because her throat's cut almost from ear to ear. I try not to scream, but a whimper leaves my mouth. I put my hand to my face, biting on my clenched fist.

'She left me no choice, you understand?' Helen Abbott's voice comes from somewhere deep within the darkness of the cellar. I look around and initially I cannot see her, until she steps out from behind a pile of stacked boxes. She's dressed in her old tatty clothes again, her new hairdo ruined by the torrential rain. She holds up the key, dangling it playfully. In her other hand is a kitchen knife.

'I found the key in your drawer, Emily. Tut-tut. Lying to my face like that. Is that any way to repay my hospitality? Your parents would be so ashamed of you. That's not how they brought you up. Did you think I wouldn't find it, hidden underneath all your underwear like that?'

I don't know what to say. I'm afraid. Terrified. I know I should probably turn and run, but my legs won't work. I keep looking down at the bloody remains of the lady who lived across the road, and I can't remember her name, not that it matters.

'Don't just stand there. Come on in.' Helen motions for me to come into the basement.

I hesitate, looking behind me.

'Don't even think about running. I'm faster than I look, as that bitch on the floor there found out.'

'Helen, I don't understand. What's going on?' I'm trying to piece things together, but nothing makes sense.

'All in time, my dear. Come on in.' She steps forward, holding up the knife towards me, and uses it to beckon me in. I walk towards her and she edges round so her back is towards the staircase, blocking my escape. She motions towards the blood-stained chair in the middle of the room. 'Sit, please, Emily.'

I look at the chair, but can't bring myself to sit on Tom's dried blood.

'Do it! Now!' she shouts, her voice hoarse.

I sit. 'Helen, I...'

'Shhhh.' She places her finger to her lips. 'You know, nothing can ever prepare you for finding out your child is dead. I know that's what people say, but it's true. When Jim came back to the party and told me what had happened, I was almost sick, but I then had to stay there, pretending that everything was fine, pretending to enjoy myself. Can you imagine how hard that was for me? Sitting, pretending to have fun, sipping champagne, all the time knowing that my little girl was–'

'I can only imagine–'

'No, don't speak. Listen. It was an accident of course. But Jim said we couldn't tell anyone. He said they would take Tom away, that he would be locked up. I wanted to tell the police there and then, but he made me keep quiet. Jim hatched the whole stupid plan. He drove her body away, wrapped in a white sheet. I don't even know where he took her. I never asked, and he never told me. Imagine that? Not even knowing where your only daughter is buried. The "abduction" was all his idea. I've never seen some- body remain so calm in such a horrendous situation. He made me do it. I didn't want *any* of this. But I didn't want to lose Tom as well. Can you imagine losing both your children in one night? So I agreed. I played the worried mother. I pretended my daughter had been taken from her bed by a man, and I did the press conferences, begging for her to be returned safe when I knew all along that that was never going to happen.'

Helen stops talking briefly, as she remembers. Tears form in her eyes. I can't really believe what I'm hearing. She's confirming what Tom told me. It *is* true. Alice Abbott never left this house alive. She has been dead all along. I stare at Helen Abbott in disbelief. She looks away.

'Don't you dare judge me, Emily. My life ended that night. Every day since that day has been a mere charade. A lie. There has been no joy for me since then. So, don't think this has been easy for me. But do you know what the final nail in the coffin was? He was going to leave me. He was having an affair with that *slut*.' Helen motions with the knife towards her neighbour's body on the floor. 'They were leaving together. But that's not the worst of it. He wanted us to come clean. Tell the world what had happened to Alice. He said he couldn't live with the guilt and the lies anymore. Can you believe that? It was all him, and then he wants to go back on it years later.'

Helen steps closer to the chair and motions for me to stand, so I obey. She spins me round and pushes me deeper into the basement.

'You're going to love this. It took me a while to get all the other boxes off from on top of it, but I got there in the end.' She pushes me towards a large trunk on the floor. It's held shut with leather straps and buckles. I look at it, and back at her. She is smiling. 'Open it.'

I crouch down on the floor, in front of the dusty old trunk and pull at the buckles. They're shut tight and it takes me a few minutes to work them loose. I lift the lid of the trunk and peer inside. At first I don't know what I'm looking at. Some old musty clothes. A pair of jeans. A tatty red chequered shirt. Some dirty work boots. I don't understand why she's showing me these things.

But as the dust settles and my eyes adjust in the darkness, I see. And I understand.

55

I see a skull with patchy grey hair on top of it. I see a skeletal hand, folded clumsily underneath the body. I see thick dried blood stains on the shirt and down the jeans. I see the body of Jim Abbott. I turn and look in horror at Helen.

'He wanted to leave, but I couldn't let him. We would all have been arrested. And Tom... poor Tom was far too damaged by then. There's no way he would have been able to handle life in prison. We had lied for many, many years, and as much as I longed for the relief of finally telling the truth, I knew it could never happen.' She points up the stairs behind her with her free hand, the point of the knife aimed straight at me with the other the whole time.

'So, he stood there in that stinking, dirty kitchen, as I chopped carrots for his fucking Sunday roast dinner, telling me he had finally found happiness and that he needed to move on. Emily, you have to understand, for the first time since the whole thing happened, I lost my temper. I *really* fucking lost it. I didn't plan it. Before I even knew what I was doing, the knife was in his chest and I kept stabbing him again and again. I kept stabbing until Tom pulled me off him and prised the knife out of my hands, but Jim was long dead.'

She stares at me. And I stare back. My mouth wide open. I try to think of something to say, but nothing comes out. My mouth closes, then opens again, but still I can't think of any words.

And then I hear it.

The creak of the top step to the basement. I hold my breath and wait, but I hear nothing else.

Did I imagine it?

Suddenly, Helen Abbott is right above me. She pushes me hard as I'm crouching, so I fall painfully onto my back, at her feet.

'And then you had to come back, didn't you, you stupid, stupid girl? After all these years. You couldn't leave well enough alone. You came back and started asking questions. And it all gets raked up again. And I realised, I'm never going to be free of this.'

She has a manic look in her eyes, and I know there's no stopping her. Behind her I see a shadow move across a wall.

Is someone here to help me?

She prods me with the point of the knife, tearing my T-shirt and breaking my skin. Droplets of blood form on the surface and soak into my top.

'I loved you, Emily. I loved you and Alice. You were like a daughter to me. Heaven knows you spent more time over here than you did in your own house. And I felt so sad for you, every time I saw you, after she was gone. That look of hope only a child can have. And the guilt I felt whenever I saw you was incomprehensible. Because I wanted to tell you that she was never coming back. But I couldn't.' She prods me again with the knife and I bite my lip from the pain. 'I was so glad when you moved away, because out of all the people I lied to, you were the hardest. I wished I could end that sadness in your eyes and give you some closure. But you know what? Then I reminded myself that–'

But the sentence never gets finished.

There is a loud thud, and something warm and wet splatters across my face as Helen Abbott falls in a heap on the floor, to reveal Adam standing beside her, a claw hammer raised in one hand. A look of hatred in his eyes.

I've never been so glad to see my brother. But before I can tell him this, he raises the hammer and hits Helen Abbott's head. Then he does it again, and again. Her head is a bloody mess. Adam screams and he keeps hitting the pulpy mess on the floor. The blood spatter hits my face again. He's covered. I'm covered.

'Adam, stop!' I scream, but he keeps going until there's nothing left of her head but a smashed-up pile of brains and skull fragments, and blood.

He stands up and the hammer clatters to the floor beside me. He looks at me.

I remain where I am, cowering on the floor, and he reaches out his hand. I take it and he helps me to my feet.

'Adam, what have you done?'

'She was a murderer, Ems. She was going to kill you too. I... had to. I had no choice.'

I look down at the mess on the floor, then across to the body of Helen Abbott's neighbour. 'We need to call the police. Now.'

'Yep, okay. Let's just get you back to Lily's first. We can call from there.' He puts his arm around my shoulder and leads me out of the blood-soaked basement for the second time in a week.

As everything starts to sink in, I sob uncontrollably.

Adam rubs my back, and I hug him tightly.

'Adam, she was dead, all along. Poor Alice. She died that night. Tom... killed her.' I can barely bring myself to say it.

'I know, I heard. It's terrible.'

'They covered it up. They lied! How? How could any parent do that?'

Adam pushes the front door of the Abbott house open and leads me out into the street, and fresh air fills my lungs.

'I think most parents will do a lot to protect their child, Ems... if they love them enough.'

56

W e walk in silence down the street towards Lily's house. Adam unlocks the door and a smell hits me.

'Excuse the stench,' he says. 'There's a problem with the drains. Whole house stinks of shite.'

He takes me into the kitchen and pours me a glass of water. I gulp it down greedily, not realising how thirsty I had been until the cold liquid touches my dry mouth.

'How did you know, Adam? How did you know I needed your help?'

He looks at me. 'I saw you get home earlier, and I felt something wasn't right. I tried your mobile but it went straight to voicemail. So I came to see you, and the door was open.'

Had I forgotten to shut the door? I don't think I did.

'Adam, can you get the phone? I want to call the police.'

He stands up straight and folds his arms in front of his chest. 'I'm afraid I can't do that, Emily.'

I don't understand, so I ask him again. 'Adam, get me the phone.' I'm almost shouting this time.

And then he punches me.

A hard balled fist, man punch, straight in the jaw.

I've never felt such force. My head whips back and my neck cracks painfully as I fall down, stunned. Everything seems to slow down and the room swirls around me. I feel blood trickle from the corner of my mouth. I try to speak, but I can't manage words. I try to stand up, but Adam pushes me back down again. I look at him, with blurred vision, and he's smiling.

'Best you stay where you are. That was quite a punch.' And he laughs. 'You have no fucking idea how long I've wanted to do that.'

He looks at me with what I can only describe as pity.

'Golden girl Emily. In a heap on the floor. I would imagine you're wanting an explanation?'

He paces up and down in front of me.

'Adam, what are you doing?' I beg, sounding far more pathetic than I intend.

He replies with a kick to my ribs. I roll onto my side and hold my torso.

So much pain.

'You just wouldn't let this go. I tried to warn you off. So many times since you arrived. I even wrote that note from that old cunt Alan Gillespie. But you still wouldn't let it go. What the hell is it with you?'

I look at Adam in disbelief.

'The necklace was a nice touch though, don't you think? Let me tell you, it was hard for me to let that go. But I thought if you saw that, it would be proof enough. But no. You still had to keep digging.'

'Adam, I don't understand,' I say, my voice weak with pain.

He kicks me again.

'No. You wouldn't. You don't know anything about me, so how could you understand? You've never taken the time or effort to find out anything about my life. So, let me lay it down for you. Borderline personality disorder. That's what they call it. Or emotionally unstable personality disorder.' He smiles as he says this. 'I was diagnosed quite young, but Mum and Dad didn't want you to know. Didn't want to risk upsetting poor little precious Emily. So that's basically my problem. I don't handle rejection well. And God knows I've been rejected and abandoned my whole fucking life. By Mum and Dad. By you...' He pauses and looks at me with a glint in his eye. 'By that fucking bitch, Alice Abbott. And you know what? If she had been a bit nicer to me, then who knows, she might still be here now. So, she's really only got herself to blame for what happened.'

I pull myself up into a sitting position. 'Alice? What are you talking about? How did Alice reject you? What happened that night?'

Adam starts toward me. I think he's going to kick me again, so I cower, but he doesn't. He just sniggers, then leans against the kitchen worktop.

'You want to know what happened to Alice? You're so fucking desperate to find out about her last moments? I'll show you exactly what happened to her.'

He lurches towards me and grabs me by my hair, pulling me up to my feet. He spins me round so I'm facing away from him, and pulls an arm painfully behind my back, still holding my hair in his other hand.

He pushes me out into the hall and towards the stairs. I try to push with my free arm on the bannisters, but he's too strong. I fall forward onto the stairs and he lands on top of me, crushing my arm in between us. I hear a crack and a tremendous pain shoots through my arm. He leans his mouth into my ear from behind me and whispers, 'Mmm, that's nice, sis. Keep that going, yeah? I like it when they put up a struggle.'

He pulls me up and I am amazed by his sheer strength.

He leads me along the landing towards a bedroom. The smell is stronger up here. And there are flies too.

Lots of flies.

He pushes me through the bedroom door and a cloud of them swarm and buzz around us.

The smell is unbearable.

As the flies begin to settle, I see the source of the stench.

Lying on the floor near to the wall is what used to be a body. The head is lodged against the wall, the neck at an unnatural angle, clearly broken. The locks of tangled stringy black and blue hair the only thing able to give away her identity. I put my hand to my face to try to block my nostrils and my mouth. I gag.

Adam throws me in a heap on the floor next to the body.

'That was your fault, you know.' He gestures towards Lily with his head. I stare back at him, defiantly.

'That morning you were here, after pussy boy blew his brains out. I told her to leave you alone. I told her I would handle you. But she wanted to find out if Tom had told you the truth before he checked out. I thought he would have done it years ago. I'm amazed he lasted as long as he did. So anyway, we got in a bit of a fight about it, and I lost it. Really lost it this time. I didn't actually mean to kill her. Her head hit the wall at the wrong angle. I was quite surprised at how easy it was to snap her neck. But she was very thin. Too much skag, I think. Stupid cow.

'I did her a favour really. She was totally fucked-up. You know, she actually found it a turn on, what happened with Alice. Lily loved it. She used to ask me to tell her about it while we were fucking. I mean, what is that? But you know what? She was the first person in my life who's not abandoned me... even after she found out about Alice, Lily stood by me. She was a real diamond. And now she's gone. Because of you.'

Adam pulls something from his back pocket and I shudder as I see what it is.

A pair of handcuffs.

He crouches down over me. I struggle. I kick. I scratch. My

nails connect with his face, and he slaps me hard across mine. It takes no effort for him to overpower me. He kneels on my arms so they're pinned to my chest, and slides the cuffs onto one wrist. I scream, and he punches me in the face again. He feeds the cuffs around a pipe on the radiator, and cuffs my other wrist. I'm powerless.

He's kneeling on my legs and straightens up, loosening his belt.

'Adam, what are you doing?' I ask, panicking.

He unbuttons the fly on his jeans, sliding them down over his thighs.

'You want to know what happened to Alice, and I said I'm going to show you.'

57

As I begin to understand what I think is about to happen, I'm sick.

'Oh, Emily. I don't want to see that. It's gonna have to be from behind now.' He slides off of me and flips me over onto my front, twisting my arms painfully in the cuffs. I feel his hands reach round underneath me, undoing my jeans. He tears them down. I'm struggling, fighting with everything I have in me for this not to happen. This can't happen. But it's useless.

He spreads my legs with his knee. I hold my breath, preparing for the horror of what my brother is about to do to me, but nothing happens. He just laughs.

I lie on the floor, crying into a puddle of vomit. He slaps my bottom and pulls my jeans back up. I hear his trousers being pulled up and his belt buckle being tightened, and I relax a little.

'Not even I would sink that low,' Adam says through his laughter. 'Bet you thought you were finally gonna lose your v-badge. Sorry to disappoint you. You're just going to have to use your imagination for that bit.'

I hear Adam exhale, a long slow drawn-out breath.

'Yeah, so that night. God it seems so fucking long ago in some ways, but in others it feels like yesterday. I still think about it a lot. Like every day. So, Mum and Dad were out at that party. The whole street was. You were being boring as always. You'd gone to bed. So I snuck over the road to see Tom. Alice was on the phone... to you, I think. So me and Tom, we were messing around, and we drank some vodka from the Abbotts' drinks cabinet. Poor little Tom couldn't really handle it and he got sick. Alice came into Tom's room to see what was going on. She was in her nighty and she was flirting with me, like she always did. And I was a bit drunk. And I thought, yeah let's do this. So I told her how I felt about her. I was crazy about her. I said it, "I love you", and she laughed at me.

'Can you imagine what that felt like, to lay yourself bare to the person you're infatuated with, and she laughs in your face? She told me to go home. And, like I said, I was a bit drunk, so I kind of grabbed her and threw her down on the bed. It was just supposed to be a laugh at first, but then her nighty rode up and I got a glimpse of her pussy. And I thought, yeah, I want that. And I fucked her. She totally wanted it, but she kept screaming, like really loud. That idiot Tom, it was his fault. I told him to shut her up, and the little twat put a pillow over her face. I felt her die while I was fucking her. That was *sick*.'

I turn my face towards him and stare at him in disbelief. I don't know who this man is. He's a rapist. And a murderer. And I need to escape.

'You bastard,' I whisper.

'What was that?'

'You're a fucking bastard. You did all of this. It's all your fault. Everything!'

'Get over it.'

'Mum and Dad would be so ashamed of you!'

He actually laughs out loud. 'Mum and Dad? You want to know about Mum and Dad? They knew, of course. The Abbotts knew too. They didn't know about the sex, but I think Helen suspected there was more to our story than I made out. She never liked me. She always used to look at me with that suspicion in her eyes. She thought she was better than us, you know... She didn't like Alice playing with us. She thought you were a bad influence. Anyway, Tom got his fucking post-traumatic bullshit amnesia, so it was down to me to tell everyone what had happened. I told them Tom got in a fight with Alice and it was an accident. But Mum and Dad, they wanted to know more. Dad used to say to me that I could tell him anything, and he would understand... that he would still love me.

'So one day, I told him. Every grisly little detail. It felt good to be sharing it with him... a real quality father and son bonding moment, you know? I really thought he would understand. He *promised* he would understand. But you should have seen the way he looked at me. It was written all over his face. He was disgusted by me. By his own son. He wouldn't even look at me after that. And then of course he told Mum, and that was it. I begged him not to tell her, but he said he had to. She went all psycho after that, as you know. We moved away, and they stopped loving me. They sent me away to that shitty fucking school. I think they were trying to protect *you*. It was always about you.'

'Adam, you're not borderline... you're a psycho... you're an actual textbook psychopath. You're not well... you must know that, right? We can get you help. We can make you well again.'

'Yes, probably... I've thought about that a lot. But really, what does it matter? And regarding making me well again... Emily, I have *never* been well. I've been like this as long as I can remember. And I don't want help. I'm getting by just fine, thanks very much.'

As Adam rants at me, I scan the room, but I see no way to escape the handcuffs. Lily's decomposing body stares at me with empty eyes.

58

'Anyway, long story short, they ended up abandoning you too, as it turns out. Fucking losers, couldn't live with the guilt anymore, it seems.'

'Don't you dare talk about them like that!'

'They did get hold of me. You won't know any of this. When they went on that holiday.' He makes air quote marks with his fingers.

'What are you talking about?'

'Dad got hold of me eventually. He told me what they were planning. They couldn't live with the guilt anymore, they had created a monster, they blamed themselves, blah blah blah. And you know what the last thing he said to me was?' Adam looks at me and cocks his head to one side. I don't reply. 'He said "look after Emily". Even in their last few hours of their miserable little fucking lives, they were more concerned about you than they were about me.'

And suddenly I understand. And I feel an overwhelming love for my mother. She was terrified of Adam. She knew what he was capable of, and she never wanted him to be alone with me. It was never me that she didn't trust, it was him. I spent so many years hating her, thinking she was paranoid after what happened to Alice, when in fact Mum was protecting me because she knew exactly what had happened.

Poor, poor Alice. Raped by her friend and buried in an unmarked shallow grave by her father. She deserved so much more.

And that's when it hits me. I feel a wave of anger unlike anything I've ever felt before.

'It was *you* all along!' I scream. 'In the woods when I first got here. You followed me? And in the house, the night my laptop got stolen, and my diary. That was all you!'

Adam smirks. 'Yeah. You looked so frightened that day in the woods, like a little rabbit. Lily said I should have just killed you there and then. But I wanted to see what you were up to, coming back here. I wanted to see what you uncovered. And you know what? You uncovered fuck all.'

'You're wrong. I knew about Tom. He told me he'd killed Alice before he shot himself. He remembered.'

'Yeah, I figured as much. It was just cos he wanted to fuck you. Little poof wouldn't have known what to do anyway. But you didn't know exactly what happened, did you? You didn't know the full story.' Adam smiles, a glint in his eye. 'But you do now. So, are you happy now, Emily? Did you get what you wanted? Was it everything you dreamed of? Does it feel good to finally have some *closure*?'

'And what about Alan Gillespie? Is he dead?'

Adam shakes his head, slowly but purposefully. 'God no. I need him to turn up after they find you. He's going to be the obligatory fall guy. But that's not going to work if they find that he died before you, is it? No... he's down in the basement. Silly old fuck. I reckon he has a soft spot for you too. Dirty old bastard. Anyway, he's been begging me not to hurt you, you know that? I couldn't take any more of his fucking moaning, so I had to knock him out.'

As I watch Adam, something occurs to me. The person I've been getting to know over the last few weeks is entirely absent. There's nothing in his eyes that I recognise. It was all lies, an elaborate act to reel me in. Cold. Calculated. And executed with expert precision.

'Adam, please. What are you going to do to me? Why don't you just let me go? I won't tell anyone. I promise. What's the point?'

I'm begging but there's no pity in his eyes. Just hatred. He despises me.

'I'm afraid I can't do that, Ems. You see, you're the last person alive who knows the truth. The only one left. I suspect Mrs Abbott has told Alan Gillespie. You know they were fucking, right? So, I'd imagine she told him at some point while she was scraping her nails down his back. The old whore. I'm so fucking close to getting away with this, and when the two of you are out of the way, then that's it. I can *finally* move on with my life. I can finally be free from Alice fucking Abbott.'

'You're crazy, Adam! You're kidding yourself if you think you'll ever be free from this. You'll feel this guilt forever. I can help you get through it. I can help you move on. Come on, Adam. We sat in a café the other day, and I felt you cared about me. I *felt* that. You can't fake that. I know my little brother's in there somewhere! It's me. Emily. Your sister. Please!'

'You're wasting your time,' he says casually. 'I know exactly what you're trying to do. You're trying to appeal to the *human being* inside me. Your little brother who played Twister with you on your birthday. You're trying to get past the hatred and anger in me, and appeal to the love I feel for you. Let me cut to the chase here, Emily. The Adam you *think* you've been getting to know these last few days, he's the one who doesn't exist. It was an act. I was trying to be the person you want me to be, to get you on side, and it worked, didn't it. All that "hey, sis" crap. You actually fell for it. Hook, line and sinker. That Adam, the one you think loves you, he stopped existing a *very* long time ago. Trust me when I say that all I feel for you is hatred, and maybe a little pity. You're totally fucking pathetic. You've wasted your whole life trying to find out what happened to some stupid kid you knew when you were twelve. *Worse* than pathetic.'

The whole time he's talking, I'm only half listening. I'm desperately scanning the room, looking for an escape route. But it's apparent that there's no way out. I need him to take off the cuffs.

'Adam, can you please just loosen these. They're too tight, I...'

He gets up and marches towards me, kicking me hard in the gut, then once more again for good measure. I wheeze with the pain, and I can't breathe for a moment.

'Shut up! Just shut up and let me think!' He then mimics me in a whiney voice, 'The cuffs are too tight.' He kicks me again. 'For fuck's sake, you're so fucking pathetic.'

He paces up and down maniacally, muttering to himself.

'I wasn't really prepared for this yet. I don't have all the things I need to pull this off. Helen Abbott's little gambit has moved things along somewhat prematurely. Fuck me though, I never thought she had it in her to kill her husband. That did surprise me. But worry not, sis. I just need to pop out and sort a few things. Now's as good a time as any to do this. You're going to absolutely *love* what I have planned for you and Alan Gillespie. It's genius!'

He looms over me, staring down at me with a smile on his face. 'Now don't you go anywhere.' And with that he stamps on my face.

His boot connects with my nose and I hear the crunch of

cartilage as blood explodes down my throat and spills down my face onto the carpet. He kicks me in the face, catapulting my head backwards against the wall, and I feel a searing pain. My whole body is weak, and the room swirls around me.

Adam steps over me and strides out of the room, slamming the door shut behind him.

As I hear his footsteps receding down the stairs, my world goes black.

59

He is coming.

The terror drives me to one final attempt at the pipe. I pull, crashing the links of the cuffs against it. I scream. I use every last bit of energy I have to try to break the pipe. I can't feel the pain in my wrists anymore. I can't feel anything but fear. Adrenaline has taken over.

As the door swings open, bashing against the wall, the flies swarm and buzz around the room, like thick black smoke. Some escape into the hall. He swats them away from his face.

He stands in the doorway, looking annoyed. As he steps inside, he kicks me hard in my ribs, twice.

'What the fuck do you think you're doing?' Adam crouches down beside me with his face next to mine. I can smell beer on his breath. He puts his hands on my breasts and I shudder, trying to block images of him and Alice from my mind. He squeezes my breasts hard and smiles.

'I hate your little boy tits. Alice had better boobs than you, and she was twelve.' He smiles. 'Now, I asked you what the fuck you think you're doing? Making all this noise. Who do you think is going to hear you? Do you think someone's going to come and save you? Because I've got news for you... that ain't gonna happen. There's nobody left. You're all alone, but I guess you're used to that by now. You've always been alone, haven't you? Poor little Emily, can't get a boyfriend. That is, if you even like blokes. You do have very short hair these days. Damn! Are you a lesbian, Emily? Is that why you've always been so infatuated with Alice Abbott? I wouldn't blame you. She was very attractive. Are you jealous that it was me who got to fuck her?'

I'm exhausted from struggling with the pipe, but as he speaks, my anger wells up inside me again. The cocky little prick is so sure of himself, and I can't let him win. I will *not* let him get away with this. I don't know how, but I *will* get out of this. I just need to bide my time and wait for an opportunity, and pray that he doesn't kill me before one presents itself. He's strong, but I'm clever. And I'm furious. I'm furious for my parents. I'm disgusted at Adam, at what he's become... is, at what he's done to me, and the other residents of Palmerston. I'm angry for Tom, who was driven mad by guilt because of my brother's actions as a boy. I'm even angry for Helen Abbott, lying dead in her basement, along-side the woman who stole her husband away from her, just yards from the skeletal remains of the man they both once loved.

But most of all I'm angry for Alice, who didn't deserve any of this. She was an innocent little girl. She was my friend. I think of how different everything would have been if Adam hadn't gone over to the Abbott house that night. I finally realise this is all my fault. If I had been paying more attention to him, to where he was, then none of this would ever have happened, and I don't know why, but I laugh.

Adam gives me a strange look. He seems annoyed. 'Why are you laughing? What do you have to laugh about?' he screams. But I can't stop. I know that this is all my own doing. One little girl's inability to make sure her brother is in bed has set all these years of events in motion. I am the catalyst.

As I laugh, I list in my head all the people whose lives I have ruined.

Alice Abbott

Tom Abbott

Jim Abbott

Helen Abbott

My mother and father

The lady, Sandie, from over the road

Alan Gillespie

Blue-haired Lily

Adam

Me.

Two whole families destroyed, three if you count Lily and her parents. And the thought of Adam being the only person to come out of this alive gives me the determination I need to beat him.

He slaps me hard across the face and I stop laughing. He reaches down, unlocking the handcuffs. He pulls me to my feet and shoves me out through the bedroom door.

60

M y wrists are bleeding and sore, and I try to stretch them, but Adam manhandles me down the stairs and into the kitchen. He forces me towards the basement door, turning the key and swinging it open. He shoves me and I scream as I fall forward down the wooden stairs. I slide on my chest with my hands stretched out in front of me, landing in a heap at the bottom, my face pressed against the cold concrete floor of the basement. I think I am so used to pain by this point that it doesn't even feel like it hurts that much anymore. Adam flicks on the light and I hear his boots clomping down the stairs behind me. I know I should try to get up, but I can't.

Every inch of me aches. I can only see out of one eye, the other is badly swollen from Adam's kicks and punches.

He pulls me to my feet and shoves me deeper into the belly of the basement. As we round the corner, I see a bloody figure tied to a chair in the far corner. Alan Gillespie. He has two black eyes, and what appears to be a broken nose. His clothes are heavily stained with dried blood. He stirs, but he's not conscious. Adam pushes me down to the floor in front of Gillespie. He grabs my hand and uses it to claw at Alan's cheek, I assume to get traces of his DNA on my nails.

Adam then walks to a workbench by the far wall. As he does, I crawl away from the chair with Gillespie on it, slowly towards the shaft of light coming down from the kitchen. I glance back towards Adam. He screws up an old rag, placing it in his own mouth before picking up what looks like a pair of bolt cutters in one hand. He places one of the fingers of his free hand between the blades and cuts it clean off. He stifles a scream, and the blood flows over the bench and onto the floor. He spits out the old rag and stumbles towards Gillespie. Adam wipes his blood down the man's shirt and onto his hands, tossing the finger on the floor, and then turns towards me, a grin on his face. He picks up the rag from the floor and wraps it around his mutilated hand, holding it tight with the other one.

'Adam! What the hell are you doing?'

'Sorting out my story. Poor little me... I must have found Alan Gillespie in my house. He had already killed my beloved Lily. And I caught him in the act as he was murdering my darling big sister. I tried to help her but I was too late. Gillespie tortures me, and then kills me too. The police will find *a lot* of my blood, and my finger on the floor. Gillespie has obviously disposed of me somewhere else. Doesn't really matter. They will search for my body. Then they will find this...' Adam pulls a note from his pocket, reading a few lines from it aloud. 'I killed Alice Abbott. I can't go on. Knowing that I have ruined so many lives, this all has to end here... Alan Gillespie.'

I stare at the mad bleeding man in front of me. 'You're totally insane, Adam. This is so implausible, nobody will *ever* believe it. For a start, I also have *your* DNA underneath my nails, you idiot!'

Behind Adam, Alan Gillespie stirs. He lifts his head and one eye opens. He looks at me, and he looks so very sad.

'Adam, your plan is so flawed nobody will ever believe it.

There are so many holes in this, it won't take them long to figure out the truth. This is ridiculous. Give up. You've caused enough pain for a lifetime. Please, give up. Kill yourself, for all I care. But fucking give up. This is madness!'

Adam pulls a gun from his leather jacket pocket, pointing it at me. 'Shut up! Shut the fuck up. I'm sick of the sound of your whinging little bitch voice. And you know what, I don't care if they believe it, because I only need enough of a head start to get away. I'm good at changing my identity. Seemingly that's part of my "condition". Lack of sense of who I am and constant reinvention, blah blah fucking blah.'

I'm sliding across the floor the whole time, almost at the foot of the stairs. I'm not sure if my leg is broken from falling into the basement, but I need to try to escape, but before I get the chance, he strides over to me, looming above me, placing the gun against my left temple.

'You're not leaving here, Emily. At least not without a bullet in your head. You think you're so fucking clever, don't you? You've always looked down your nose at me with that superior smug expression... like you're better than me, like you pity me. Now look at you. I don't need your fucking pity. Who's winning now you little fucking–'

Before he can finish the sentence there is a guttural roar from behind him. I see Alan Gillespie, on his feet, launch himself towards Adam. The sheer force of the mountain of a man colliding with Adam sends him flying across the floor. Adam is strong, but Gillespie has the advantage of an unexpected attack. He may be old, but he still has a lot of bulk behind him.

The gun goes off with a deafening bang and I hear glass smash. Adam is stunned by the unexpected turn of events. My ears ring and I can't hear anything else momentarily.

Alan Gillespie runs towards the side of the cellar, smashing the chair between him and the wall. It breaks into pieces with a loud crash. While he still has the upper hand, he runs at Adam, kicking the gun out of his hand. It clatters across the basement floor into the shadows. Adam tries to get up but Gillespie kicks him hard in the face. His hands are still tied behind his back, so he has to improvise.

Adam's head bounces off Gillespie's boot and impacts hard with the concrete floor of the basement with a loud crack. Gillespie's foot comes slamming down onto Adam's face. I watch as Gillespie stamps on Adam's head again and again. He tries to get up, but Gillespie delivers a hard kick and I hear Adam's neck snap. Gillespie continues to stamp on the bloody mess of Adam's face, long after he's dead. Bone crunches under his foot. Something fleshy and pink bursts and splatters across the concrete.

Tears stream from Gillespie's eyes, and he screams, and screams, until finally he stops and falls to his knees, sobbing, and I sob too.

Alan Gillespie turns his blood-soaked face towards me, and in that split second we both know.

This is *finally* over.

EPILOGUE

I am standing at a grave. Alice's grave. With the information I was able to provide the police, they reopened the search for Alice's remains. It took them a few months, but eventually they found her, or what little was left of her, in some dense woodland on the South Downs. Miles from anywhere.

I called Dave a few days after the events unfolded in Palmerston. Of course by that point it had already been all over the news. He had left me countless voicemails, peppered with his usual colourful language, and the odd threat. I told him I wouldn't be returning to work. The events with my brother had made me take a good long look at my life, and I didn't feel that working for a shitty gossip magazine was what my parents would have ultimately wanted for me. He was furious. I don't care. I have enough savings to keep me going for a while. Maybe I'll go travelling. See the world.

Alan Gillespie stands next to me. The rain pours down on us as we stand in silence. We are soaked but neither of us care.

I hang Alice's necklace, and my half of it, over the corner of the shiny new marble headstone, and trace Alice's name engraved into the face of the stone softly with my index finger.

My hand is drawn to my neck. It feels naked without the chain around it, but I know it's finally time to move on.

I have found the closure I was looking for, for so very long. They may not have been the answers I wanted to find, but nevertheless, they are the answers.

We both stand quietly in the rain for what feels like an age.

Finally, I break the silence. 'I take it you heard about Becky Clarke?'

Gillespie looks at me and takes a deep breath before he answers. 'Hiding at her uncle's house? What sort of people would do that? Lie about something like that, and get a child involved.'

'Desperate people, it would appear. The Clarkes were up to their eyeballs in debt. They were about to lose their house... they were terrified that the kids would be taken away from them if they ended up homeless. Seems Mr Clarke remembered that a lot of money was donated in the early days to try to find Alice. They thought they could keep Becky hidden for a while, benefit from the donations, then all of a sudden she would turn up, wandering in the street or something. Becky didn't know anything about the plan. As far as she knew, she was just having a sleepover at her uncle's house. It was all a game to her. Although she did think it was odd that she wasn't allowed to leave the house or watch TV. Anyway, when all the shit hit the fan about Adam and me, they kind of got cold feet, felt guilty or something, and changed their minds. But then they couldn't keep Becky from saying she had been at the uncle's house all the time, so the whole thing fell apart.'

'Bloody idiots,' Gillespie says, shaking his head.

'At least her story has a happier ending,' I say, looking down to Alice's grave. I look back at Gillespie and open my mouth to speak, but I think better of it before the words come out. I shake my head, closing my mouth again.

Gillespie gives me a sideways glance. 'What?'

I reason to myself that after everything we've been through together, I can be honest with him, so I ask him the question that has been playing on my mind. 'Did you know?'

He looks at me blankly.

'Did you know about Alice? That she was dead. Did you know the real story?'

Gillespie shakes his head, then looks down at the grave in front of us. 'I didn't know for sure, but yes, I suspected. I spent a lot of time with Helen over the years, and one thing that always occurred to me was that she *never* believed that I had anything to do with Alice going missing. Even my own sister asked me if it was me. She called me and she said, "Alan, you're my brother, and I love you, but did you do it?", but the Abbotts, they never asked. They never accused me. They showed me nothing but compassion from day one. And that was a little odd. You touched on that when we were talking once, and I wondered if you had figured something out. But on top of that, even back in the very early days, in public they stuck to their line that they believed Alice was alive, out there somewhere, and there was some hope that they might find her.'

Gillespie sighs. 'In the press conferences and interviews, Helen always referred to Alice in the present tense, as if she was alive, but behind closed doors, when we were talking privately, she always used the past tense. "Alice was such a good girl", and so on. I always thought that was peculiar. It was as if she *knew*. She knew that little girl was never coming home. I knew about Jim of course. She came round knocking at my door in the middle of the night. She was distraught; she wanted to go to the police. I managed to calm her down, and then I convinced her that going to the police was not going to help anyone, especially not Tom, who would be left to look after himself alone. I think that's what changed her mind in the end. I helped her put the body into the trunk, and we hid it behind all of Alice's boxes. Then after Jim had been "missing" for a few months, we put his stuff into boxes and piled them in front of it too. The smell was horrendous for a while, but that's when she came up with the story about rats.'

I let that little nugget of information sink in and take some time to digest it before I ask my next question. 'What will you do now?'

'I really don't know,' he replies after some thought. 'The house is on the market, but the estate agent doesn't think it will sell. Not with everything that's happened on that street. I don't really know where else to go anyway. Helen... she was the only person I had, you know. And now she's gone...' He trails off, a sad look in his eye, and I get the feeling that, for a moment, he's no longer here with me.

He shakes his head and looks at me. 'What about you?'

I don't answer immediately. I think about the options, then smile. 'I'll live my life.'

He raises a grey eyebrow.

'My brother stopped a lot of people from living the life they deserved, including me. All I've ever known is the sadness of losing Alice and the pain of not knowing what happened to her. And now we know, and as shitty as everything that happened is, I'm not going to let Adam's actions stop me from living one more day of my life. I'm going to enjoy every new day, and be glad that I'm alive, because if it hadn't been for you, Alan, I might not be standing here right now.'

Embarrassed, he swats a hand towards me, in a 'shut up' gesture.

'I'm going to live my life for Alice, and Helen, and Tom, and Jim, and Sandie Jackson, and Lily. I'm going to live my life for my mum and dad, who felt so wrapped up with guilt about everything that Adam did, that they drove their car off a cliff. But most of all, I'm going to live my life for me.'

Alan Gillespie stands in the rain staring at the two half-heart shaped pendants on fine gold chains, dangling from the corner of a child's gravestone, and after a few moments he replies, 'Miss Blake, that sounds like a *really* great plan.'

-THE END-

ACKNOWLEDGEMENTS

I have to say thanks to Carole for all the help and advice, and also for bullying me into sending this to a publisher. I also have to thank both my brothers... Phil, for endless texts for advice about police procedures and legal matters, and Matt for reading it and making me believe that it wasn't terrible. And, of course, thank you to Colin, for his unwavering support.